ANOTHER LITTLE DRINK

Jane Ellison was born in Yorkshire. She worked as a journalist for several years, on *Vogue*, the *Standard* and *Private Eye.* Currently she writes articles and reviews for a number of leading newspapers and magazines. Her first novel, *A Fine Excess*, was shortlisted for the Yorkshire Post Prize for the best first work.

Jane Ellison is married with two small children. She lives in London.

ALSO BY JANE ELLISON

A Fine Excess

Jane Ellison

ANOTHER LITTLE DRINK

ARENA

An Arena Book
Published by Arrow Books Limited
62-65 Chandos Place, London WC2N 4NW

An imprint of Century Hutchinson Limited

London Melbourne Sydney Auckland
Johannesburg and agencies throughout
the world

First published in Great Britain by
Martin Secker & Warburg Limited 1987
Arena edition 1989

Made and printed in Great Britain by
The Guernsey Press Co. Ltd., Guernsey, Channel Islands.

ISBN 0 09 960300 4

ACKNOWLEDGEMENTS

The publishers wish to thank Gerald Duckworth & Company for permission to quote from Edith Sitwell, *Facade and Other Poems 1920-35* (Duckworth). 'Lines to Christopher Isherwood' is reprinted by permission of Faber and Faber Ltd from *The English Auden: Poems, Essays and Dramatic Writings 1927-1939* by W. H. Auden

And there the pearl-ropes fall like shawls
With a noise like marine waterfalls
And 'Another little drink wouldn't do us any harm'
Pierces through the Sabbatical calm
And that is the place for me!

Edith Sitwell

Let us honour if we can
The vertical man
Though we value none
But the horizontal one.

W. H. Auden

For Peter

· CHAPTER · I ·

The uniform was ill fitting.

'Do you have anything longer?' said Florence Barge, looking doubtfully at her thighs exposed to public view below the short red hem.

'It's supposed to be short,' said Mrs Crisp. 'That's the point of the dress, darling. Anyway, there's nothing wrong with your knees. Not really. You're just not used to showing 'em.'

Florence looked at herself in the mirror, then turned hastily away.

'Anyway,' said Mrs Crisp, drawing heavily on her cigarette. 'This isn't a model agency, darling. Take it or leave it. It's up to you. Although, I can tell you I have girls it looks a lot worse on.'

Florence stared at Mrs Crisp's face. Her eyes were black and inexpressive, although disconcertingly bright. Lipstick had leaked from the outline of her mouth, so that bright red rivulets ran up the deep gorges of her lips towards her nose.

'Here's your sheets,' Mrs Crisp said in a deep, rough voice. 'And here's your vouchers. If you run out come back for more, but most girls find they last 'em a week.'

'They're rather heavy,' said Florence Barge, staggering beneath the weight of the bundle.

'Nothing a strong young girl like you can't manage,' said Mrs Crisp counting through the forms with a bright orange finger. 'You get your money at the end of the week. All right?'

'Right, Mrs Crisp,' said Florence Barge.

'You do this lot and see how you get on and then we might get you on to promotions,' said Mrs Crisp encouragingly. 'It's more interesting work, really. I've got some fruit pies coming along which should be just up your street.'

'What do I do with them?'

'You offer samples, darling. People are not averse to taking half a dozen, usually, if you can get them to swallow a mouthful.'

'How exciting. Am I allowed to eat my own pies?'

'You'll be on commission, dear,' said Mrs Crisp seriously. 'You'll be consuming your own profit. But it's up to you. Now, any questions?'

'No. I feel terrified, Mrs Crisp. But I'll do my best.'

'Righty-ho. On with the show,' said Mrs Crisp, waving her cigarette with enthusiasm.

'Wish me luck,' said Florence Barge.

She picked up her shoulder bag, a white plastic hold-all emblazoned with a red diamond and the word RIGHT-O written in red letters.

'Go out there and break a leg,' cried Mrs Crisp hoarsely.

Florence Barge left the cramped office in the Edgware Road and stepped self-consciously into the crowded street. It was early October, and too mild to wear a coat. In any case, she was designed to be a walking advertisement for the RIGHT-O brand of groceries. Several people turned to stare at her as she walked to the number twelve bus stop; some changed their direction or stepped carefully across the pavement to avoid her. A woman pushing a plastic shopping trolley giggled as Florence passed her; a small child raised its arm and pointed at her. Once she had gained the safety of the bus she sat hunched by the window hoping to avoid attention. The scarlet uniform rode up over her thighs.

The bus wound slowly round Marble Arch and set off down the Bayswater Road. The leaves of the trees were starting to show the first impure colours of autumn. Florence, still unfamiliar with the London streets, stared out with excitement across Hyde Park, hoping for a glimpse of the royal helicopter arriving at Kensington Palace. The scene was vaguely familiar. She remembered a childhood visit to see *Peter Pan*; and, many years later, a shopping trip to Harrods. With these two exceptions, however, Florence had been brought up in the comforting safety of Herefordshire, leaving its rural peace only for the reassuring fastness of her girls' boarding school. The bus stopped ten minutes later at Shepherd's Bush, which was Florence's destination. Standing at the stop she saw it recede into the distance with an alarming finality. She walked down the street, turning left into the Charles Dickens estate, where her first vouchers were to be distributed. The concrete facades of the cramped flats rose in uniformity, heavily stained with long, dark streaks. 'No ball games,' a notice said. 'The exercising of dogs in the recreation areas is not permitted.' Concrete ledges rose at sharp angles giving access to the upper storeys. The doors were all exactly alike, painted in a series of repeated colours – red, blue and orange. All the windows were covered, screened from onlookers by nylon net curtains. As she walked along Dorritt View, Florence Barge saw the large, overflowing communal dustbins, piled to the top with half-consumed packets of Kentucky Fried chicken, tins of baked beans and greasy paper. Some of the litter overflowed onto the path before her. Conspicuous in her bright red dress she advanced into Chuzzlewit Walk and struck the doorbell of number fourteen. There was a long silence. In the distance she could hear a dog barking. No one came to the door. Disappointed by this unpropitious start, she went on to number fifteen. Here there was no doorbell. She banged loudly on the door.

After some time she heard shuffling footsteps and the sound of a key being turned in the lock. The door opened slightly and she saw, in the dark hall, a pair of eyes staring at her through the gloom.

'Good morning,' she said brightly. 'I wonder if you have any RIGHT-O products in your home. If so, you are entitled to some free grocery vouchers.'

The door opened a little further to reveal an old man, wearing splashed trousers and a discoloured vest. His skin was pale and hung in creases under his armpits, from which long, grey hairs descended. Although his hair was scant, his nostrils sprouted a profusion of black bristles.

After a moment's silence, Florence smiled encouragingly at him and pointed to her RIGHT-O bag. 'Do you have any products in the house?' she said slowly and clearly. 'If so, you are entitled to a voucher worth one pound.'

The man stared at her and said something indistinct.

'I'm sorry, I can't hear you,' said Florence Barge.

The man mumbled again and pointed to his mouth. It became clear that he was temporarily toothless.

'Pur 'em in,' said the man, pointing to his wet gums. 'Pur mi teeth in.'

He disappeared into the dark interior. Florence stood uneasily on the doorstep. 'Whar 'er wan'?' he said, coming back, his speech scarcely more distinguishable now that he had regained his teeth. 'Are yer from the council?'

'Do you have a RIGHT-O product in the house?' said Florence Barge. 'A tin of RIGHT-O baked beans, bath cleaner, washing-up liquid . . .' The man stared at her, his mouth slightly open, a little saliva dribbling from the side of his mouth. 'Go on then,' he said at last. 'I'll 'ave a couple. Whar's er damage?'

He reached into his back trouser pocket and produced a surprisingly large roll of bank notes.

'No, no, the vouchers are free,' said Florence.

The man narrowed his eyes in suspicion.

'Just produce any RIGHT-O product and . . .' She gave up the attempt and took a voucher from the vinyl shoulder bag. 'Here is your voucher,' she said. 'Now, if you would just sign here in exchange –'

'Free?' said the old man in alarm. He looked in doubt at the voucher. 'Naa, I don wan' . . . It's all righ', love, I don wan' . . .' He backed hastily into the hall and the door shut firmly. Florence Barge put the rejected voucher back into her shoulder bag. When she knocked at the next house, an Alsatian leaped at the glass door panel and barked ferociously, its white teeth and pink tongue clearly visible. The vouchers were increasingly heavy. Florence decided that the inhabitants of the Charles Dickens estate were unlikely to have any RIGHT-O products in their houses and walked quickly out towards the main road. She turned off into Artesan Road, following Mrs Crisp's instruction sheet. A line of plane trees bordered each side of the street and behind them a terrace of Victorian houses. Once of noble proportions, they were now divided into flats, with portions of their stucco peeling onto the gardens below. Many had yellowing milk bottles and cartons of orange juice arranged on upper floor window sills, precarious refrigerators for the upstairs tenants. On the ground floor, pieces of dirty material were tacked to the windows, forming temporary curtains.

Like a scarlet signal, indicating danger or a similar hazard, Florence progressed down the street with distaste. She passed a stall offering a selection of poor quality vegetables for sale. 'Corgets, 60p per lb,' one sign declared. 'Fresh brocli.'

'Stand back,' one stallholder shouted. 'Fire! Got a bucket of water, anybody? Don't stand too close, gel, or the stall'll go up.'

Florence ignored the trader and went up to the front door of the next house. It still bore the signs of its former grandeur, with two chipped and crumbling urns on the front porch and cracked black and white marble tiles leading up the front steps.

She pressed the top of a list of five bells. No one answered. Systematically she worked down the list of bells. Still no one seemed to be at home. She was about to go on to the next house when someone down below said quietly, 'Yes, what do you want?'

Florence looked down. A head was visible in the basement area and, next to it, a hand which gripped the railings. Then the head looked up and Florence saw a man staring up at her. He had short, almost razored hair and wore an earring in one ear. She turned and climbed down the steps to the basement. 'I wonder if you have any RIGHT-O products in the house,' she said, feeling certain that he would have none at all.

The man stood on the step and looked at her suspiciously. 'Is this a survey?' he said. 'Are you from the Government?'

'Dressed like this?' said Florence, laughing nervously. 'No, no. I'm promoting RIGHT-O products. One jar of RIGHT-O pickle, for example, could earn you a pound's worth of groceries.'

The man looked at her again. 'Just a minute,' he said, and disappeared inside the house, shutting the door behind him. Florence stood on the doorstep. The door had a piece of frosted glass in it, behind which she could see dark shapes moving backwards and forwards. She had decided to remove her vouchers and go when the door suddenly opened again, and the young man said. 'This is what I've got.' He had a large Sainsbury's plastic bag which was filled with tins of RIGHT-O baked beans.

'Goodness,' said Florence. 'What a lot.'

'I make it nineteen,' said the man, 'but you can count them.'

'Oh,' said Florence. 'Shall I?' Under his unflinching gaze she turned the beans out onto the path and began to pile them up in pyramids.

'You must eat a lot of beans,' said Florence, counting the tins. The man said nothing. 'Of course, they are delicious,' she said. 'Cheap and nutritious. Beans on toast. Scrumptious. It was my favourite meal when I was a child.'

The man still maintained an aggressive silence.

'Yes, nineteen tins,' Florence said. 'Quite right. That entitles you to nineteen pounds' worth of groceries.'

'OK,' the man said.

'Would you sign here please?'

'Sign?' said the man. 'What for?'

'Just to acknowledge the vouchers . . .'

The man stared at her sheet of paper. 'I don't want to sign anything,' he said. 'The point is, you never know who's going to look at all this, do you?'

'Well – no one's going to look at it. It's not official or anything.'

'It's not going on a computer?'

'Oh, no.'

'Or to the DHSS?'

'Certainly not.'

'I have to be careful,' the man said. 'I'm –'

'Well, I can't give you the vouchers if you don't sign the paper.'

The man considered. Then he stretched out his hand. 'Can you lend me a pen?' he said.

Florence offered him her biro. With concentration the man wrote his name on the form. Florence handed over the bundle of vouchers.

'I'll just count them,' he said.

'They're all there, you know.'

'Can't be too careful.'

Laboriously he thumbed through the pile.

'Yes, that's all right.'

'Good. Enjoy exchanging them.'

The man stared at her and shut the door. With relief Florence climbed the steps and fled the basement. For the next hour she wandered up and down the streets, occasionally parting with some vouchers, more often confronting mute and suspicious householders who shut the door immediately in her face. The bag grew heavier. The bright auspicious day had become cloudy and a soft rain was falling. She walked slowly, wandering across intersecting avenues until she found she had drifted towards Holland Park and the great broad avenues, canopied by the interlocking branches of the London plane. Here the houses were white and their facades immaculate. The porches and steps shone from diligent polishing. Wrought-iron railings, shiny and painted black, screened their gardens; metal grilles barred their windows; and burglar alarms were displayed on their walls like plaques denoting that someone famous once lived there. Florence turned to the grander spaces with relief. She pulled her skirt towards her knees and knocked on the door of a house that had a bay tree in a Grecian-style pot by the front door.

At first there was no answer. Florence was about to put several vouchers – unsigned for – through the letter box when the door opened several degrees and a man said 'Yes?' in an aggressive manner.

'I am sorry to interrupt you,' said Florence. 'I –'

'Yes?' said the man loudly. 'What is it? If you're trying to sell me something, I don't want it. Nothing. Is that clear? I don't want to buy anything. I haven't any money.'

Florence had expected better manners. 'I'm not selling anything,' she said crossly. 'Now, produce a RIGHT-O product and . . .'

The door opened further. Florence Barge confronted the speaker. He was tall, slightly stooping, with luxuriant, prematurely grey hair and a highly coloured complexion. His bones protruded aristocratically from his wrists. His hands were long and, Florence noticed, shook slightly. The man licked his lips, as if his mouth was dry. His eyes, when he stared at her, were startlingly blue.

'RIGHT-O?' the man said, looking bewildered. 'What kind of a bloody stupid name is that?'

'Everyone knows what they are,' said Florence. 'Don't tell me you've never heard of them.'

'Why are you wearing that silly dress?'

'For fun,' said Florence in irritation. 'I am advertising my products.'

'It looks ridiculous.'

'What a charming compliment.'

'Laughable.'

'Your opinion is of no interest to me,' said Florence, furiously picking up her voucher bag, 'Goodbye.'

'Don't go,' said the man. 'Please . . .' He regarded her with an expression of entreaty.

Florence put her bag down again. 'Do you have any products?' she said coldly.

There was a short pause. 'Products?' the man stared at her helplessly. 'I don't know what there is. I don't – ' He raised a trembling hand to his head and pushed back a section of hair that had fallen over his eyes.

Florence moved impatiently on the step.

'You can have a look,' he said hastily. 'God knows what there is in the kitchen. Come in and look for these strange products. I suppose you know what they look like?'

'Red, with yellow lettering,' said Florence who was not inclined to move from the safety of the doorstep.

'Dear God,' said the man. 'The kitchen's down there. Why don't you see if you can find some? Please?'

Florence looked into the hall and hesitated. She had hundreds of vouchers still to give away. Reluctantly she stepped inside.

'Straight ahead,' said the man, 'and down the stairs.' Uncertainly she led the way. He shut the door with difficulty and followed her.

'That stuff looks like plastic,' he said.

'What stuff?'

'Your dress. It looks like plastic.'

'It's not my idea to look like this,' said Florence. 'It's a uniform. It's made of Crimplene. You can wash it and it's dry in an hour.'

'What's the good of that?'

'I've no idea,' said Florence.

The man laughed. 'Here's the kitchen.'

There was a strong smell of fat in the kitchen which was surprisingly large and comfortably arranged, with a central scrubbed oak table and an extensive arrangement of expensive cupboards, built-in appliances and an Aga. A quantity of plates, all of them used, were arranged over every available surface. All seemed to contain the remnants of the same meal, which appeared to be bacon and egg.

'What time is it?'

'Nearly ten-thirty.'

'Christ.'

'Would you like me to look in the larder?'

In reply the man waved his arm vaguely in a gesture of approval. 'You'll have to look around in the cupboards. I've no idea what . . .' He became abruptly silent and sat down rather suddenly on the pine bench that ran the length of the table.

Florence opened one of the leaded glass cupboards. Inside were many tins of tomato soup. Unfortunately the tins were not of the necessary RIGHT-O brand. Another cupboard yielded exactly the same cargo.

She opened some more cupboards. These were empty, apart from an opened packet of cocktail biscuits and a box of Brillo pads. 'You don't seem to have any RIGHT-O products at all.'

She saw the man was not listening, but staring at the table.

'Do you want a drink?' he said suddenly.

'A drink?'

'Yes.'

'It's much too early.'

The man got unsteadily to his feet. He opened one of the unexamined cupboards which, Florence saw, contained a great many bottles of gin. With exquisite care and deliberation he fetched a cut glass tumbler from another unexplored cupboard and filled it with ice cubes, then applied a generous portion of gin to the glass which he filled up with fresh orange juice. He carried it carefully in two hands back to the table and sat down before it. After a moment's contemplation he emptied a third of its contents.

'What did you say your name was?' he said, squinting at her through the facets of the glass.

'Florence.'

'What are you doing here?' said the man, obviously puzzled.

'I'll just let myself out, shall I? Obviously you're busy.'

'Have a drink,' said the man. 'My name's Tarquin de Vere Colefax-Jones.' Florence smiled uncertainly.

'Actually it's Gude,' the man said. 'Jerry Gude. What did you say your name was?'

'Florence.'

'Have a drink, Florence.'

Gude finished his gin and orange. Rather more steadily he got up from the bench and carefully refilled his glass. Then he filled another crystal glass and handed it to Florence.

'Why are you sitting here in the kitchen,' said Gude, 'dressed in that extraordinary costume? Have I met you before? Did I invite you round for coffee? Did I – by any chance – fuck you last night?'

Appalled, Florence blushed in confusion.

'Where have you come from?' Gude said, looking puzzled. 'Tell me, er – '

'Florence.'

'Florence, where have you come from?'

'Shepherd's Bush,' said Florence Barge still blushing. 'I must go.' She made a rush for the door.

Gude, who had been staring hard at her, took a deep breath and said, 'Please don't go. Please don't abandon me to my own tedious company again.'

Florence Barge held her bag of vouchers defensively before her.

'Come back,' said Gude. 'You remind me of a shy, startled fawn.' He smiled at her in a sentimental manner.

Florence giggled. 'You can have these,' she said, opening her bag and taking out a handful of coupons.

'What are those?' said Gude.

'Your vouchers. You don't really qualify for any.'

'Oh, please,' said Gude. 'Please give me a voucher. Can't you see I deserve one?'

'All right. You have to sign here to say you've received it.'

'I can't, without my glasses.'

'Well – '

'You sign it for me.' Gude sat back in his chair and finished his drink.

'I'm not used to visitors,' he said. 'Not at this time in the morning. What time is it, actually?'

'Nearly eleven.'

'Would you like some bacon and egg?'

'No.'

'I cook it bloody well,' said Gude. 'Particularly the fried bread. I don't know – I can't remember whether I cooked it this morning or not.' He looked at the cooker which housed a collection of used pans. 'What do you think, Florence? Have I had breakfast?'

'It's hard to tell.'

'Yes.' Jerry Gude got up and walked down the kitchen. He was wearing jeans which hung stiffly on his long thin legs and a pair of blue espadrilles. 'Well, what's going on in the world?' he said. 'Have I missed anything of importance this morning? Anyone dropped a bomb? Anyone assassinated the Prime Minister? Anyone sent me a cheque?' He took out a pair of spectacles and with difficulty put them across his nose.

'Where's the paper?' he said. 'You know, you haven't got bad legs, Florence. Are you sure you wouldn't like me to make some breakfast?'

'Quite sure.'

'Well,' said Gude heavily, and sat down again. 'Sometimes I write to the papers, Florence,' he said. 'I write long letters which they always print. It amuses me. I can't remember if I wrote any this week.'

He picked up the *Times* off the floor and turned to the Letters page. 'No, nothing from me today.' Gude laughed in a sudden, explosive way. Then he leaned forward suddenly and took Florence's face in his hand.

'Have you come to save me from myself?' he said, in a low voice.

Florence, her face captured, stared into his azure eyes. Gude continued. 'Have you come to pick up the pieces of my life? You can, if you want. They are lying in broken shards at your feet. Or you can tread on them. Think of the power I am assigning you. My whole destiny is in the palm of your hand.'

Jerry Gude released her face and brushed the back of his hand softly across her cheek.

Florence opened her eyes wide.

'Are you a romantic?' said Jerry Gude.

'I don't know.'

'Yes, you do. Are you a romantic? Do you believe in the possibility of falling in love with a perfect stranger? Or are you a sensible girl who has a boyfriend, and a job, and buys her own round of drinks?'

Florence had a boyfriend, though no job, and never went into pubs. She believed she was fervently romantic. 'I'm sensible,' she said.

'What's his name?' said Gude, leaning forward and lifting strands of her hair which he then gently dropped over her face.

'Who?'

'Your boyfriend.'

'Well, he's – '

'You see him twice a week and stay at his place every Saturday night? It's what they call a stable relationship. Am I right?'

Annoyed by his accurate analysis of the relationship, Florence stared at Gude. 'I don't see why I should tell you.'

'Is he a banker?'

'No, he's a writer. He edits a magazine. He's terribly clever.'

'Are you clever, too?'

'No,' said Florence.

'I don't like clever women,' said Gude. 'I did once, but that was in the days when I was braver. They've left me battle-scarred and unfit for active service. You don't need to be too clever. I expect you're just being modest. How long have you been walking around in this ridiculous costume? Do you do it every day?'

'It's just a temporary job,' said Florence. 'I'm unemployed.'

'No job?'

'No. I'm just doing this to earn some money.'

'I like a girl to be financially independent,' said Gude. 'Did you say you bought your own drinks?'

'Well – '

'I suppose your boyfriend always buys them. Are you engaged?'

'It's none of your business.'

'But you're going to marry him?'

'I'm not going to marry anyone,' said Florence with decision.

'That's bloody right,' said Gude. 'Marriage is a greatly overrated activity, Florence. I did it far too often. I advise you against it.'

'Did I ask for your advice?'

'It's bloody expensive, too,' said Gude grimly. 'At least that's my experience of it. You'd be all right, though. You could marry your bloody banker, fuck off somewhere later, and get paid for the rest of your life. Sounds marvellous, doesn't it?'

He drained his glass.

'I have to go,' said Florence.

'I want to talk to you,' said Gude. 'How much do you get on the dole these days?'

'I've no idea,' said Florence loftily. 'I've never claimed it.'

'How do you pay the mortgage?'

'I haven't got one.'

'Don't tell me mummy and daddy bought you a nice little flat in town?'

'Yes they did – you're just sneering because you're envious.'

'Private means,' said Gude gloomily. 'Christ, I'm a pauper compared to you. So much for a life of letters.'

Florence wished she had not rung Jerry Gude's doorbell. 'I'm going now. I have to get on with my job.'

Gude sat in his chair and lit a cigar. 'You think I'm a shit but you'd really like to go to bed with me.'

'You'd be lucky,' said Florence. 'What a frightful person you are. I'm not listening to any more of this.'

She stood up. So did Gude who walked unsteadily over to the oven, where a small electronic dial registered the time in glowing green digits. He peered for some time at the shining figures.

'Christ,' he said. 'They're open. I'm late.'

Florence gathered up her bag. 'Go and powder your nose or something,' said Gude, 'and let yourself out. I'm bloody late.' He put on a blazer which hung on the back of the kitchen door. 'Just slam the door behind you when you go. Alternatively you can stay here if you want and I'll give you a fuck when I come back.' He went down the hall towards the door. Florence seized her bag of vouchers. The front door slammed and all was silent.

She stood for a few minutes in the empty kitchen. Then she wondered if Gude had been telling the truth. Perhaps the house was not empty. Perhaps someone even more startling and unpleasant might suddenly come into the kitchen. Hurriedly she left Gude's house and, in the warm rain outside, stopped a taxi. Inside, she regained her determination to finish the job and she bravely rode to Kilburn High Road. She spent the next four hours visiting the uniform terraces of Brondesbury and West Hampstead, and after a long afternoon, found to her surprise that she still had over half her bag of vouchers left.

The sky was darkening when Florence returned to the mansion flat just off Baker Street which her family had thoughtfully provided for her out of the ample Barge resources. It was convenient and serviceable, housed in a large block and maintained by the services of a porter. Florence shared the flat with her best friend from boarding school, Marigold Few. The kitchen was empty when she looked round the door. The room was dark, facing out into a tiled courtyard and illuminated only by a north-facing window.

In a warmer country, the courtyard would have been filled with ornamental plants, perhaps an orange tree or a vine climbing up whitewashed walls to the distant sky. As it was, however, the enclosure was walled with white ceramic tiles, chipped and cracked, resembling the decoration of a gentlemen's lavatory. Those washing dishes at the sink looked out at the opaque net curtains of the opposite flat, behind which occasional shapes moved as its occupants performed their kitchen duties. More interesting was the flat one storey below, seen dimly through the gloom of the courtyard, whose windows were screened by curtains more flimsy than most. This flat was occupied by a chiropodist and the burden of washing-up was often enlivened by the spectacle of toenails being clipped, callouses filed away and corns dug out of their horny beds.

Today there was no one reclining on the leather couch. Florence carefully put down her bag of vouchers and looked round the kitchen in search of something edible. In the bread bin she found nothing except a small, blackened crust on which a blue, powdery fungus bloomed. She opened the door of the refrigerator and found it empty too, except for a small bag of wilted, yellowing lettuce and a bottle of milk, already separating into a pale, yellow liquid at the top and a darker, lower sediment. Marigold, neglectful of the household rota, had not done the shopping.

Florence put the bag of vouchers on the kitchen table and took out the forms. She had collected only twenty names and disposed of over sixty vouchers. Clearly there was a discrepancy. Staring at the empty forms, Florence decided to improve her numbers by inventing the names of grateful householders. She wrote 'John Smith' in a backward sloping hand. 'D. H. Evans' sloped forward. 'Peter Jones' was written in block capitals. Inspiration began to fail her. She wrote her own name in an indecipherable scrawl. She wrote the names of her parents, boyfriend and flat-mate. She wrote as many of her school contemporaries as she could remember. Glancing through the forms completed by genuine voucher holders, she saw the name 'Norman Crisp' printed clearly in red ink. She looked at it with curiosity. The coincidence was remarkable. Had she, by chance, given a voucher to one of Mrs Crisp's own relatives?

· CHAPTER · II ·

'The thing is,' said Maurice Earish, 'the thing is, I don't see why anyone should want to do a programme about Jerry Gude. I'm amazed there's so much interest in him.' His voice rose high and peevish above the muted conversations in the pub.

Lucinda Harpie-Kerr breathed out a long gust of smoke which hung over Earish's head for a moment then slowly sank in a grey cloud around his eyes, causing them to brim with momentary tears. 'Cheer up, lovey,' she said, grinding her cigarette into the overflowing ashtray. 'You're looking a bit downtrodden. It can't be as bad as all that.'

Earish ignored her. 'I mean, I could understand it if he was a famous person, like a film-star or one of those actors in a soap opera, but Gude hasn't done anything for years. Why should anyone want to know about him?'

Lucinda Harpie-Kerr took out her compact and studied her face in the mirror with close attention. She passed her tongue over her front teeth and made a smacking noise with her lips.

'Of course, you're right, Maurice,' said Vernon Corner, emptying his glass. 'But that's because we know him. We see him in here, day in day out, sometimes a little more than human, and sometimes a little less, so – it stands to reason – we think of him as just an ordinary bloke. For us, he has no aura of mystery. But for the rest of the world – ' Corner spread his arms wide, indicating the great mass of humanity outside the walls of the Dog and Biscuit– 'for the great British public out there, he is an enigma.'

'I shouldn't think many of the great British public have ever heard of him these days,' said Earish. 'Try stopping a few in the street out there and saying "Who is Jerry Gude?" No one would have any idea who you were talking about.'

'That's not the point, Maurice,' said Corner. 'Same again, mate? Same again, Luce?'

'Yes, thanks.'

'Bless you, Vernon.'

Corner went over to the bar where a tall, dark-haired man behind the counter was waving his arms in the air and shouting wildly into a telephone.

'You know,' said Lucinda Harpie-Kerr, 'it's been proved that something like ninety per cent of the British public don't know the name of the Prime Minister. So where does that leave poor Jerry?' She laughed raspingly.

'Two large whiskies, please, and a gin and French.'

'I want my usual table,' the tall man was shouting. 'Ten-thirty, usual time.'

'After all, he hasn't written anything for years, has he? Apart from those letters to the *Times*, which I found pathetic rather than amusing, you know. Is he really interesting at all?'

'When you have a moment, Galen.'

'I don't care if you are fucking full up. I've spent a thousand pounds on you this year, which is a complete bloody rip-off, considering the fucking awful food you serve.'

'Thank you, barman!'

The man whirled round from the phone with sudden speed. 'Just fucking shut up and wait your turn,' he shouted at Corner. He turned back to the telephone. 'Fetch the manager. Who are you? I'm not speaking to you a fucking minute longer.'

'I suppose it will be one of those minority interest programmes, you know, Maurice. He's going to be on Channel Six, isn't he? Not Terry Wogan.'

'Yes, but the whole programme is about him, isn't it?'

'Well, who's going to watch it, Maurice?'

'People do watch these programmes. Influential people.'

'Two whiskies, if you please.'

'Right, you can cancel my booking and that's the end of your restaurant, as far as I'm concerned. I happen to be in the trade myself, so I know what I'm talking about. From now on you're finished. And what's more, I'm going to write to that fucking Egon Ronay and tell him not to include you any more.'

'Is this a pub or a cabaret?'

'Right, fuck off then,' shouted Galen Bone slamming down the phone. He spun on his heels. 'And you can fuck off, too, standing there shouting for drink when I'm trying to have a conversation.'

Corner banged on the counter. 'I want some service around here.'

Galen Bone took three glasses from under the counter and reached up behind the bar for the bottle of whisky. Neglecting to measure the contents he rapidly poured a random amount into three glasses. 'Five pounds fifty,' he shouted.

'I wanted two whiskies and one gin and French.'

'You'll have to have what you've fucking got.'

'What about ice?'

'There's the bucket,' said Bone leaning forward over the bar. 'You can fucking well put your hand in and help yourself.'

'What's fame, anyway. You're probably more famous than Jerry Gude.'

'Don't be ridiculous.'

'Well, lovey, people see your name in the papers.'

'Occasionally,' said Earish. 'I find it very difficult to get regular work these days.'

'Three whiskies,' said Corner, shuffling forward with a handful of glasses. He put them down clumsily on the table and some of the whisky spilled over.

'Cheers, boys,' said Lucinda.

'I wanted a gin and French, actually, Vernon,' said Earish.

'That's all I could get. Galen's having a funny turn. Won't it do?'

'I don't actually like whisky very much.'

'Stop complaining, darling.'

'Cheers.'

'Drink up.'

'Cheers.'

'I was just telling Maurice to cheer up a bit,' said Lucinda. 'I was saying he looks a bit glum.'

'Unlike yourself, dear lady,' said Corner.

Lucinda Harpie-Kerr sparkled with animation. Her crimson-rouged cheeks took on a darker flush of red and her scarlet nails flashed and glittered in the light of the dull wall lamps. 'Oh, I've seen better days, Vernon,' she said, pushing a strand of her surprisingly yellow hair back over her face. It was true that she had.

'Never lovelier, dear lady,' said Corner gallantly. 'Never lovelier.'

She laughed vivaciously.

'What are you writing at the moment?' said Earish, morosely.

'Confessions of a sex-change vicar,' she said. 'It's quite a long time since I did one of those.'

'Is it a good story?' said Corner with professional interest. He was chief staff writer for *Prankster*, the most successful and profitable pornographic magazine in Morton Minitz's publishing empire. Corner composed his features in an office near the Dog and Biscuit.

'Not really. Peaceful country town. Everyone very respectable. Of course, I'm trying to make it a bit more meaty. This poor old bloke just likes wearing women's clothes. Someone claimed they saw him wearing a dress under his surplice in the pulpit. There's the outraged wife's story, of course. Unfortunately she's in her fifties. We'll say forties, I think. And lots and lots of shocked and disgusted parishioners.' Lucinda Harpie-Kerr laughed loudly.

'God, how depressing,' said Earish.

'Does he like any particular style of clothes?'

'Very keen on pleated skirts. Don't ask me why.'

'What has it all come to?'

'It's just a job, lovey. Don't get too upset about it.'

Earish looked at his watch. It was nearly six-thirty.

'I've got to write an article tonight,' he said, unhappily. 'I think I'd better go and make a start.'

'Just the one?' said Corner.

'No, no, my round,' said Lucinda Harpie-Kerr reaching for her handbag. 'Same again, boys?'

'Could I have a gin and French instead of whisky?' said Earish, pushing his untouched drink across the table.

'Don't you want it?'

'No. I said I don't like whisky.'

'Well, Lucinda and I will share it then.'

'It's the introduction that I find the hardest bit,' said Earish. 'I spend hours trying to get the introduction right.'

Lucinda Harpie-Kerr stood up. 'Just start straight off,' she said. 'That's what I always do. First thoughts are always best. You can't improve upon what first springs into your mind.'

'She's right,' said Corner.

'Well, I can't write quite like that,' said Earish loftily. 'After all – when you're trying to set out rather complicated arguments . . .'

'What's your article about?'

'The disintegration of the idea of fidelity in marriage.'

'Who's it for?'

'The *Commentator*.'

'I wouldn't waste much time on that, mate,' said Corner. 'Not many people will read it.'

'Nevertheless, it's an important weekly. Small circulation, yes, but highly influential.'

'Do they pay well?' said Lucinda Harpie-Kerr, shouting from the bar.

'Well, no, not particularly. No. Not at all well. Very little, actually.'

'The thing is,' said Corner, 'I find I have no ideas at all if I start writing first thing in the morning. But if I have a few whiskies, and make a start after lunch, all sorts of things come springing into my head.'

Earish listened with a miserable expression.

'Do they? Do they really?'

'Straight up. No problem.'

'What sort of things?'

'Ideas, inspiration.'

'Oh.'

'Yes. Now, I'd got into a very difficult patch with 'Confessions of a Side-Saddle'. No ideas. Nothing at all. Whenever I sat down in front of the typewriter, yours truly just spent hours and hours staring at a blank sheet of paper.'

'Yes,' said Earish. 'That terrible sensation of panic, that terrifying blankness of the mind . . .'

'Then, after a few drinks, bingo! Things just seemed to flow. The side-saddle, you see, suddenly had all kinds of luscious, perfect bottoms sitting on top of it. Whisky loosens the mind, gets the brain cells working. Do you no harm at all, my son.'

Lucinda Harpie-Kerr came back with the drinks. 'Here we are gentlemen,' she said. 'Here's to the sexy vicar.'

'Cheers.'

'Cheers.'

'Of course, once I get started, I'm all right,' said Earish. 'It's just the first paragraph I find so hard. By the way, did you hear that Hilary and Rupert are splitting up?'

'I don't believe it,' said Lucinda.

'Yes, apparently the marriage has been on the rocks for some time.'

'She'll get the house, naturally.'

'And a great deal more,' said Earish.

'It would have been cheaper to stay married.'

'Well, I wouldn't know anything about that,' said Earish, staring gloomily into his gin and French.

'Are you going to see Brayne tonight?'

Marigold Few was sitting at the kitchen table writing with concentration in a school exercise book.

'Well, yes. It's Tuesday,' said Florence Barge.

Marigold looked up from the notebook. 'Do you really like Brayne?' she said in a disbelieving voice. 'Or are you just stuck with him?'

Florence looked at her with irritation. 'Of course I like him.

What's wrong with him? Lots of people like Alexander. He's already quite famous.'

Marigold raised her eyebrows and said nothing.

'Anyway he's been sweet to me,' Florence went on defensively. 'He's introduced me to lots of interesting people.'

'All exactly like him.'

'He's very clever,' Florence said seriously. 'I can't understand half of what he says. And yet, he can be very funny too. Sometimes.'

'I have yet to see his lighter side,' said Marigold. She regarded Florence critically.

'Well, you don't see him in his private moments. He's good fun.'

Marigold yawned. 'He's a grey man,' she said. 'And a frightful prig. I think you must be mad.'

Florence shouted crossly at her, 'You introduced us, after all.'

'I can't be blamed for the consequences. Anyway, I only work for his horrible magazine for the money. I'm in a dreadful rut there.'

'How is the novel going?' said Florence, anxious to change the subject.

'I'm stuck at chapter three,' said Marigold. 'I seem to have too many characters all over the place and I can't think of what to do with them.'

'Perhaps Alexander would help.'

'He's not interested in that sort of book, Florence. He only reads books that no one buys. This is going to be a best-seller. It's going to have lots of sex in it. That wouldn't appeal to Alexander at all.'

'At least that's one good thing about him.'

'What?'

'Well, he's very . . . considerate.'

'You mean he doesn't – '

'He doesn't behave like an animal,' said Florence hastily. 'You know how horrible some men can be like that.'

'I wouldn't know,' said Marigold grimly. 'Men seem reluctant to show me their animal tendencies.'

'For example,' said Florence, 'I met a man yesterday who said the most horrible things to me and actually started stroking my hair.'

Marigold looked interested. 'Who was he?'

'I can't remember his name. I gave him some vouchers.'

'How old?'

'Oh, really old. Over forty.'

'Attractive?'

'No – except in a worn-out sort of way.'

'Tell me more,' said Marigold. 'This sounds excellent material for the novel.'

'I must go and pack Alexander's basket,' said Florence retreating hurriedly out of the kitchen.

Every Tuesday she made her regular visit to Brayne's house in Clapham, travelling nervously on the Underground bearing a straw basket brimming with delicacies bought specially to tempt Brayne's robust appetite. Their evenings were usually quiet. Occasionally some of Brayne's intellectual friends came round to share their expensive supper. On such evenings, they would shout round the dinner table, banging their spoons and wine glasses, heated and voluble. Florence, a mere spectator at these displays, would often find her mind wandering. Brayne and his friends paid her no attention at all.

More often they ate alone. On such evenings, Brayne would talk for hours to Florence about his forthcoming book – a collection of essays awaited with high excitement by his contemporaries and colleagues. If Brayne was too tired to talk, they would listen instead to music, or watch a television programme on his small black and white set.

Tonight Brayne and Florence were not expecting company. As Jerry Gude's friends ordered another round of drinks, Florence Barge rang the doorbell of Brayne's terraced house, situated in a leafy street recently made fashionable by the arrival of young, professional people like Brayne himself. She did not have her own front-door key.

'My dear Florence,' said Brayne, appearing in the hall. 'Here you stand bringing good things to cheer the faint-hearted.'

'Hello, Alexander. What on earth are you listening to?'

The small Victorian house resounded with loud, straining sounds of lush chords and opulent orchestration. Brayne lifted his head and stood silently for a moment. He raised his right hand. 'Just listen, Florence. Just listen.'

They stood in the hall, listening. Florence tried to take her coat off.

'Be still,' said Brayne. 'Still and silent.'

Irritably Florence stood in her coat, holding the heavy basket.

'Now,' said Brayne. 'Isn't that the most ravishing sound you have ever heard?'

'No. I think it's ghastly. Who is it by?'

He smiled distantly. 'Always trying to categorise things. What does it matter who wrote it, if the music is beautiful?'

'Well, who did write it, Alexander?'

'Let us continue your education, Florence. Who do you think wrote it? Who does it sound like? Think. Listen. Who could it be?'

Florence walked past him into the kitchen. 'I'm going to put this basket down,' she called back. 'It's terribly heavy. Wagner or something? What time would you like to eat?'

'Not bad,' said Brayne, as if marking an examination paper. 'Not bad, but not quite right. Stay in that century – but further forward.'

'No idea. He's the only one I know.'

'Give up already?'

'Yes.'

Brayne sighed. 'Florence, it's Schoenberg the early period, of course. You've heard of him, haven't you? *Verklärte Nacht*. Isn't it the most marvellous, transcendent thing you've ever heard?'

Florence made a face.

Brayne came into the kitchen and put his arm round her waist. 'What have you brought to eat tonight? Yum, yum, let me look in the basket.'

'There's quails eggs, scallops, duck breast – '

'That sounds appallingly trendy,' said Brayne. 'Good solid stodge is what I like. What about pudding? Is there a pudding?'

'Spotted dick. I had to buy it from Marks & Spencer. There wasn't time to make one.'

'Dear girl, I have no quarrel with Marks & Spencer. This looks delicious.' Brayne removed his hands from Florence's hips. 'I'll open a bottle of Fleurie, I think. Would you like that?'

'Delicious. Is it red or white?'

Brayne laughed, as if the question was not worth answering. 'Now come and sit by the fire and tell me all about your day.'

'Well, Mrs Crisp gave me – '

'A drop of sherry?'

'Yes, please, I – '

'I must tell you my latest triumph,' said Brayne in excitement. 'Evelyn Fragment is lunching at the *Commentator* next week. He's accepted our invitation. This is the first member of the cabinet we've persuaded to come. It's a real bonus for the magazine.'

'Who is Fragment?'

'My dear girl, he's a member of Parliament,' said Brayne. 'He is junior minister at the Home Office. He's one of the coming men. A very keen intellect and tremendously ambitious.'

'I've never heard of him.'

'You amaze me,' said Brayne. 'What a funny creature you are.' Brayne sat back in his chair and drank his sherry. The music shimmered and moaned in the distance. After some time he said, 'And how goes the job-hunting?'

'No luck, so far,' said Florence.

'Mmm?' said Brayne vaguely.

'I thought I might go into business,' said Florence decisively. 'I think I'd rather like to run my own company. One could dress up in a smart suit and have business lunches and sit behind a desk. I think I'd enjoy being rich and powerful.'

Brayne regarded her with benign amusement. 'And tell me, how would one O-level in art – '

'And English,' Florence interrupted.

'And English,' Brayne said, 'equip you for the life of big business?'

'Not in the least,' said Florence. 'But qualifications on paper aren't everything.'

'No.'

'I had to go round a housing estate yesterday.'

'Poor thing. Was it ghastly?'

'Quite. I met an old man in a vest.'

'Anyone else?'

'Well, there was another man who . . .' She hesitated at the thought of mentioning Jerry Gude.

'Florence,' said Brayne lifting his head slightly. 'I think those scallops will be absolutely done by now. You might just take a look at them . . .'

'The glasses seem to be empty.'

'Well, I really must make a move.'

Earish stared at the row of empty glasses on the table in front of him. Lucinda Harpie-Kerr had filled one ashtray with cigarette ends, and was busily stubbing out a cigarette into an adjacent ashtray stuffed with two empty crisp packets.

'Just another for the road?' said Corner.

Earish said, 'I believe it's my round.'

'Is it?'

'Well, I think it's my turn – '

'I'm drinking whisky,' said Lucinda loudly. 'Let's have a toast to my dear old TV vicar.'

'God bless you, Rev,' said Corner.

'There is a depressing vulgarity about the English addiction to smut,' said Earish, rising suddenly to his feet. 'It was precisely this prurience I was trying to write about in my book, *The New Hedonists*. This compulsion to gaze into the sewer.'

'Steady.'

'He's up. He's all right.'

Earish set off unsteadily for the bar.

'Never eat at fucking Oberon's,' said Galen Bone coming from behind the bar and sitting heavily beside them. 'It's diabolical. It's a rip-off for what they charge.'

'Never tried it, Galen. Beyond my pocket, old chap.'

'I just tried to book a table and they say they're full up. I've spent thousands in that place and they don't know my bloody name. It's appalling, setting that standard in a place like that,' Bone said seriously. 'And they're in that *Good Food Guide*, too. It's a disgrace.'

'Who have you been to Oberon's with, Galen?' said Lucinda, leaning forward across the table and stabbing Bone's shoulder with her finger. 'Someone we don't know about?'

'With a companion,' said Bone.

Lucinda and Corner sniggered at each other.

'I am a single man,' said Bone quietly. 'At least, since my divorce. I am completely free to take out anyone I choose.'

'Of course you are.'

'Is it anyone we know?'

'She has not made your acquaintance,' said Bone with dignity. 'And I have no intention of bringing her in here.'

'Oh do.'

'We want to see her. Is she a lady?'

'She's a fucking old slag,' said Bone suddenly, shouting at the top of his voice. 'I took her to Oberon's last week and she ordered the most expensive thing on the menu.'

'What do you mean?'

'They gave her the menu without prices. Naturally. That's quite in order in a place like that. "Choose whatever you like, my dear," I said to her. "Whatever you desire shall be yours." Of course, I didn't expect her to pick the fucking lobster. It's crude, isn't it, behaving like that. She should have had a steak – that's all she knows about, anyway. But no. "I'll have the lobster," she says. "I've never had it before." It was quite humiliating. An embarrassment for me because I am known quite well in first-class restaurants like that. Of course, when they brought the fucking thing, she hadn't a clue how to eat it. I can tell you I got a lot of pleasure watching her fiddling around with it on her plate, trying to use her knife and fork.'

'You're appalling. Why didn't you show her the right way?'

'Why fucking should I? She chose it. I thought, she can fucking well sit there and eat it. She didn't even like it. She left most of it.'

'What's her name, Galen?'

'I do not wish to disclose her identity,' said Bone loftily. Earish came back with the drinks.

'You still here?' said Bone.

Earish sat down heavily. 'It was a book that tried to analyse our elevation of self-gratification into an end worth pursuing for itself. It sold nothing at all. A mere hundred copies or so. That is the story of my life.'

Corner sighed. 'It wasn't your fault, Maurice, old mate,' he said. 'They didn't sell that book. They didn't work for you. Those publishers – they're all bastards, excepting old Minitz of course. They could have turned it into a best-seller if they'd pulled their fingers out and got off their arses.'

Lucinda put her arm round him. 'Don't brood on it, lovey. It was a fabulous book. We all loved it.'

'No one bought it.'

'The world was not ready for it,' said Corner. 'We can all think of books like that – disregarded at the time, but which history has judged differently.'

'It was a bloody boring book,' said Bone loudly. 'That's why no one bought it. A waste of ten quid, if you ask me. Who wants to read about him, anyway, airing his views on brothels and underwear?'

'You're a hard man,' said Lucinda Harpie-Kerr.

'You're a harder woman. You're the hardest woman in the world.'

'I may look hard, but under this brash exterior, there is a sensitive and shrinking heart of gold.'

'Look, I've got to go and get this piece done,' said Earish, trying to rest his head on his hand.

'If you sit here any longer you're going to be too pissed to write a word,' said Bone. 'Your article will be late and they'll give you the sack. Serve you right, too.'

Earish sank lower in his chair.

'Don't shout at him,' said Lucinda.

'Every word I say is true.'

'If I could just think of the intro, I feel I'd be all right. I could just polish it off then in a matter of minutes.'

'Of course you could.'

'It's just so hard to get the thing started. It's just the first paragraph I can't quite manage . . .'

'More Fleurie?' said Brayne, refilling his own glass.

'Lovely.'

'Are you sure you want some?' he said, eyeing the amount remaining in the bottle.

'Quite sure,' said Florence, emptying her glass quickly.

'You shouldn't drink too much, you know.' He poured her half a glass. Then he refilled his own glass to the top. 'Would you like to go and see *The Slag* next week, Florence?' he said. 'I intend to write a column about it for the *Commentator*.'

She looked at him blankly.

'It's a play,' said Brayne with exaggerated patience. 'The King's Court are putting on a revival. It's twenty-five years since they first staged it. Should be well worth a look.'

'Who's it by?'

Brayne sighed in humorous exasperation. 'Jerry Gude, dear girl. Never heard of him?'

'Never.' Florence frowned. The name seemed strangely familiar.

'You're such a child,' said Brayne. 'One forgets how young you are.'

'I squandered my time at school,' said Florence. 'That's why I don't know anything now.'

'It matters not,' said Brayne looking at his empty plate. 'I don't insist on brains and beauty. In fact, you don't need to know very much, Florence. You might start to argue with me. And I shouldn't like that.' Brayne laughed, amused by his joke.

'I wonder if I might be an actress,' said Florence thoughtfully. 'It's rather an appealing idea. I think I'd like standing there in the middle of a stage, holding an audience spellbound. Do you think I'd be any good?'

Brayne laughed indulgently.

'Have you trodden the boards before?'

'In the school play. I forgot my lines.'

'What part did you play?'

'It was something by Shakespeare. Can't remember now.'

'I'm sure you were charming,' said Brayne. 'I wonder, is there by chance any more of that duck . . .?'

'Do you think I'll be on the television?' Galen Bone slapped his hands down on the table, excited by the thought.

'I should think so. Not in a starring role, of course.'

'You're not talking about Gude again, are you?' Earish swayed miserably over his glass.

'They'll have to interview everyone who's known him,' said Lucinda. 'Galen knows him very well. Almost as well as I know him.'

'The point is this,' said Bone, leaning forward. 'He could have been a millionaire.'

Lucinda laughed raspingly.

'No, no, hear me straight,' said Bone. 'All that money he's earned – he could have made a fortune. Instead – he's completely skint.'

'He didn't earn all that much,' said Lucinda.

'He did when he was famous. There was that book that everyone read,' said Bone. 'And there was that play he wrote.'

'They're reviving it,' said Lucinda. 'As a sort of twenty-five-year anniversary present.'

'He has not been particularly active for some time, though,' said Corner, 'unlike the rest of us, toiling away to earn our daily crust.'

'If he'd saved all his money, instead of throwing it around like a fucking madman,' said Bone, 'he'd be richer than all of us put together.'

'I'm amazed about Hilary and Rupert,' said Earish meditatively. 'So many of my friends have got divorced recently. In fact, practically everyone I know is divorced. People don't bother to stay married much these days, do they?'

'He's thinking about his article,' said Corner. Bone's face grew dark and brooding as he reflected upon the acrimonious ending of his own marriage.

'Don't ask me,' said Lucinda. 'I've had a lot of practice at matrimony. I don't think men are up to much these days.'

'Will you be in Jerry's programme?' said Corner.

'I suppose they'll want to interview me, as his most recent wife. I could write a column about it.'

'We all know him better than he knows himself,' said Bone. 'We could all be fucking stars. We could all go on chat shows and talk about him.'

'How long is it since you parted company?' said Corner.

'I became a free woman two years ago. No hard feelings. No big deal.'

'Do you think he'll write anything else?' said Corner. 'Myself, I reckon he's just about past it.'

'He thinks he's fucking burned out,' shouted Bone. 'He's lost confidence in himself. He could be a fucking genius if he did any work.'

'He never did anything at all,' said Lucinda. 'That was the trouble.' She laughed in a vulgar way, and nudged Corner.

'Mark my words,' said Bone darkly. 'When he goes we'll discover how wrong we've been. I bet you there's millions there.'

'Is Maurice all right?' said Lucinda suddenly. 'He's gone quiet.' She turned to examine him. Earish's head seemed to have sunk into his shoulders. His eyes were half-closed.

'OK, my old mate, take it easy,' said Corner. 'Time to go home.'

'He's having a bad week,' said Lucinda.

'Aren't we all, dear lady. Aren't we all.'

In a surreptitious gesture, which Florence noticed, Brayne looked at his watch. 'Come and sit by the fire, dear girl,' he said. They each assumed a chair opposite each other, while Brayne lit a pipe. He yawned loudly.

'Are you working tonight?'

'Sadly, I must.'

'How is the book going?'

'Well, in parts. Its just a little too soon to say just how good it's going to be.'

Florence said, 'Why don't we go and have a drink somewhere?'

'A what?' said Brayne in astonishment.

'A drink. You know, in a pub.'

Brayne gaped at her. 'But Florence, you don't like pubs.'

'Well, I haven't been in that many. Only one with you, Alexander, which was horribly crowded. All those men were carrying drinks above their heads and spilling beer all over me.'

'All pubs are like that.'

'No they're not.'

'The ones I like are.'

'I'll buy the drinks,' said Florence, remembering Gude's preferences in women.

'Dear girl, I must get on with the book.'

Florence stood up abruptly. 'Don't let me delay you.'

Brayne sucked noisily at his pipe. 'See you next Saturday, then.'

'Landlord, some more drinks please. The night is still young.' Corner took out a roll of twenty-pound notes from his hip pocket.

'I'm supposed to be meeting a man in here,' said Lucinda Harpie-Kerr, 'but I've forgotten what his name is.'

'God,' said Earish, suddenly sitting up. 'What's the time?'

'Would you be interested,' Corner asked Bone, 'in stocking copies of the magazine behind the bar – you know, for interested customers.'

'Time. Time gentlemen please.'

'Is that man looking for you, dear lady?'

'I've never seen him before in my life.'

'Time. Fucking drink up.'

'Oh God, I feel . . .'

'Watch him, he's fallen over.'

'He's gone.'

'Steady on there.'

'Poor love. He's very depressed tonight.'

Florence put on her coat. She and Brayne stood together in the hall. She gathered up her empty basket. Brayne bumped clumsily against her and lunged towards her intending an embrace. Involuntarily Florence stepped back, knocking Brayne's spectacles from his nose. His lips came into contact with her ear.

'See you on Saturday, Flo.'

'Goodbye.' With relief Florence fled out into the darkness of the street. 'It's what they call a stable relationship.' The cruel words of Jerry Gude reverberated in her mind as she walked towards the Underground.

'He's banned. He's flat on the floor. We don't serve drunks in this pub.'

'He's never done it before, Galen.'

'He's never going to do it again.'

'He's upset about things.'

'About Jerry Gude.'

'Are you going to take him home?'

'I'll put him in a taxi, darling.'

'I wonder why Gude didn't come in tonight.'

'He'll be in tomorrow.'

'That's right.'

'Take his legs and I'll hold his head.'

· CHAPTER · III ·

Once every fortnight, the *Commentator* invited a selection of guests to its regular lunch. Those who were invited were invariably flattered, supposing that they had been chosen for their special qualities of sagacity and wit. This was far from true. Some lunchers were invited for their capacity to keep the conversation going, rehearsing familiar though entertaining anecdotes. Others were asked for their notorious indiscretion, encouraging an atmosphere of gossip which Brayne liked to foster. Still others were asked because they would invariably come at the last moment without taking offence. Most of the journalists invited fell into this last category.

The lunch was held in a third-floor room of the Georgian terraced house in which the *Commentator* was housed. Marigold Few was retained to provide sustaining food which she cooked in a small kitchen on the floor below in surroundings which were badly lit and poorly ventilated. Here she prepared the filling food which Brayne and his colleagues liked to eat for lunch – stews, pies, casseroles and puddings. Marigold did not enjoy her work and provided the food reluctantly; she longed to cook for a merchant bank in the City where they would provide better facilities and really appreciate sophisticated cuisine.

Guests who came expecting to admire the proportions and furnishings of the building were taken aback when they arrived. Inside, shabbiness prevailed. They first encountered an untidy reception area, which housed an old, overstuffed sofa, one desk and a telephone switchboard held together by pieces of black insulating tape. From there they were directed up two floors of winding, narrow stairs until they reached the dining room. At the first landing they encountered an overpowering smell of boiled cabbage which followed them with its green, gaseous odour to the top of the stairs. Here was a door whose yellow paint was cracked and peeling, from behind which came the muted sounds of conversation.

The contributors to the *Commentator* were standing at angles and talking to each other. They stood crammed together in front of the fireplace as most of the room was occupied by a large, rectangular table where places had been set for lunch. A passageway could, with difficulty, be negotiated round the room, but this could only be done by crawling over a large, inconveniently placed sofa which jutted out from one wall. In the opposite corner, a pile of wooden collapsible chairs were stacked, which threatened at any moment to overflow into the room. The mantelshelf, once marble, but now a shade of melancholy blue, was all that remained of the original fireplace. The grate and surround had been ripped out; and someone had replaced the cavity with a sheet of hardboard, tacked to the surround. Above the fireplace a picture of the Crying Boy gazed dolefully out over the room.

Throughout the whole of London it would have been hard to find a more inhospitable and unattractive room. But the young men who worked on the *Commentator* loved its ugliness, its gloom, its inconvenience. Their guests too, for the most part, were thrilled by the unpleasant nature of the room and spent some time commenting on its peculiarities. It was one of the talking points of a *Commentator* lunch.

The contributors, crowded up by the mantelpiece, talked to each other while they waited for their guests to arrive. They were mostly young, at least few of them were over forty, but an onlooker might have mistaken them for middle-aged men. While their contemporaries ranged the streets of Bloomsbury outside in vivid, box-shouldered jackets and tight, brightly coloured trousers, in shiny unstructured suits and expensive Italian shoes, Brayne and his friends wore second-hand clothing – the full-cut trousers and jackets of an earlier age which they hunted with diligence in fashionable shops in Chelsea. While the young men outside combed hair which whirled and rippled into peaks of meringue-like confection, Brayne and his friends were neatly brushed into short, smooth waves. While youth outside was thin and lean, Brayne and his friends were comfortably covered with flesh – their rounded bottoms protruding gently through the vents in their tweed jackets. They looked confidently out on the world which they addressed in loud voices.

A shaft of sunlight entered the room and illuminated the streaked windows and the dusty net curtains that hung from the windows in dipping loops. It shone on the grey carpet and the wine glasses laid on the table, indicating that some were smeared as though they had been hurriedly and imperfectly washed.

'My dear Bunsen,' said Brayne as the door opened and a tall young man came in wearing a second-hand Crombie and a large felt hat. 'Good to see you. How are you?'

'I have left my bicycle chained to the lamppost outside,' said Gerard Bunsen in a high-pitched voice. 'I hope it will be safe out there.'

Bunsen removed his Crombie and his hat and dropped them onto the plastic sofa. Brayne and he went over to the window, edging round the table with some difficulty. The bicycle was opposite the building, chained to its lamppost. They regarded it with concentration.

A young man dressed in black leggings and a black woollen cape walked past. Bunsen shuddered. 'I wanted to bring it inside,' he said, 'but that very rude young woman downstairs refused to let me.'

'Marigold, I'm afraid,' said Brayne.

'My dear, what a harridan,' said Bunsen with an exaggerated shudder.

Two more contributors arrived, pushing their way confidently through the stained door. One of them was wearing a bow tie and spats. The other, considerably older, had a creased, shabby appearance and wild bushy hair.

'Brayne, how do you do,' said the man in spats, joining the crowd by the mantelpiece.

'Ah, Jasper,' said Brayne, shaking his hand.

'My dear Brayne,' said the man with bushy hair, nodding and smiling at the group by the fireplace. The sun illuminated his spectacles and temporarily rendered him eyeless, substituting two winking, flashing orbs beneath his luxuriant hair.

'Hallo Quintin,' said Brayne. He was too far away to shake hands and there were too many people in the room now to permit him to move easily round it. 'How grows the broccoli?'

'Magnificent this year, dear boy,' said Quintin Plugge. 'I have had a tremendous crop. Not so the runner beans. A poor showing this year. I suspect it is something to do with the rainfall, or the effusions of the sewage plant near Brickmanstead, which regularly contravenes the Pollution Act with impunity.'

'Ah ha, Plugge, good to see you're still keeping your fingers green,' said Aldous Watmough, a political columnist. Plugge disagreed with his opinions. 'Still pouring out all that Trotskyist rubbish?' he said pleasantly. 'Still trying to persuade us that you really are a true man of the Left?'

'I must earn my crust,' said Watmough. 'I'm willing to let the proletariat judge us, when the revolution comes.'

More guests came into the room.

'What an amazing room,' someone said. 'I've never seen anything like it.'

'Just look at the wallpaper.'

'And that dreadful picture.'

The lunch was going well.

Few women attended the *Commentator* lunches. Few were invited. Those who did come were regarded with a mixture of fear and admiration by the *Commentator* staff. Today there was a fat woman called Pauline, who was a television researcher; and a girl who worked for the publisher, Morton Minitz, in some unspecified capacity. She was, for once, astonishingly attractive and earned the admiring gaze of the surprised, but timid, *Comment-*

ator lunchers. She was talking to the man in spats, Julian Jasper, who wrote a wine column for a fashion magazine.

Brayne saw Quintin Plugge looking at the girl wistfully. After a few moments he began to climb over the sofa, now piled with a great heap of coats, in a determined move towards her.

'Quintin, come and meet Gerard Bunsen,' said Brayne forcefully, arresting him in his progress. 'He's particularly interested in your plan for restoring the rural counties.'

Plugge's face registered disappointment. He climbed back with difficulty over the sofa.

The guests slowly arrived and greeted each other with cries of recognition and surprise. Brayne, watching for the arrival of Evelyn Fragment, was relieved when the door opened and revealed the Government minister, wearing a dark blue overcoat and a dark blue suit. Brayne strode forward to meet him.

'May I welcome you to the *Commentator* lunch.'

Fragment removed his overcoat and ran a hand through his luxuriant, slightly greying hair. His sharp, fastidious face remained impassive as his lips extended in a faint, thin smile.

'A curious room,' he murmured, 'but preferable, I assure you, to my own dreary office.'

'You're in the Norman Shaw Building aren't you, Sir?' said Julian Jasper who had swiftly climbed over the sofa to greet the celebrity.

'Not since I became a Minister,' said Fragment, sighing. 'Alas. It takes me a full half hour to drive from my new office at the Elephant and Castle to the Commons. All highly inconvenient. But then, London is becoming impossibly full of traffic these days.'

'It is because of all these dreadful housewives who go shopping,' said Gerard Bunsen. 'Have you noticed that they all have their own cars? Why can't they travel on the buses?'

'I want to sit at the end of the table,' Pauline said to Brayne. 'I'll have to slip out early. I've got to go and meet a murderer at two-thirty and I don't want to miss him.'

'A murderer? How peculiar.'

'He's in my latest programme. He's fantastic television.'

Brayne looked at his watch. 'I think we might as well sit down,' he said.

'Just a minute. We can't sit down yet.' Harry Horlick, a tall young man of dissolute appearance, suddenly shouted across the room. 'Don't sit down, anyone. Stay where you are.'

Brayne looked up in annoyance. 'Sit down, Horlick,' he said.

Julian Jasper said to the attractive publishing woman, 'Mr Horlick has already taken a drop too much, it seems.'

Watmough sat down heavily in the far corner of the room. He was hungry and wanted his lunch. The quality of the *Commentator*'s wines left a great deal to be desired. He filled his glass.

'Don't sit down,' Horlick shouted.

'I want some grub,' said Watmough.

'We are thirteen,' said Horlick.

'What are you talking about, Horlick?'

'Thirteen at table.'

'. . . he's started drinking in the mornings, I understand.'

'So what?'

'It's terribly unlucky. We can't sit down.'

'Are you superstitious?'

'. . . particularly because he's likely to get the sack quite soon. He works on Man of the World but he never gets any stories.'

'Look, I really am serious. Thirteen is a desperately unlucky number. Something terrible will happen to us if we sit down,' said Horlick.

'Accident, do you mean?' said Watmough. 'Broken ankle, run down by a bus? Struck by lightning?'

'It's just awfully bad luck.'

'After all,' Watmough went on. 'Death comes to us all. So your superstition will come true eventually whether we sit down or not.'

'I think I'll just check my bicycle,' said Bunsen going over to the window. 'Look there's Earish walking down the street.'

'We could get him to make up the number,' said Quintin Plugge. 'Not that I believe in all this superstition business at all.'

'Oh, no, not Earish,' said Julian Jasper. He turned to the rest of the room. 'He's the most frightful old bore. All he talks about are how his friends are all getting divorced and how he never earns enough to live on any more.'

'Oh, come, I think that's a little unfair,' said Plugge. 'Poor old Maurice. A little harsh? Yes, a little harsh, I think.'

'Is he outside?' said Brayne.

'He's just going past the door,' said Bunsen.

'He was a very good writer once,' said Plugge. 'He had a column in the *Guardian*. He used to write some very interesting stuff.'

'Right,' said Brayne. 'Get him in.'

'Are we going to eat at all?' said Watmough. 'Just as a matter of interest.'

'Well, go and get him, Horlick.'

Horlick rushed off down the narrow stairs.

'I've never heard of thirteen being unlucky at table,' said the fat woman, Pauline.

'My own guest hasn't turned up yet,' said Jasper. 'If he did, it would solve the problem.'

'Who have you asked?' said Brayne suspiciously.

'It's that – '

Marigold appeared suddenly with thirteen plates containing halves of melon. She walked round the room, dumping them loudly on the table so that the glasses rattled. 'If you don't sit down now,' she said, 'the steaks will be ruined.'

'Ah, our delightful hostess,' said Julian Jasper. 'And what do you propose to place before us today?'

Marigold considered him coldly. 'Same as usual. If you don't like it, complain to Alexander. He's so mean with his budget he won't even pay for bread and butter.'

'Steak and chips?'

'Steak and chips,' said Marigold, without enthusiasm.

'Are we going to get it at all?' said Watmough staring at his melon. 'I thought this was supposed to be a lunch.'

'Are you going to sit down,' said Marigold. 'Because I'm not cooking any more steaks once these are ruined.'

She went towards the door. Julian Jasper took her on one side. 'I don't suppose you saw any sign of my guest downstairs did you?'

'Who is he?'

'A man called Pleasant. Writes dirty books.'

'What does he look like?'

'Awful. A walking nightmare. Smooth and smarmy, sort of oily face.'

'Has he got a frightful sun-tan and lots of teeth?'

'Certainly,' said Jasper.

'I told him he'd come to the wrong place,' said Marigold. 'I didn't like the look of him at all.'

'So that's where my mystery guest has got to,' said Jasper.

Horlick came running up the stairs. 'Earish won't come.' Watmough's stomach rumbled audibly round the room.

'Right, we're going to sit down now,' said Brayne forcefully.

'Wait. I know,' cried Horlick running to the mantelshelf. While the rest of the lunchers looked on in surprise he seized the picture of the Crying Boy and placed it on the empty chair. The face, with its trembling lip, looked over the table, its eyes welling over in watery tears, fixing the rest of the lunchers in silent appeal.

'It's a bit off-putting,' said Pauline.

Greedily, Watmough started to eat his melon.

Downstairs, Norris Pleasant had come back into the reception area with a baffled expression. The room was now quite empty. Three or four flashing lights on the switchboard indicated a number of unanswered calls. Pleasant walked up and down in the shabby room and inspected the walls. He went to the bottom of the staircase and peered up. He coughed several times very loudly. Then he rapped his hand sharply on the reception desk. A profound silence answered him.

Upstairs they had finished the melon. 'Mine wasn't particularly good,' Watmough said to the person next to him, who happened to be the strikingly attractive girl. The placing was haphazard. Watmough had secured for himself the coveted seat next to her by the simple expedient of sitting down first. From time to time

Evelyn Fragment, forced to sit next to Brayne and Jasper, gave him resentful glances.

'Avocados are better at this time of the year,' said the girl, whose name was Venetia. 'Do you know that there are thirty-eight essential vitamins and elements in an avocado. It's the perfect meal.'

'How do you know?' said Watmough. 'Are you an avocado expert?'

'As a matter of fact we've just published a book about avocados. It's called *The Amorous Avocado*. Did you know they were an aphrodisiac?'

'Ah now,' said Plugge leaning forward eagerly. 'An avocado expert. Then you can solve the perennial problem for us.'

'What's that?'

'Fruit or vegetable?' said Plugge. 'Now – what's your verdict?'

Watmough yawned and put his elbows on the table.

Evelyn Fragment toyed with his melon and poured himself a glass of mineral water.

'What do you think about Ralph Spring-Greene as next leader of the party?' Jasper asked Fragment loudly. 'I gather he's highly regarded.'

'Yes, he's a sound man,' said Fragment

'Intensely able, I believe?' Jasper shouted.

'His wife is quite brilliant. It is she who should be in politics, not he. A remarkable woman. She gives the most marvellous parties, you know.'

'They are marvellous, aren't they' said Jasper, who had not been to any.

Watmough sighed. He had heard it all before.

'He has a limited imagination, of course,' said Fragment. 'But imagination is not always to be desired in political life.' He smiled sensitively.

'I think there's something odd about his private life,' said Horlick, eating fast. 'Something to do with his marriage, I think.'

Fragment frowned slightly.

'Do you know anything about it?' said Horlick, turning to Fragment.

'I can't help you there, I'm afraid.' Fragment's face was like a mask.

'Something about his wife having an affair . . . Can't remember who with, though.'

Watmough leaned forward. 'For a diarist, your grasp of detail seems rather poor.'

'That's why I never get any stories,' said Horlick. 'It's hard to remember all this stuff, isn't it?'

'By the way, Alexander,' said Bunsen excitedly. 'I want to talk to you about a feature I have in mind. I think it could prove to be enormously controversial . . .'

Downstairs Marigold had found Pleasant in the reception area again. He was investigating the contents of her desk. 'What do you want?' she said fiercely. 'I thought I told you to go away. You've got the wrong address.'

'This is the *Commentator*,' said Pleasant. 'I was right first time. You seem pretty uptight over the situation. Why this negative behaviour?'

'There's a lunch going on here. I'm extremely busy. And I'd like you to leave the office this minute.'

'Of course there's a lunch. I am a guest.'

'Prove it.'

'What do you mean?'

'Where's your invitation?'

'Let's talk this through,' said Pleasant. 'Let's try and relate to one another as reasonable adults.'

'I don't like your tone,' said Marigold.

'Clearly we have a communication problem here.'

'Are you going to go quietly?'

'No,' said Pleasant.' I am not.'

'Now the point is that the GPO are going round the country laying waste the country's telephone boxes. These are absolute antiques.

Priceless unique monuments to a vanished age.'

'You mean those old red boxes?'

'Precisely,' said Bunsen. 'They are disappearing at an alarming rate, only to be replaced by dismal, plastic abominations.'

'I quite like those new boxes,' said Watmough. 'At least they don't stink of piss, if the young lady will excuse my language.'

Venetia gave him a demure smile.

'There is a nineteen-thirties box under threat in Somerset at the moment,' Bunsen said to Brayne. 'There's not very much local interest in it, I'm afraid, indeed no one down there seems to care whether it stays or goes. But that's the sort of thing you expect with these boxes. They very often are not appreciated by people who have simply no interest in their surroundings. Who merely want to make a telephone call.' He looked condescendingly at Watmough.

'Of course, I've seen it all before,' said Watmough. 'There was that terrific scandal with old Harry MacCleod when his wife ran off with a member of the Communist Party. Then there was old Dawson who ran off with a woman who served lunches in the Members' Dining Room. Abandoned his wife and four young children and went to live in a basement in the East End for quite some time. Everyone's forgotten all about it now.'

Fragment shifted in his seat uneasily.

'I thought it would be an excellent campaign,' said Bunsen in a high, excited voice. 'Save these telephone boxes. It has, I am sure, an almost universal appeal for *Commentator* readers.'

Brayne took out a leather-bound notebook. 'I like it,' he said, noting down Bunsen's idea. 'We could have an illustration of a telephone box on the front cover. It's the sort of thing that people would respond to.'

'Absolutely, my dear,' said Bunsen. 'Everyone's interested in telephone boxes.'

'It's a documentary,' said Pauline, 'in thirteen parts.'

'For the religious affairs department?'

'Yes.'

'What's it about?'

'Well, it's quite an original idea. We get a murderer, a sex offender, a rapist, a child molester – that sort of thing, and we get them to talk about their crimes in the light of their subsequent religious experience.'

'Sounds fascinating,' said Horlick. 'Did they all have a religious experience?'

'Yes, that's the point of the programme. They were visited with divine inspiration while they were inside.'

Plugge's eyes gleamed behind his spectacles. 'That's very interesting,' he said. 'I myself was affected by a similar experience when I – '

'Pauline, you must write about it for us,' said Brayne. 'Could you do us an article?'

'OK,' said Pauline.

'What's the programme called?'

'Sorry, God.'

'Yes, I like it.'

'I think it could be quite controversial.'

'I might write a piece about that,' said Horlick, 'for the diary.'

'I thought a piece of about two and a half thousand words just to start with,' said Bunsen, 'naming the guilty men at the GPO.'

'Terrific stuff,' said Brayne. He turned to Fragment who had been sitting silently at his side, toying with his steak and chips. 'I tremendously admired your stand on the Bishop of Brigg,' he said. 'It's absolute humbug to say that the Government shouldn't interfere with the Church. You just can't get away with saying nothing any more. People expect politicians to concern themselves with the heretical ravings of progressive churchmen. I thought you put the case for orthodoxy extremely well.'

Fragment arranged his features into an expression of seriousness. 'He is a frightful chap,' he said. 'You know the Government are seriously worried about the effect he is having on the faith of millions of ordinary, everyday people, who are genuinely distressed to see the clergy behaving in this radical way, and undermining our moral standards.'

'Is there any chance of another bottle of this?' said Watmough, holding up a bottle of claret.

Brayne looked down the table where Jasper and Watmough were shouting loudly. 'They want more to drink,' he said to Plugge. 'Give Marigold a shout.'

'I think it's interesting,' said Brayne, 'that no one had ever heard of the Bishop of Brigg until he started to go on the television.'

'Yes, quite. Exactly who is he?' said Plugge.

'His wife is a bit of a raver,' said Horlick eagerly. 'We've got quite a few stories about her and her coffee mornings. Unfortunately I haven't been able to check them out yet.'

'Isn't he an academic?'

'Yes, he was buried away at Brigg University for years,' said Watmough from the distant end of the table, 'until he suddenly discovered that he didn't believe in God. Since then he's been writing articles all over the place – then he happened to get picked up by his local radio station. One of his vicars is a transvestite. He's been unearthed by the popular press. Harpie-Kerr's done a lurid exposé.'

'How dreadful for the church,' said Plugge.

'No, apparently the Bishop approves.'

'To committed Christians, such as myself,' said Fragment, with a pained expression on his face, 'this sort of thing simply will not do.'

'I understand he is enthusiastic about women priests,' said Brayne.

Bunsen groaned.

'And why not?' shouted Watmough. 'There's absolutely no liturgical reason why women should not be ordained. Very good thing too, in my opinion.'

'Well, you would think that, wouldn't you?' said Plugge wearily. 'Always rehearsing these dreary, Leftish opinions you perfected at Cambridge. Come on, Aldous. Admit you don't believe one word of all this rubbish you're spouting.'

'I admit nothing,' said Watmough.

'We should get a piece on this Bishop,' said Brayne, 'before everyone writes about him.'

'Oh, no,' said Bunsen, in a shrill voice. 'Not Brigg. Oh, he's a dreadful fellow. It's all kissing in the pews and guitar music every Sunday. He's put a microphone down in the nave and hung a ghastly great orange banner in the choir painted by some local women's group.'

'Splendid man,' said Watmough. 'The C of E could do with more like him.'

'I wish I could stand up that story about his wife,' said Horlick. 'It would be a really good exclusive, if I could check it out.'

'I think I might tackle him myself,' said Brayne. 'I think he merits a profile.'

'Absolutely,' said Bunsen. 'You must mention all those dreadful deaconesses with positive moustaches he entertains every Sunday.'

Marigold came in with two more bottles of red wine. 'Where are the drinkers?' she said, staring round the table.

'There are the flushed faces,' said Brayne, indicating Watmough and Jasper.

'I suppose they're Socialists,' she said scathingly, putting the wine down in front of Watmough. 'They always drink more than anyone else.'

'Yes, Watmough is a dreadful wild man of the Left,' said Plugge.

'And proud of it,' said Watmough. 'When we were young we waved banners and marched at the head of the beautiful people. All the radicals were beautiful then, at least the women were.'

'What did you march about?' said Venetia.

'What about? My God, how old it makes me feel to hear you sitting there asking questions about the movement as though it was part of history. Well, my young friend, we marched because we cared about the future of the world. We wanted abortion on demand, gay rights, free love. We wanted to spread the revolution. We wanted to stop the war.'

'Which war was that?' said Venetia. 'I'm hopeless at history.'

Jasper yawned loudly. 'Not all that dreary stuff again,' he said.

'We stopped the war in Vietnam,' said Watmough forcefully. He poured himself another glass of wine. 'We marched to Grosvenor Square. We demonstrated outside the American

Embassy. We were brutally assaulted by policemen and trampled by horses' hooves.'

'You poor thing,' said Bunsen.

'He's making it all up,' said Jasper.

'But we could not be stopped. We had youth and justice on our side. We had a cause and we fought for it,' said Watmough, leaning on the table.

He shouted:

'Hey, hey, LBJ,
How many kids have you killed today?'

Brayne and Plugge laughed loudly.

'We shall fight,' Watmough declaimed,
'We shall win
'London, Paris,
'Rome, Berlin.
Good stuff, good stuff. Of course, the young don't believe in anything like that these days. All they want to do is make a lot of money and vote Conservative. But we fight the fight as best we can.'

'I don't see you fighting much these days,' said Plugge. 'You've changed a bit since those days when you stamped about in your donkey jacket, waving your banner. What about your comfortable salary, your expensive house in Islington, your smart car . . .'

'You were there, comrade. You were there,' said Watmough, pointing an accusing finger at Plugge.

'I haven't changed. The party changed, not me.'

'You're still here, are you?' said Marigold, coming down the stairs again and finding Pleasant standing angrily in the middle of the room with his arms folded and his legs wide apart.

'Naturally.'

'I don't know what you're waiting for.'

'Perhaps this is some publicity stunt?' said Pleasant.

'What do you mean?'

'Famous author kept waiting for lunch.'

'I've never heard of you in my life.'

'Young woman,' said Pleasant. 'You could certainly benefit from studying one of my manuals.' He smiled, exposing a row of white teeth, the result of complicated and expensive dentistry. 'Your trouble may be hormonal. Do you have a regular monthly cycle?'

'You're disgusting.'

'You see, your skin seems heavily congested with impurities. Do you have a vigorous and active sex life, for example?'

'Just clear out of here at once.'

'I would advise a course of folic acid tablets.'

Marigold came out from behind the desk. 'This way,' she shouted, pointing her arm. 'Through that door, now.'

Pleasant smiled. 'We are all at the mercy of our bodies. I advise meditation. You are clearly the victim of acute premenstrual inner tension.'

'Piss off,' said Marigold.

In reply, Pleasant promptly lay down at the foot of the stairs. 'This is the first TM exercise I advocate in my manual, *Take it Gently*. It makes your body more responsive to the signals of sexual arousal. Breathe in. Feel your body float into an area of inner tranquillity. Lie down, young woman. Feel what your bio-rhythms are trying to tell you.'

Supine on the floor, Pleasant gave a demonstration of his technique.

'We shall not forget,' said Watmough happily. 'Come the revolution we shall not forget.'

'Who wants pudding?' said Marigold, appearing at the door, flushed from her encounter with Pleasant.

'What is it?' said Pauline.

'Treacle sponge,' said Marigold.

Several of the lunchers banged their spoons with excitement on the table. The Crying Boy slipped from his chair onto the floor.

'Can I have extra treacle?' said Horlick.

'No.'

'Oh, please,' said Horlick loudly.

'You can have my treacle,' said Pauline. 'And the sponge, too, if you like. I'm on a diet.'

'I say, is there any cheese?' said Watmough.

'No.'

'No cheese?'

'You heard me.'

'Why not?' said Watmough, putting down his wine glass with a serious expression. 'I'd just like a small piece of Blue Brie or Camembert. Nothing special.'

'You're not going to get anything special,' said Marigold. 'Because you're not going to get anything at all.'

'Cheese is a perfectly reasonable request,' said Watmough. 'Why can't we have cheese?'

'Because Alexander doesn't like cheese. It's off the menu.'

'He doesn't like cheese?'

'He doesn't like cheese,' said Marigold. 'He doesn't want cheese. So none of you lot can have cheese, either.'

Watmough stared at Brayne in indignation.

'You can have cheese if you want,' said Brayne. 'But you'll have to have English cheese. We don't serve French stuff at *Commentator* lunches.'

Venetia giggled.

'English cheese then,' said Watmough sulkily. 'What have you got? A bit of Wensleydale, perhaps? Or a spot of Double Gloucester?'

'Cheddar,' said Marigold.

'Cheddar then,' said Watmough. 'With biscuits.'

'So what have we got for the next issue?' said Brayne in a businesslike tone of voice. 'Telephone boxes. The Bishop of Brigg and – Quintin – what about you? Any ideas?'

'Well, dear boy,' said Plugge, taking off his glasses with an oratorical flourish. 'I thought it might be time for a new analysis of the family. You know – asking whether the traditional, nuclear family group is a thing of the past.'

Fragment nodded. 'Awfully important,' he said. 'A subject many of my constituents feel particularly strongly about. I myself hope to play an important part in developing the Government's concern for the restoration of family life.'

'Good stuff,' said Brayne. 'How would you develop the theme?'

'I shall look to the contraceptive pill,' said Plugge importantly. 'I would trace the social significance of family planning in terms of the grave devastation these free hormones have wrought on our national life. By this, I mean that the attitudes promulgated by the "family planners", born out of the notorious Sixties ethic – I want it now – have seeped like poisoned drops into the consciousness of our youth, until today it is commonplace to hold in mockery the ideals and standards which have always characterised the British way of life.'

Watmough drained his glass. 'That seems a fairly major charge to lay at the door of the Pill,' he said. 'Can you make it stand up?'

'I most certainly can,' said Plugge with vigour. 'For youth to admire and, certainly, imitate a moral code founded on promiscuity leads inevitably to an easy, flip denial of all human dignity and the sort of demoralised attitudes we see today. That is, an inability to form lasting relationships, a totally casual attitude to sexual activity, promiscuity and defiance of all forms of authority.'

'I personally thought the Sixties attitude to sex rather refreshing. I certainly profited by it, in my day, and I rather think the same was true for you, comrade.'

'What do you mean?' said Plugge.

'Free love,' said Watmough. 'Chastity did not play an important part in your earlier life, Quintin. It was all before your time,' he added to Jasper and Venetia, 'but Plugge here was a great success with what we used to call the Dolly Birds.'

Venetia giggled at some length.

'Indeed,' Watmough went on. 'Having met them it was a matter of pride to him how quickly he could get their knickers off.'

'Good God,' said Plugge, turning red. 'This is merely a figment of your diseased imagination. You're simply making the whole thing up, Watmough.'

'I'd like to know what's wrong with sex anyway,' Watmough said challengingly.

'Oh God, can't you give it a rest,' said Plugge.

'Yes, yes. Whatever you like. Subject closed.'

'I must be going,' said Evelyn Fragment, getting up hurriedly from the table. 'Thank you so much. A most entertaining lunch.' He gathered his coat and closed the door behind him. At the foot of the stairs he stepped over the recumbent form of Pleasant, and absently apologised to him.

'Is that the time?' said Pauline. 'My murderer will be waiting. Must dash.'

'What's wrong with sex?' said Watmough quietly. 'What's wrong with love, what's wrong with women?'

'I thought Fragment was awfully dull,' said Brayne. 'He didn't say much to pay for his lunch, did he?'

'Terrible stuffed shirt,' said Jasper.

'He's not that bad for a Tory, when you get to know him,' said Watmough. 'He's an old chum of mine. He seemed rather ill at ease in his surroundings.'

'I thought he was rather sweet,' said Venetia.

Bunsen got up from the table. 'The piece about the boxes will be with you tomorrow,' he said. 'I'm going to do it now, while I feel inspired.'

'I wonder what happened to Pleasant?' said Jasper.

Brayne frowned at him. 'Who?'

'I invited Pleasant to lunch but he never turned up.'

'Why did you invite him? I'm supposed to see all the invitations before they're sent.'

'I thought he'd be good for a laugh. His new book's about to come out. Bound to be dirty like all the rest.' Jasper brayed with laughter. Brayne chewed his lip. He got up from the table with a sour expression.

'Didn't know you felt so strongly about it. Have I overstepped the mark?' Jasper leered in apology.

'Anyone staying on for stickies?' said Watmough, at the end of the table.

'I'm game,' said Venetia.

'Tell Marigold to send up the brandy,' Watmough shouted to Brayne.

'Back to the grindstone,' Jasper said, standing up unsteadily. He walked down the narrow stairs with care. 'Can I give anyone a lift to Westminster?' His spat-clad foot trod heavily on Pleasant's leg. Pleasant cried out in pain.

'I say, there's a man lying here on the floor.'

'What's he doing,' said Brayne.

'Lying down.'

'How eccentric,' said Horlick. 'That would make a very good paragraph for my diary.'

'Has he been here all the time?'

'Do you know who he is?' said Horlick. 'I suppose I ought to get a quote.'

Brayne stood behind Jasper and looked down at the recumbent figure.

'Yes, I know who he is,' he said coldly, and stepped over the body of Pleasant. 'I should get up, if I were you.'

Pleasant eyed him with malice.

'Just practising a little meditation technique,' he said.

'I say, do you know each other,' said Jasper.

'No,' said Brayne, who was white with fury.

'Intimately,' said Pleasant, 'in a manner of speaking.'

· CHAPTER · IV ·

'A world famous sex guru has just staged a lie-in at a well-known magazine,' Horlick typed laboriously. 'I hear that Norris Pleasant, author of the famous *Joy through the Day* manuals, is worrying friends by his increasingly strange behaviour. A recent guest at a *Commentator* lunch, he was discovered by members of the magazine's staff lying at the foot of the stairs in what he called a peaceful demonstration. Alexander Brayne, editor of the *Commentator*, said: "I was amazed to discover Mr Pleasant, who refused to get up. We greatly regret the incident." When I telephoned the eccentric sexpert, he replied: "We are all giving out physical stimuli through our body language. In my latest book – " Horlick yawned and stretched his arms behind his head. The diary editor looked at him critically.

Horlick finished the piece and put it, with a casual air, on the diary editor's desk.

The diary editor read it without comment.

'Don't you think it's an amazing story?' said Horlick excitedly.

'Not very. It might do as an overnight filler.'

Horlick went through an extensive pantomine of bafflement. He raised his hands in the air, puffed out his cheeks and made a whistling noise through his lips. 'If that's not a cracking story,' he said, 'well, frankly I don't know what is.'

The diary editor handed him a piece of paper. 'Evelyn Fragment's doing a walkabout in Soho,' he said, 'protesting about the porn shops. Get down there and give us four hundred words by midday.'

'Right,' said Horlick. He took the piece of paper and returned to his desk. He sat down and picked his nose.

'Well?' said the diary editor. 'Are you going?'

'What now?' said Horlick. 'Today? This morning?'

'This minute.'

'Oh God. I thought you meant tomorrow. I say, it's already ten-thirty. That's a bit sudden. I'll have to look at the cuttings before I go.' And Horlick set off slowly for the files of the newspaper library.

In the middle of Turkey Street, Evelyn Fragment was addressing a crowd of press photographers and reporters. 'I feel most strongly,' he said softly, 'and most passionately about this degradation and corruption which surrounds us.' He indicated, with his right hand, the object of his displeasure. THE LOCKER ROOM a sign above the shop declared. Inside the window, a male dummy sprawled provocatively clad in a tight, shiny leather vest. On its head was a German-style peaked military cap. Photographs of male models in muscular poses gazed out naughtily at passers-by, displaying impossibly brief undergarments. Fragment went closer to the window. 'Do you see,' he said, 'how this blatant display of sexually explicit material revolts and disgusts the ordinary person, and moreover is an insult and degrading to women.'

The crowd of press photographers followed him obediently over to the window.

'It's a gay shop,' one of the reporters said.

Fragment peered closely into the window.

'Oh. So it is,' he said. He stared for a moment at the goods displayed, then moved hastily down the street. The pressmen followed him. Fragment looked across the street for another example of offensive and provocative display and came to rest by the Girls Unlimited Club. 'Here again,' he said, with sorrow, 'we see these salacious and offensive pictures for everyone to see. Do you have children? I know I do. And would you want your children to see such a terrible sight as this? I know I would not.'

'How old are they?' a reporter shouted from the crowd.

Fragment paused. 'There are three little ones,' he said,

temporising while he remembered their ages. 'They range from fourteen to eight. They are at the most impressionable stage of their young lives; and what would I say to them – my own children – if we were to find ourselves confronted by material like this?' (Photographs of Fragment's children duly appeared in the next day's newspapers wrongly named and several years out of date.)

Fragment began to move slowly down the street at a thoughtful, reflective pace. Horlick, coming down the street towards him saw the lights of the cameras and the photographers and joined in the rear of the party.

'I know I do not speak just for myself,' said Fragment with sincerity, knotting his eyebrows together in an expression of anguish. 'I speak as a parent and for all the parents in this country. And that is why, in my new role as Minister for the Family, I intend to speak out on behalf of those decent men and women who are doing their best to raise wholesome sons and daughters with a respect for traditional values.'

Horlick discovered he had left his biro behind. 'I say,' he said to a man who was holding a microphone up to Fragment's mouth. 'Could you lend me a pen, please?'

The man pushed him out of the way as he tried to thrust his instrument closer to Fragment's mouth.

'Steady on,' said Horlick. 'I only wanted a pen . . .'

But Fragment was moving off again. After a few moments he came to rest outside the Dog and Biscuit where a group of people were standing outside the door. As the reporters approached they saw that they were bearing placards and banners. One of them was shouting.

'Censorship kills,' bawled Corner, who was leading the demonstration.

'Oppose Government control.' The placards endorsed his recommendations. 'Big Brother is Back,' one of them said. 'Mind Control at Work.'

'Adult reading for adult minds,' Corner shouted. 'The Thought Police will come for you next.'

Fragment stared at the demonstration then turned to the

reporters. 'There you see the porn profiteers,' he said, 'who are attempting to defend this sordid business. They claim they want freedom. But what about those in our society – the children, the women, the pure in heart – who have no freedom to resist such filth?'

Corner advanced towards him. 'Fragment! Fragment! Fragment!' he shouted, waving his banner.

'Out! Out! Out!' the demonstrators cried in response.

Fragment gave a theatrical shudder. He turned to the reporters and said, 'Suffer the little children . . .'

'Got any kids?' a reporter said to Corner.

'Four, bless their hearts,' said Corner, 'and all of them little girls.'

(This too, was reported in the papers, inaccurately as it happened, since Corner was without progeny.)

Horlick said to a girl on his left, 'I say, could I borrow a pen.'

Silently she handed him one.

'Thanks. How long is all this going to last?'

'He's going down to the Commons after this,' the girl said, 'to meet a delegation from the Mothers' Union. Then he gives a press conference with the Prime Minister to launch his new role.'

'Ah ha,' said Horlick. 'And what new role is this?'

The girl regarded him critically and turned her back. Fragment was speaking again. Horlick took out his notebook and wrote down: 'I intend to demonstrate the Government's . . . importance of maintaining . . . values and make it my business to . . . utmost severity.'

'What was that bit about values?' Horlick said to the man in front of him. 'I didn't quite catch that bit.'

'You'll have to write a bit quicker then mate,' said the man.

'Charming!' said Horlick.

'Fragment! Fragment! Fragment!' Corner shouted.

'Out! Out! Out!'

The minister moved on up the road. Corner looked at his watch. 'OK, time for a quick one,' he told his band of demonstrators. They moved briskly through the doors of the Dog and Biscuit.

Further up the street Fragment's voice could be heard intoning his message. He stopped outside Minitz House and once again the cameras flashed as he began to speak about family unity.

Horlick said to Corner, 'Did you hear what he was saying?'

'Only too clearly, my boy,' said Corner.

'I'm Horlick from the *Reporter*.'

'Here's the press, lads,' said Corner, 'eager to hear our side of the story. Come inside and you can buy us all a drink.'

Later that evening Florence Barge and Alexander Brayne stood on the steps of the King's Court theatre waiting for their companions to turn up. Brayne had the uneasy air of someone who had arrived too early for an appointment. He stood, ill at ease on the pavement, looking at his watch, shifting his weight from one leg to the other. Excited by the television cameras and the crowd of press photographers, Florence inspected the faces of the arriving crowd, eager to spot a celebrity. 'Isn't that Marius Grope,' she said, naming a celebrated chat show host, and squeezing Brayne's arm in excitement.

He lifted up his head and gazed beyond her. 'I haven't the faintest idea.'

A couple in matching sequinned jackets were met by an explosion of bright lights and flashing cameras.

'I wish you'd worn your dinner jacket, Alexander,' said Florence. 'You'd have looked sensational.'

Brayne smiled distantly. 'No one dresses up to go to the King's Court,' he said. He had not dressed specially for the occasion, but wore his customary corduroy jacket and brown lace-up shoes. Florence had gone to some lengths, however, and was wearing a bright red hat.

Brayne looked at his watch again. 'What time did you tell Marigold to be here?'

'I said six-thirty precisely, but it's often difficult for her to get away on time. You give her so much work to do.'

'Here's Julian Jasper,' said Brayne. 'Do you know him?'

Jasper came up and said in a loud, braying voice, 'My dear Alexander. How goes it?'

Florence regarded him with disappointment. He wore small gold pince-nez, a bow-tie, and a loudly-checked three-piece suit. She was surprised to notice, a few moments later, that he was wearing spats.

'May I introduce Miss Florence Barge,' said Brayne.

'Greetings,' said Jasper, shaking her hand. 'Are you by any chance – '

'We lack the third member of the party,' said Brayne. 'Another moment, Florence, then we must go in without her.'

'Are you by any chance a Barge?' Jasper said to Florence.

'Yes, she is,' Brayne interrupted. 'One of the Hereford ones.'

'Jolly good,' said Jasper. 'Do you know Alexandra and Adrian Rosebery?' he went on. 'He's got the finest private cellar in the country. They've got a place in your neck of the woods.'

'I've never heard of them,' said Florence. She looked across the square.

'Are you listening, Florence. We must go in now.'

Brayne took out a leather notebook, bound at the corners with gold.

'Look, there's someone famous,' Florence suddenly said. 'I know that face. Who is she, Alexander? Isn't she the woman who reads the news? Don't you think it's exciting to see all these photographers?'

'I have no interest in television personalities,' said Brayne. 'There's something impossibly vulgar about all this thirst for publicity.'

'Oh, here's Arabella Spring-Greene arriving,' said Julian Jasper. 'Look, they're rushing towards her taxi.' Brayne's eyes registered sudden interest.

'They're fighting each other,' Florence exclaimed. There was a loud noise of shattering glass and Brayne flinched. At the corner of the street, two photographers were wrestling, pushing each other backwards and forwards across the pavement. 'They're going to kill each other,' said Florence, running down the steps to get a better view.

'It's the battling Rileys,' said another photographer on her right. 'Father and son, locked in combat. They've fought on more street corners than you've had hot dinners.'

'Why are they fighting?'

'They were both trying to get a picture of Lady Arabella as she went in, but now they've both missed her, haven't they.'

Brayne called down the steps to Florence. 'We are going inside this minute.'

'So sorry,' said Marigold Few, arriving breathless. 'No taxis. Had to get a bus.'

'You know Julian Jasper?' said Brayne.

'Greetings,' Jasper shouted. 'I believe we met at the *Commentator* lunch.'

Marigold looked at him without enthusiasm.

She and Florence embraced.

'We must go in absolutely now,' said Brayne, marching into the foyer. Inside, the theatre was crowded with people talking in loud excited voices. Florence looked eagerly at the faces.

'Oh, *there's* Arabella,' said Brayne in an admiring voice. He pointed to a tall blonde woman who was smoking a cigarette in a long ebony holder. Although she was in her mid-forties, her face was smooth and blushed with the delicate texture of a peach.

'She's on that panel game, isn't she?' said Marigold.

Brayne winced and nodded. 'Among other things. She is, actually, a brilliant woman and the most marvellous party giver.'

'Oh quite,' said Jasper. 'No one gives parties like Arabella.'

Brayne regarded him with annoyance. 'They're the most marvellous parties,' he said.

'Marvellous,' said Jasper. 'When's the next one, do you know?'

'She's giving one for me next month,' said Brayne. 'To celebrate the first anniversary of the magazine.'

'Ah,' said Jasper, who had not been invited.

'It's just a small, rather intimate affair. The numbers, otherwise, . . . you understand – '

'Oh quite, absolutely.'

As they went down the stairs towards the stalls, Florence inspected the photographs of the cast and director which decorated the walls. At the end of a line of portraits, she saw, with a shock of recognition, the face of Jerry Gude. It was pinched and white; the eyes stared out at her with a hungry, fierce expression. There were crevices etched down either side of the mouth which drooped in a fastidious sneer at the world.

'Come on, Florence.'

Florence stared at the photograph. This was the man in Holland Park who had said such dreadful things to her. Amazed, she stared at the face again. The portrait erased the blemishes of time which had ravaged Gude's face. He seemed almost handsome. She looked round the foyer wondering if the playwright was lurking amid the crowd. What if he recognised her? She lingered in the foyer until Brayne pulled at her arm.

'Would you like a programme, Florence?'

'What?'

'A programme?'

'Yes. Yes.'

Clutching the programme she followed Brayne into the row of seats and turned hastily to the biographical information about the author. Here she found another picture of Gude in his younger days. There was no doubt, thought Florence, that he had once been very good-looking. The audience took their seats. Half of them had seen the play the first time it was performed when they were twenty-five years younger. These people tried to remember the occasion, and whether they had liked the play or not. 'An epoch-making statement for the permissive society,' Brayne read from the programme, 'which set the style for a whole generation. A play which irrevocably changed the dramatic language of its time.'

'Bound to be worth a laugh,' said Jasper, offering Marigold a box of peppermint creams. 'I'm not a great theatre-goer, myself.'

'I prefer musicals,' said Marigold. 'Something amusing, at least. This looks awfully dreary.'

'Alexander is writing an article about the play,' said Florence.

She lowered her voice. 'How are you getting on with Jasper?'

'He's terribly boring,' said Marigold. 'He seems to be some kind of wine writer.'

'Those spats are a bit much.'

'He looks ridiculous.'

'What has Gude done since?' said someone in the seat behind them. 'I remember he used to be quite well known, but I haven't heard of him for years.'

Brayne said: 'Look, I'm just going to say hello to Arabella.' Abruptly he rose from his seat and pushed his way heavily down the aisle towards her.

'How rude,' said Marigold. 'Look at him climbing all over people. I'd put my foot down.'

'He does it all the time,' said Florence. 'He's always looking for someone more interesting to talk to. I'm getting sick of it.'

The conversation behind them resumed. 'I don't know what Gude is doing now, do you?'

'I haven't heard of him for years. He was quite famous in the Seventies, wasn't he? Everyone was talking about him then.'

'Don't you remember – he was the first man who said fuck on the television.'

'Oh yes. You're right. Everyone was quite outraged at the time.'

The group of people with Lady Arabella Spring-Greene were elaborately dressed in clothes designed to make them look younger.

'My God,' said one of them. 'Doesn't it make you feel old. Just think, we were only twenty-one when we saw this first time round.'

Lady Arabella nodded her head and smiled.

'It got the worst reviews a play's ever had.'

'At first.'

'Then it got the best.'

'Do you think it was any good?'

'I don't know.'

'What do you think, Arabella?' said Brayne crouching at her feet as people pushed past him in search of their seats.

Arabella did not hear him. 'A man from Channel Six,' she was saying to someone else. 'They want me to talk all about Jerry. They're doing a special programme about him.'

'Will you?'

'Why not? I was his first wife. They'll have to let me have first go.'

'I think that's terribly brave.'

Arabella laughed lightly. 'It's hard to forget Jerry. I still think of him as a friend. Oh, Alexander, I didn't see you crouching there. How are you, my darling?' They exchanged kisses with a smacking noise.

On the end of the row behind them, Pauline was sitting with a box of chocolates. She ate her way savagely through the box, putting the next sweet into her mouth before she had finished the first. She made notes on her programme and looked around her in a pugnacious way. She saw Jasper, who looked up and waved at her. Pauline nodded back abruptly. When she was working she did not like to be distracted.

The lights came down. Brayne came climbing back clumsily down the row. He trod heavily on Florence's foot as he sank into his seat.

There was a long silence, then some harsh, dissonant music filled the auditorium. A fretwork of light lit a backcloth illuminating the stage, which was revealed to contain a gas stove and a large pile of newspapers. In the centre of the stage a man stood motionless, wearing a dirty raincoat and wellington boots. The music faded into silence. The man raised his head and stared at the audience.

'Brenda?' he shouted. 'Brenda? What's for my tea? Are you there you stupid cow? Oh fuck. Brenda? Bloody get in here this minute.' There was a burst of nervous laughter from somewhere at the back of the auditorium. The audience stirred.

'You can see why he didn't write anything else,' said Jasper.

'Be quiet,' said Marigold.

The actor strode up to the footlights and stared at the audience. Then he laughed wildly in a series of short cries and walked over to the gas stove.

'Where the fuck is that stupid bitch?' the man continued. A woman wearing a dressing gown and holding a carving knife entered the room and went out again without speaking.

After a few seconds she came in again.

'So you're back,' the woman said.

The man stared at her. 'You're a fucking stuck-up patronising bitch,' he shouted. 'Just because you've got a bloody title and a private income you think you can lie in bed all bloody day.'

The woman started to remove her curlers.

'There's a boil on my neck,' said the man. 'It's bloody painful.' Several people giggled in reply.

Some latecomers moved self-consciously to their seats, near the front row. There was some confusion. Two of the women remained standing, blocking the view of those behind them.

'Sit down. Sit down.' Florence heard a loud voice hissing with fury at the standing women. It seemed to come from someone beside her right ear. She turned round to see, with a shock, the face of Jerry Gude, a little distance from her own, contorted with fury. 'Sit down, you fucking cow,' he hissed again, crouching in the aisle. 'Sit down.'

Unaware, the women continued to fumble for their places. Gude waved his arm in a gesture of fury. As the women still took no notice, he advanced towards them in a crab-like, sideways crawl down the aisle, until he was level with their row. 'Sit down, you silly fucking bitches,' he muttered hoarsely. Alarmed, they turned to look for the origin of the voice. As one of the women looked down and saw Gude's crouching figure, she exclaimed softly in fear. The latecomers stared at him in horror, wondering if he was part of the dramatic plot. Gude retreated, still crouching, to the back of the auditorium, where he stood nervously, chewing his lips.

The man and woman sat down on the stage and stared at each other.

'I'm nothing more than your bit of rough,' the man said. 'Slumming, that's what you're bloody doing. Why don't you go back to mummy and daddy.'

'You're such a bore,' the woman said. She picked up the carving knife and pointed it at the man's throat. There was a loud bang off stage.

'Who's in the bloody bedroom?' said the man picking up a lump of coal. 'You're nothing but a fucking tart.'

This time the audience laughed quite loudly, gaining confidence from each other.

'To think this was hailed as a masterpiece,' said Jasper. Brayne twisted his pencil in the half-light and made quick notes in his leather notepad.

Outside the auditorium, another party of latecomers found their way into the theatre barred.

'I'm sorry, sir,' said the house manager. 'No latecomers admitted after the curtain goes up until a suitable break.'

'You're fucking joking,' said Galen Bone, waving his arms in the air. 'It's not our fault we're late. Blame the stupid, fucking traffic round this theatre. Why don't you build a car park next door, instead of expecting people to walk miles because they can't get anywhere to park? These are complimentary tickets, too. Look. A present from the author, with whom we are on intimate terms. We are privileged customers. I demand immediate admittance.'

The house manager bowed his head firmly. 'I apologise for the inconvenience. But it is a rule of this theatre that patrons may not be admitted until – '

'Oh, never mind, Galen,' said Lucinda Harpie-Kerr. 'Look we can watch the play in the bar until they let us in. There's a little television screen up there.'

Maurice Earish and Vernon Corner looked up and saw two tiny figures shouting at each other on the flickering screen.

'This has never happened to me before,' said Bone. 'It's fucking humiliating.'

'I'll get some drinks,' said Corner.

'I knew we'd be late,' said Earish. 'It's impossible to go anywhere in London without sitting in a traffic jam. I didn't particularly want to come anyway.'

'Never in my whole life,' said Bone, 'have I watched a play from the fucking bar.'

'Be quiet and drink your brandy,' said Lucinda. 'I can't hear what they're saying if you keep talking.'

'I thought those pictures of Jerry were very flattering,' said Earish. 'He looks much worse than that in real life.'

'Cheers.'

'Cheers.'

'To Jerry.'

'The famous author.'

The party in the bar turned their attention to the television screen. For some moments they watched engrossed, as the two tiny figures strode furiously backwards and forwards across the stage.

'Hard to get a grasp of it, watching like this,' said Corner, staring hard. 'You know, I think it's a bit out of focus. I can see wavy lines going across it.'

'You're pissed,' said Bone. 'You had too many before we came out.'

'No, no, he's right,' said Lucinda. 'There are wavy lines going across it.'

'Complain,' Bone shouted. 'Complain to the fucking management. First of all they make us sit out here, watching this set, then they can't even get a proper picture.'

'Let's have some more drinks, first,' she said brightly.

'I'll get them this time,' said Earish reluctantly. He had been sitting silently for the last few minutes, staring beyond the screen into the distance. 'I suppose this will make Jerry famous all over again.'

There was the sound of distant laughter from the auditorium.

'They love it,' said Lucinda.

'I still can't hear what they're saying.'

'It's not supposed to be fucking funny,' said Bone with contempt.

'He should know,' said Lucinda Harpie-Kerr. 'He was there first time round.'

'I was here, in this very same theatre, twenty-five years ago,' said

Bone. 'No one laughed then, I am here to tell you.'

The tiny figures shouted and swore at each other.

Inside, the audience had started to enjoy the play, sustained by the sense that they were witnessing an irretrievable disaster. After the first initial giggles, the more audacious among them now dared to laugh out loud, after the man in wellingtons made a particularly long and violent speech. People exchanged glances with their companions. There was a smirk of complacency on their features. The middle-aged shifted uncomfortably and prepared angry speeches of self-justification for when the lights came up; the young nudged each other and giggled.

Brayne wrote in his notebook with a supercilious expression.

'Laughably inept is what I'd call it,' said Jasper in a piercing whisper. 'Amazing that people thought it was the greatest work of the decade, isn't it? Completely lacking in any content or idea, I'd say.' He turned in alarm as a voice hissed in his ear: 'Keep your fucking mouth shut or I'll break your head open.'

Florence, too, turned sharply, to see Gude kneeling by their row again, white-faced and irate. 'Just shut up,' he said. 'Just keep your fucking mouth shut.' He glared at Jasper then at Brayne and then at Florence. Their eyes met in a fixed, locked stare. Florence looked into his intensely blue eyes, uncertain whether there was an answering sign of recognition. For a few seconds, Gude stared fixedly at her, then he doubled backwards and retreated down the aisle. Florence strained her eyes in the darkness for another glimpse of him. She felt sure he had recognised her. Vivid memories of their Holland Park encounter distracted her from the play.

'You can go in now,' the house manager told the friends of Jerry Gude, who were drinking in the bar. 'There's a short change of scene. If you'd like to come this way please?'

They looked at each other for a moment. No one rose to their feet. Lucinda Harpie-Kerr picked up her glass reluctantly. 'I suppose we can't bring these in with us?'

'I am afraid not, madam. No glasses in the auditorium.'

'The screen has gone blank,' said Earish. 'What's happening?'

'Fucking poor quality,' said Bone to the manager. 'Can't you get better pictures? It's all covered with wavy lines.'

'Interference,' said the manager. 'It's the police cars. Would you be kind enough to – '

'Maurice, old son?' said Corner, getting up slowly.

'Where's everybody going? Aren't we going to watch the play after all?'

'We're going to sit down. There's a scene change.'

'I think I'll stay out here, if that's all right,' said Earish. 'I don't want to go inside much. I like this little screen.' There was a short silence, as they looked at each other.

'We'll stay put, guvnor,' said Corner, 'if it's all the same to you. Unless Galen here wants . . .?'

'I'm not fucking going in there,' said Bone. 'Sitting in those terrible seats. Give you a real pain in the bum.'

The house manager shrugged and went away.

'Anyway,' said Lucinda, 'we can get the gist of it all out here. We'll be able to tell Jerry we saw everything.'

'Have you seen him, dear lady?'

'Not a glimpse. I suppose he's watching it inside.'

'Not a good wheeze,' said Corner, 'considering his emotional state.'

'Mark my words, we'll have to fucking carry him home,' said Bone darkly.

After another half-hour, the lights went up, indicating the interval. Gude's friends waved and smiled to familiar faces.

'Isn't it marvellous, lovey?' Lucinda Harpie-Kerr said to lots of people.

'Are you going to the party?' someone shouted.

'Have you seen Jerry?'

'. . .awfully talented.'

'. . .can't understand a word.'

'Look, we must have lunch some time.'

In a circle, beneath a pillar, Lady Arabella stood surrounded by a group of her admirers. Fragrant and cool, she smiled and looked around her with a serene expression. Every time she spoke, the admirers burst into enthusiastic laughter.

Eagerly, Florence looked round the bar, wondering if Gude might emerge. What would she say to him if he suddenly appeared? She found, to her consternation, she could remember nothing about the play except for the woman with the carving knife. If they met, Gude would undoubtedly be rude to Alexander. Florence found herself looking forward to the confrontation with relish.

'I quite liked it,' said Marigold. 'I thought it was an absolute scream.'

'What do you think, Florence?' said Jasper.

'The author must be a fascinating man,' said Florence, attempting to steer the conversation towards Gude.

'In need of a straitjacket, if you ask me,' said Jasper.

'What do you know about him?' said Florence crossly.

'Look at Arabella,' said Brayne in an admiring voice. 'Doesn't she look absolutely marvellous tonight?'

'There he is,' Lucinda Harpie-Kerr pointed to a small door behind the bar which had suddenly opened and closed.

'Jerry, I love it!' she shouted. 'Fantastic. Marvellous show.' Several people turned to stare at her.

'Who are you fucking shouting at?' said Bone.

'Jerry just came out of that door.'

They looked in the direction she was pointing.

'Well, he's not there now,' said Corner.

'He was there. I distinctly saw him.'

'You're fucking seeing things.'

'Are you sure he was there?'

'Of course I am. He's gone back in again. He's too nervous to face us, poor love.'

'He's probably next door in the pub,' said Corner. 'Having a few quick ones. All right, Maurice?'

They looked at Earish, who was gazing with a fixed stare at the television screen. 'When's the picture going to start again?' he said.

'Ladies and gentlemen, please take your seats.'

The audience filed back into the theatre.

Gude's friends smiled and waved as they were slowly left in the privacy of the bar.

'Doubles all round?' said Corner. 'Perhaps our friend here had better miss out this round.'

'He'll be all right,' said Lucinda. 'He's still fighting his depression.'

The figures began shouting again on the tiny screen. After a few moments, Lucinda Harpie-Kerr said, 'It is difficult to hear what they're saying isn't it? Do you think we'd miss a lot if we went on to the party now?'

'We've got the gist,' said Corner. 'We can guess the rest.' Lucinda leaned over and gripped Bone's elbow. 'Can you remember what happens in the end, Galen?' she said. 'Since you're the only one who's seen it before?'

'Nothing fucking happens,' said Bone loudly and laughed at some length. 'That's why it's such a fucking awful play.'

'That's all right then,' said Corner. 'We won't have missed anything.'

'What about Jerry?'

'What about him?'

'Won't he be upset if he knows we've left early?'

'He won't know. We'll see him at the party.'

'Come along, Maurice lovey. He's looking a bit tired, Galen. Can you give him a hand.'

Slowly Gude's friends made their way out through the empty foyer into the street.

· CHAPTER · V ·

'It was terrible,' said Pauline, eating a bar of chocolate wafer. 'The audience laughed, in all the wrong places. A lot of that *Commentator* crowd were there.'

'I should have gone,' said Charlie Enever, yawning. 'Perhaps I'll go next week. What do the reviews say?'

'They all love it. A triumph. The rediscovery of a masterpiece. Stood the test of time brilliantly.'

'That's lucky.'

'Oh, yes.'

'After all, our programme might lack a certain credibility if the play was a complete disaster.'

'It was a complete disaster.'

'Yes, but no one's actually said that, have they?'

'Brayne's mounting an attack on it, this week.'

'Oh Brayne . . . Everyone would expect him to hate it.'

'I suppose so.'

'So Gude's booked for next week?'

'Yes. He's got a working script, just some lines he's written down. He wants to say all his lines straight to camera, with the tele-prompter going past.'

'Yes, I'll buy that.'

'The interviews are all set up. I'm seeing all his wives over the next few weeks.'

'Should we actually see them in the programme, I wonder?'

'Oh, I think so. You could also use their voices in the middle of Gude's narrative – if you wanted to.'

'Yes, it sounds good.'

'The thing is to let him ramble.'

'Yes.'

'So that his particular qualities will emerge . . .'

'Precisely.'

Harry Horlick sat at his desk on the Man of the World column, and stared out of the window. He looked at the clock and yawned in an exaggerated manner, then he sat back in his chair and stretched his arms out behind his head.

He wondered if he had any stories for the diary. Inspiration was slow to dawn. He yawned again and sat back in his chair. He thought about his book. He wrote the title, *Shooting Stars*, on a piece of paper and underlined it, several times. The title looked excellent, he thought; he would have a wide field of research, selecting the brightest and most talented of today's youth for prominence in his book. Horlick wondered if he might include himself. He wondered if he knew any bright and talented young people. He had once interviewed a brilliant young novelist who had become famous after a first, glittering, applauded book. The novelist refused to meet Horlick for lunch, claiming he worked every day until three. They met, instead, for a cup of tea in a small Italian café. At four the novelist stood up and said he had to go back to work; Horlick couldn't remember his name any more.

'It's important to get Gude in here first thing in the morning. He's no good later on.'

'He must be able to read his script.'

'How's your murderer?'

'Norman Crisp?'

'Yes.'

'He's rung me up four times this week. I think the documentary has gone to his head. He wants to do another programme.'

'Can't you get rid of him?'

Pauline screwed up her sweet wrapper thoughtfully. 'He's interesting. I find his philosophy of life rather fascinating.'

'Do you intend to trouble the typewriter this afternoon, Horlick?' said the diary editor.

'Bit short of stories, as a matter of fact.'

'Go through the invitations. Find something to go to.' Horlick read out the list. 'Bishop of Brigg launches his new book, *God Wants to Change the World*. Julian Jasper's wine tasting at the Lower Depths Cellars. Pipeman of the Year. *The Englishwoman's WC*. I say, that wine tasting looks rather interesting.'

'Go to *The Englishwoman's WC*,' said the diary editor. 'It's Arabella Spring-Greene's first book. You should find someone there to write about.'

'Sounds good,' said Horlick, yawning. He picked up the invitation and returned to his desk. He gazed at the clock again. 'I suppose I could ring up the Bishop of Brigg and ask him if his wife is having an affair?'

'Yes, why don't you,' said the diary editor sarcastically.

Horlick looked up the bishop in the Church Directory and dialled the number. 'Hello,' he said. 'Could I speak to the Bishop of Brigg please? Horlick from the *Reporter*.' After a short pause he said, 'Good afternoon your Grace. I wondered if I might just put a few questions to you about – er, about your new book. Yes it seems very interesting indeed. Certainly we'll do a few paragraphs about it . . . Yes. Where exactly did you get the idea from . . .'

Later that evening, Horlick stood at the doorway of Minitz House, looking up at the tall Georgian building which was conspicuous among the shabbier offices in Soho. He was reluctant to go inside and embark on the tedious round of introducing himself to the assembled celebrities. He felt in his pocket for his notebook. In the foyer a group of attractive girls took his coat and invited him to sign his name in the book. Horlick stared at them enviously. Reluctantly he got into the lift.

The scent of flowers assailed him nine floors up as he stepped out into a world of glittering lights. Thick carpet absorbed his footsteps; chandeliers dazzled his eyes. Low sofas round the walls were piled with satin cushions. Prints in matching colours covered the ivory walls. A chrome and glass cocktail bar was built into one corner of the room, behind which a white-coated barman was in attendance.

At the centre of the room, Lady Arabella Spring-Greene stood surrounded by her customary crowd of admirers. She was dressed entirely in pink, in a shimmering dress which hung in folds from a low neck to her calves. Her blonde hair fell in a cascade of curls over her back and shoulders. Her lips were full and wide and slightly parted. From time to time she laughed softly, whereupon the admirers, as if on cue, laughed too, much more loudly and for much longer. As they did so, Arabella set her lips together and lowered her pearly eyelids.

'Would you like a copy of the book?' Horlick turned and saw the girl who had sat next to Watmough at the *Commentator* lunch.

'Ah ha,' said Horlick. 'We've met before.'

Venetia smiled without interest. She seemed unimpressed.

'At that boring *Commentator* lunch,' Horlick persisted. He looked across the room and saw Norris Pleasant, Evelyn Fragment and Alexander Brayne at the heart of the adoring crowd.

'I am from the Man of the World,' said Horlick. 'I'm supposed to write a piece about all this.'

Venetia smiled at him vacantly.

'Anyone interesting here?'

'Mr Minitz is over there,' she said, pointing to the far corner of the room where a crowd of people were talking loudly. Horlick went over to the bar. 'Up the workers!' said a voice at his side. He turned to see Aldous Watmough drinking white wine.

'Oh, hello Watmough. What are you doing here?'

'Strictly pleasure, comrade. Make the most of it. Come the revolution everyone in this room will be digging potatoes.'

'Oh.'

'Covering the event, are you? A few pars for the diary?'

'I'm afraid so.'

'Arabella's looking grand, don't you think.'

'You're a friend of hers?'

'Oh, for many years. Here we are – Pleasant, Fragment, myself – all middle-aged men, still rivals, after all these years, for her affection. We would have killed for her at Cambridge, yet she turned us all down. What did Jerry Gude have that we didn't? This isn't much of a party,' Watmough went on. 'It's like a ladies' powder room in here.'

'Horrible, isn't it?'

'Of course, Arabella gives pretty serious parties. An embarrassing display of wealth and privilege, but highly enjoyable all the same,' said Watmough. 'Have you ever been to any of them?'

'No,' said Horlick.

'She's pretty smart at organisation. This isn't much of a party.'

'Who's that dwarfish man with a cigar?' said Horlick, looking across the room.

'That's Morton Minitz.'

'Looks like a crook.'

'These press barons are all evil men,' said Watmough. 'Oppressors of free speech and haters of socialism. Dig into his background and you'll discover a real can of worms, my young friend.'

'This is a glorious party,' said Lady Arabella softly, exhaling cigarette smoke through her nose. 'It's a fine party. Are you enjoying yourself, Evelyn?'

'Yes, thank you,' said Fragment, standing stiffly at her side, as though at attention.

'I think I need another drink,' Arabella said. 'Would you be an angel, Evelyn?' Fragment nodded and bowed slightly from the waist. He strode across the room to the bar, passing Watmough on his way.

'Good evening, Aldous. This is a marvellous night for Arabella.'

'Indeed it is. Her first book. An original work – not an exalted theme perhaps, but every word her own.'

Fragment leaned forward slightly. 'She has worked so hard on this book, Aldous,' he said, his voice shaking slightly with emotion. 'So hard that you or I would have simply given up under the strain. She has put herself into it. She has eaten, drunk and slept this book for the last year. You couldn't tell from her appearance – how ravishingly lovely she looks tonight – but it has taken a terrible toll on her.'

Aldous stared at Arabella with his mouth slightly open. 'She looks all right to me,' he said.

'It has drained her emotionally,' said Fragment. 'Thank God, the book is over, now. I think it's a marvellous, wonderful book, don't you?'

'I have yet to have the pleasure of reading it.'

Fragment noticed Horlick standing at Watmough's elbow obviously listening to the conversation. He looked at him in silent curiosity.

'No, I haven't read it yet, either,' said Horlick, grasping Fragment's hand.

'This is young Horlick. He's writing about the party for the papers,' said Watmough.

'Are you going to write about Arabella's book?'

'Oh, definitely.'

'You must say how brilliant it is. Would you like me to give you a quote about it?'

'Er – yes.'

'Yes. Well, you can say the following: "I think it is a marvellously entertaining book, brilliantly written and most amusing." ' Fragment paused while Horlick's hand laboured slowly across the paper. ' "It is a book I shall treasure and I urge everyone to buy a copy." That's the end of the quote.'

'Thank you very much.'

'Don't mention it.' Fragment went away to the bar to refresh his glasses.

'What is Fragment doing here?' Horlick asked Watmough.

'We admirers of Arabella do our best to support her.'

'Oh.'

'Besides, one of his own lavatories features in the book.'

'That's quite a good story, don't you think?' Horlick picked up his notebook. 'I can't read what I've written.'

'I should make it up.'

'It wasn't a very good quote, anyway, was it?'

'Piss poor, comrade.'

Arabella was talking to Norris Pleasant. His face was bronze and glistened as if oil had been applied to its surface. 'It's such a difficult decision,' she was saying. 'Of course, I'd do anything for Jerry – but I couldn't say anything dreadful about him.'

Pleasant smiled, and raised her hand to his shiny lips.

'I think the director is rather sweet,' she said. 'He seems a very clever and artistic boy. I suppose it will be all right.'

'What do you still feel for Jerry?' said Pleasant.

'Well,' said Arabella, 'we've kept in touch.'

'In a physical sense,' said Pleasant. 'In terms of body language . . .'

'I'm going to take up more exercise next summer,' said Horlick. 'I feel like exercise. Yes, I'm definitely going to get into shape again.'

Watmough looked at Pleasant's sleek and shapely figure. 'It's odd thinking so much about your body.'

'I suppose it depends on the kind of body you've got.'

'Isn't it curious,' said Watmough, 'that the young go round talking so much about their bodies? I can't remember ever thinking about mine, when I was your age. It merely functioned – maintained life – and was subjected to all kinds of dreadful abuse without giving me any trouble at all.'

'Well, in your day everyone abused their bodies frightfully.'

'They did. Everyone smoked and drank and – well, we had a good time,' said Watmough lamely.

'Yes.'

Pleasant walked past them leaving a faint odour of cologne. Arabella came up to Watmough and said: 'How are you, Aldous? How stout you're becoming these days.'

Watmough regarded his stomach with irritation. 'It's nothing to do with me,' he said. 'It just keeps on growing.'

'You're a naughty man,' said Arabella. 'You've been bullying Evelyn terribly.'

'What have I done?'

'You've been writing the most unkind things about him in your newspaper.'

'That's my job,' said Watmough. 'He doesn't mind.'

Arabella shook her head and leaned towards him. 'He's very upset,' she said softly. Her hair swung forward over her eyes. Horlick stared, greedily, down the front of her dress.

'You must stop it,' she said, hitting Watmough playfully and rather hard on the shoulder.

'What do you take particular exception to, Arabella?'

'That piece about Evelyn's new job. You made him look silly.'

'It's a silly job.'

'Oh, I do hate you,' said Arabella. 'Why can't you write something nice about him?'

'He could write to the editor and complain.'

'Well, of course he couldn't. He'd look even sillier.'

'We should definitely publish it.'

'Now, you must promise not to do it again.'

'What about my integrity as a writer, Arabella?'

'Promise. Never another unkind word?'

'Too ruthless,' said Watmough.

Arabella slapped him, rather harder this time, and went away. Horlick looked on open-mouthed. Watmough stared at him. 'Why don't you go and circulate, comrade? Find someone else to talk to?'

Morton Minitz stood like a fixed point at the centre of the room and looked with satisfaction at his guests. He caught the eye of Venetia, who was moving among the guests with a tray of drinks. Obediently she came and stood beside him.

'Venetia, are the press here?'

'Well, there's some man from the *Reporter*. I think he's writing something.'

'Take me to him,' said Minitz.

'It's him,' she said, pointing at Horlick.

Minitz regarded him silently.

'It's the best I can do, at the moment,' said Venetia apologetically.

'Venetia, I want to read about this book on every front page tomorrow,' said Minitz. 'OK, let's start with him.'

'I'm fascinated by the programme,' said Brayne. 'I think it's terribly brave of you to do it.'

'What did you think of Jerry's play?'

Brayne twisted his features into an expression of regret. 'I thought it was awfully poor,' he said. 'It just has nothing to say.'

'Oh how sad. Can't I persuade you to like it?'

'Not even you, Arabella.'

'Poor Jerry.'

Minitz grasped Horlick by the hand. 'Mr Horlick. I understand you represent the press here tonight.'

'Well, Man of the World, actually.'

'Let me refresh your glass,' said Minitz.

'Oh, thanks.'

'Tell me about yourself, Mr Horlick. What kind of stories do you write?'

'Well,' said Horlick, 'I – '

'That's very interesting,' said Minitz. 'Let me give you an outline of the most interesting items in the book,' said Minitz. 'First, and of especial interest to you, are the famous people who invited Lady Arabella into the privacy of their own bathrooms . . .'

Horlick half-closed his eyes and stifled a yawn.

Arabella smiled sweetly at Brayne. 'Alexander,' she said, 'I must talk to you about the party. Can we agree on our list of guests? I must send the invitations out soon.'

Brayne smiled at her. 'I'm sure I can leave all that to you, Arabella. It's bound to be a marvellous party, like all the others.'

'I thought we might ask everyone to dress in black and white.'

'Oh, how amusing,' said Brayne. His face clouded slightly as he wondered how effective he would look in fancy dress.

'You could come as Hamlet.'

Brayne blushed with pleasure. 'I've asked Plugge to write a short piece about your book, by the way,' he said confidingly. 'It will be in next week. He'll say something nice about it.'

'Oh, how adorable of you,' said Arabella. 'One feels so nervous with one's first book . . . tell me, what did you really think of it?'

'Terrifically entertaining,' said Brayne promptly. 'I think you've done a brilliant job.'

'But what about the writing?' Arabella persisted.

'I thought it was marvellous.'

'Did you really, Alexander?'

'Absolutely . . .'

'You see, Aldous,' said Fragment earnestly. 'People have lost faith in the idea of the family. They no longer feel that society has any respect for that all-important, autonomous unit which is able to resist all pressure from state intervention. The father, the mother, the children. There they are – they have existed for thousands of years, inviolate, undeterred, invincible.'

'It's a ridiculous mission, old friend. I advise you to have nothing to do with it.'

'It is critically important that we take the initiative in reasserting the goals of discipline and restraint.'

'Don't say I didn't warn you.'

'The family is an important unit,' said Fragment. 'In my own case, too. My wife, as you know, does wonderful work in the community. She is a pillar of the local church and maintains a stout presence in the – ah – family home. Indeed, were it not for the lone lance-corporal there, keeping duty at her post, I could not, of course, carry out my public duties.'

'She doesn't come to London?'

'Infrequently – with the children, of course. Anyway, she prefers the country. She hates London,' said Fragment, looking depressed.

'I like you, Mr Horlick. I like your style.'

'I say! Thank you.'

'I feel sure that you have a great future in journalism.'

'I can't say I'm convinced.'

'One hundred per cent confidence,' said Minitz seriously. 'Without that, Mr Horlick, you are nothing. Whatever you write, without one hundred per cent confidence, it will come to nothing.'

'Well,' said Horlick, emboldened by this advice, 'I was thinking of writing a book.'

'Don't think about it,' said Morton Minitz. 'Do it.'

'Yes,' said Horlick. 'Well, I thought I might do a book about successful people – you know – young, talented people who were likely to be famous in the future. I think it would be jolly interesting to find out who they were.'

'Go on, young man,' said Minitz.

'Well, that's all I'd thought of so far,' said Horlick. 'I'd go off and talk to all these people, and then I'd write down what they said.'

'Young man!' said Minitz. 'I like the sound of this book. You've just got yourself a publisher.'

Horlick gaped at him. 'What?'

'I like it. I'll buy it.'

'Oh, well, that's frightfully good of you.'

'I am keen to publish all kinds of works by young and talented people.'

Horlick flushed with pleasure.

'Shall we say an advance of five thousand pounds?'

Horlick blinked rapidly. 'Yes. Yes, that sounds fine.'

'OK, Mr Horlick. Start right now.'

'I say, thanks very much.'

'I have felt recently that a new tide has turned,' said Evelyn Fragment. 'It is my task to shape and form the great swell of public opinion.'

'What do the opinion polls say?' said Alexander Brayne.

'They indicate a great swell of popular opinion, as I said.'

'That's very interesting.'

'The entire nation is behind us in this campaign.'

'A vote winner?'

'One hopes, naturally . . .'

'The magazine is behind you all the way in this one. We'll back you editorially.'

'I'm so pleased to hear that. So often, the young have no idea – '

'I think what you're doing is absolutely right,' said Brayne with sincerity.

'You mean he bought it just like that?'

'Yes. He's offered me five thousand pounds.'

Watmough smiled with an insincere expression. 'I'd thought of doing a book myself. I thought I might put together a book of essays, loosely based on my columns, you know, but not just a rehash of all the old stuff I've written before.' He laughed. 'I thought I'd call it *Left Foot Forward*. Has a good sort of ring about it.'

Horlick nodded. 'I just said I wanted to write a book and he immediately offered . . .'

'I think I might just mention my book to him.'

Over by the gleaming cocktail bar, Pleasant and Brayne were glaring at each other. 'I really can't understand why you're here,' said Brayne. 'I think it's most unfortunate. Had I had any idea – '

'Ravello is unpleasantly cold at this time of the year,' said Pleasant baring his gleaming teeth. 'Besides, I'm an old friend of our charming hostess.'

'Are you indeed,' said Brayne.

'Are you a friend of hers too?'

'I simply don't want to discuss it,' said Brayne. 'I've nothing to say to – '

'My latest book is out next week,' said Pleasant with an expression of triumph. 'I wondered if you'd like to review it. In your own inimitable style, of course.'

'No, I would not,' said Brayne. 'I don't give space to pornography.'

'It's particularly up your street,' said Pleasant. 'It advances the ideal of high monogamy. A return to fidelity and – wait for this one, Alexander – prolonged chastity. Now, that's something you approve of, isn't it?'

Brayne half-closed his eyes in a shudder.

'I really must make a move,' he said. 'We have nothing to gain from further communication. If you would excuse me. . .'

'America the week after next,' said Pleasant. 'I'll leave you my address if you like. By the way, I advise some extra supplement of the B2 complex, Alexander. Your skin is looking just a little cloudy. That's one of the risks of prolonged chastity, as it happens. The circulation becomes a little sluggish. I recommend a herbal preparation called – '

Brayne turned on his heel and walked angrily through the crowded room. Pleasant watched him with an expression of curiosity.

Lady Arabella moved through the groups of guests, offering to sign their books and shaking their hands. 'Tell me,' said Horlick, anxious to obtain a quote for his diary piece. 'What gave you the idea of writing about lavatories.'

Arabella smiled at him. Horlick felt himself blushing and smirking in response. 'You don't really want to know, do you?' she said.

'Oh, do tell me,' said Horlick.

'Well, it's a long story. I first had the idea last summer when . . .' As Arabella spoke on, Horlick gazed at her in silent admiration.

'He's bought it.' Watmough stared in excitement at Horlick. 'He's bought mine, too.'

'Your book, too?'

'Yes.'

'*Left Foot Forward?*'

'*Left Foot Forward.*'

'That's incredible.'

'I owe you a lunch or two for tipping me off.'

'Oh, not at all.'

Watmough and Horlick drank each other's health. Horlick stared at his notebook. 'There's not much here,' he said. 'Just a few useless quotes from Fragment and a long story from Lady Arabella about how she had the idea for the book which I simply can't remember.'

Watmough wrinkled his forehead. 'If you want a good story,' he said, 'it might be worth your while to look into the more intimate life of the evening's most gracious couple.'

'Who do you mean?'

Watmough narrowed his eyes. 'This is strictly off the record, but were you to investigate the early history of Arabella and that dear old prig, Fragment, you would find that they shared some wilder moments together in their youth.'

'Really,' said Horlick, his eyes wide with excitement.

'Yes. In view of all this Family Life ethos that Fragment is extolling at the moment, it might be amusing to discover what he was doing in nineteen sixty-five, month August, place Isle of Wight. There, I can't tell you more than that.'

'Oh.'

'Strictly between ourselves, comrade.'

'Of course.'

· CHAPTER · VI ·

Florence Barge stood outside the Happy Girls Agency in Hanover Square and looked at the jobs displayed on postcards inside the window. 'Experienced Girl Friday, £9000,' said one notice. 'Friendly, efficient secretary for happy-go-lucky office,' said another. She went inside and stared at the notice boards demanding secretarial skills or attractive temperaments. Three girls were waiting to be interviewed for suitable appointments. 'First Rupert got it, then I got it, and then I discovered that Algy had got it too,' one of them was saying in a loud whisper to her companion.

'Are you sure?'

'The doctor said there was no doubt.'

'Poor you. Sounds beastly.'

'Rupert's absolutely furious.'

'What does Algy think?'

Florence stood half-heartedly at the end of the queue for several minutes. 'I think I'd like to work in public relations,' one of the girls said. 'I really want a job where I can meet people.' Florence suddenly made up her mind. She opened the door quickly and stepped out onto the street in the direction of Soho Square. The decision made, she felt as though a load had been lifted from her shoulders. She would go back to Mrs Crisp, who would certainly offer her another job. A slight rain began to drift in the wind as Florence turned into Turkey Street, looking for the Underground. There were restaurants on each side of the road and a sex shop between them. The remains of a pigeon littered the gutter. She stepped aside quickly and continued to walk on.

At the corner of the street three derelict old tramps sitting on the pavement shouted at her. As she hesitated, one of them gave a wild cry and tried to rise to his feet. Florence looked away in alarm but, to her horror, the man succeeded in getting up, and started waving at her. He was shouting wildly and was clearly intending to come across the road to her. Heedless of the stream of traffic, the tramp stepped out bravely into the middle of the road. A messenger bike swerved sharply to avoid him, sending its rider sprawling at the side of the kerb. The bike lay on its side, its wheels spinning in the air. A woman screamed. From the nearby restaurant several waiters came out to stare. Undaunted, the tramp came on, shouting more loudly.

Florence turned and ran quickly away from the dreadful scene. In her haste, she collided with a person standing against the wall, outside the Dog and Biscuit, at a precarious angle. 'Help,' said Jerry Gude. 'I think I'm having a heart attack.' He reached out and grabbed Florence's shoulder, making it impossible for her to go on. 'It's a coronary,' Gude gasped. 'It's my heart.'

'Lie down,' said Florence. 'Don't panic. I'll call an ambulance.'

'No, no,' shouted Gude wildly. 'I don't want to go in one of those. I want to go home.' He sat down on the pavement and whimpered quietly. 'I want a drink.' Then he said, 'Oh, God, I am a very wicked man.'

'Are you?' said Florence, looking round for help. A small crowd had collected outside the continental butcher's shop.

'He's been run over!' an old man observed. 'One of those bikes ran him down in the road.'

'Is he dead?'

'No, he's shouting.'

'He's concussed. He should lie down.'

'You're concussed,' said Florence. 'I think you should go to hospital.' In the distance they heard the sound of an approaching ambulance siren.

'For God's sake,' said Gude, struggling to his feet. 'I'm not going to die in an ambulance. Taxi! Taxi!' He lurched out into the middle of the road and waved his arm at an approaching cab. The taxi stopped.

'Let me get in,' said Gude, gasping for breath.

'Where to, guv?' the driver said.

'He wants to go home,' said Florence. 'Holland Park, please.'

Gude gained the back seat with difficulty. Then he reached forward and grabbed Florence's wrist.

'Please,' he said, rolling his eyes wildly, 'please don't leave me alone.'

Florence hesitated, wondering whether to commit herself to the danger of the taxi or retain the safer ground outside.

'Please,' said Gude. He gazed at her in terror, then jerked at her wrist and pulled her onto the seat. The door closed and the taxi set off down the narrow, interlocking streets. Inside, they sat in silence, except for the laboured breathing of Gude. Florence hoped he would not die in the taxi.

'How are you feeling now?' she said cautiously.

Gude leaned back on the seat and closed his eyes.

'Funny sort of weather for October,' observed the taxi driver as the cab swung up past Soho Square towards Oxford Street.

'I don't want to die,' Gude whimpered. 'A hundred women are longing for this moment, but I don't want to go yet.' He held on to her hand tightly.

'Although, as I was saying to the last geezer in the cab, I blame it all on this radioactive cloud that's hanging over Britain.'

'Oh, yes,' said Florence.

'I'm a complete SHIT,' said Gude. Florence sat back to distance herself from the alcoholic fumes wafting from his breath.

'I am worthless. I don't deserve to live, any more. I am – '

' – and every time it rains it washes down this great layer of dust from the sky which gets into the water supply.'

'Yes, it's terrible.'

'I am a boil on the neck of humanity. I don't deserve to be called a man.'

'What's your line of work then?'

'I'm staring at the wreckage of my life. I want to say I'm sorry. I'm very, very sorry.'

'Still at college, are you?'

'I have ruined so many lives, and brought happiness – '

'Working in London? This your first job?'

'Brought happiness to no one.'

'No, I'm – ' said Florence, straining to hear the taxi driver's words.

'Yes, funny old place, London,' the driver went on, his hunched black back impassive. 'Good if you've got the wherewithal to enjoy it, know what I mean, but very hard if you haven't got the readies. Very hard.'

'Arabella, Amanda,' said Gude staring down at the shiny, plastic seat. 'And Lucinda. Dogs every one. Oh God, they're coming to exact retribution. They're coming for me. Their eyes are shining with vengeance.'

'That's what I always say.'

'Yes?'

'Bless them all,' cried Gude wildly. 'All good girls till they met me.'

'Keep smiling and you'll be all right.'

'Yes.'

The cab spun round the narrow streets, stopping abruptly from time to time at red lights or congested junctions. After ten minutes, Florence was alarmed to see that they had not progressed beyond Bloomsbury and seemed to be moving very slowly.

'Where are we?' said Gude, suddenly gripping her hand.

'Charlotte Lane.'

'Right,' shouted Gude very loudly. 'Stop the cab at once.'

'I had that Evelyn Fragment in the back of the cab once,' the driver said, unstoppable in his reminiscence. 'Very expensively dressed, and wouldn't you like to know where he was bound for an evening of excitement?'

'Why do you want him to stop?' said Florence in alarm. 'You must go back home and have a rest.'

'None of my business where he wants to go, naturally, or who he's with, if you catch my meaning. Suffice it to say I did not form the impression she was his lady wife. Still, a fare's a fare. I take them where they want to go. No questions asked.'

'Stop,' Gude shouted again. His voice, weak and emotional, made no impression on the driver's stolid back.

'British jobs for British workers,' said the cabbie. 'You see, I've nothing against the blacks myself, but I won't take no one further south than Victoria. They can run their own cabs down there can't they for their own kind.'

'I want to get out,' said Gude, 'I am a professional. I want to stop.'

'Mind you, those terrorists,' the driver went on inexorably. 'Only one thing they understand, the way I see it. Hanging's too good for them. Personally, I'd string them up by the – '

Florence struggled to free her wrist from Gude's grip and tapped on the driver's back. He swung his head round from the wheel.

'We would like to stop here,' she said.

The driver braked. 'Right you are. Gent all right, is he?' he said. 'Looks a bit peaky to me.'

'He's rather upset,' said Florence. 'He doesn't feel very well.'

'That's six pounds fifty,' said the driver, 'if you please.' Florence looked at Jerry who was standing against the wall with his eyes closed. He showed no sign of paying the bill. Surprised by the amount, Florence opened her handbag and took out two five-pound notes. She handed them over to the driver, who leaned over in an exaggerated manner and began to delve into his cash box for change.

Florence stood in confusion trying to calculate the tip. After a few moments of the cabbie's prolonged rummaging she gave up the attempt. 'That's all right,' she said quickly. 'Thank you.'

'And thank you,' he replied. He looked at Gude. 'Hope your friend picks up a bit. What he wants, if you take my advice, is a few cups of strong black coffee. No offence. Keep smiling. Cheerio.'

The cab disappeared into the distance. Florence regarded Gude with some anxiety.

'Where do you want to go?' she said.

Gude opened his eyes with a jerk.

'Who are you?' he said suddenly.

Florence looked at him in surprise.

'Who are you?' Gude shouted again. 'Where have you come from, you unspeakably beautiful creature?'

'Outside the Dog and Biscuit,' said Florence.

'Let me take you out to dinner,' said Gude. 'Tell me all about yourself. But first, I have to finish my business.'

He took a slim envelope from his pocket and began to walk unsteadily up the road in the direction of the *Commentator* office.

'What about your heart attack?'

'The spasm has passed,' said Gude, smiling at her.

'Are you sure you're all right?'

Gude stopped by the *Commentator*'s shiny black railings.

'Oh,' said Florence, recognising the building. 'You don't want to go in here, do you?'

In reply, Gude struggled to open the heavy black door. Inside, Marigold looked up in surprise as Gude stood before her, breathing heavily and gripping the table.

'Yes, can I help you?' said Marigold pugnaciously, fingering her pearls. 'What are you doing here, Florence?'

'Who are you?' said Gude loudly.

'Who are you?' said Marigold. 'Kindly state your business.'

'Look here, you toffee-nosed bitch,' said Gude leaning forward and breathing into her face. 'It's none of your fucking business who I am. I'm going upstairs to deliver this piece, OK? Now move out of the fucking way.'

'Is he a friend of yours?' said Marigold accusingly to Florence.

'He's the man,' said Florence, whispering in excitement. 'The man I met in Holland Park. The one who wrote the play.'

'Why have you brought him here?'

'He wasn't very well. He pulled me into the taxi. I haven't brought him.' As she spoke, Gude pushed past her and began to climb the narrow stairs unsteadily, colliding with the walls as he did so.

'I just met him in the street,' said Florence. 'I think he's feeling better now.'

'What a disgusting person. I shall call the police. Does he have any business here?'

'He wants to see Alexander,' said Florence. 'Don't call the police, Marigold. He's perfectly all right now.'

'Where is he going?'

'Upstairs. Should I follow him?'

'He smells abominably of drink.'

'Well, don't blame me,' said Florence. 'I couldn't stop him coming here.'

At the top of the stairs there was a loud crash as Gude collided with a cupboard, containing bound copies of the magazine. He pushed open the editor's door and found Brayne sitting behind a huge oak desk inlaid with brown leather.

'Mr Gude,' said Brayne, looking up from a pile of letters. 'An unexpected pleasure. Please sit down.'

Gude stood rocking at the door.

Brayne looked up and saw Florence standing at the door. His mouth sagged in amazement. She waved brightly at him. 'What a surprise, Alexander.'

'What are you doing here?' said Brayne.

'Oh,' said Florence, thinking quickly. 'I was just passing, and I wanted to look something up in *Who's Who*. So I just dropped in.'

'Have you come with Gude?'

'Who? Oh, Gude. No, no, we just happened to arrive together,' she said evasively.

Gude looked about him. The room was in fashionable chaos. Old piles of yellowing newspapers littered one corner; in another corner a small, stuffed dog lay beneath a battered lectern. Oak bookshelves had been fitted along one wall, containing a random collection of books, mostly sent free for review to the office. A pile of unframed cartoons leaned against one wall and several silver cups, awarded for merit and achievement, decorated the top shelf of the bookcase. A canvas bag, green and shabby, lay underneath Brayne's desk and on one shelf of the bookcase a pair of brown walking shoes were lined side by side.

'Are you the fucker who rubbished my play?' shouted Gude. Brayne nodded in silence. 'I've brought my reply,' said Gude. 'As requested. Here it is. Two thousand words explaining why you're completely and utterly wrong.'

'Splendid,' said Brayne, taking the envelope. 'Delivered in person.'

'I am a professional,' said Gude.

Florence went to the bookcase and took down the copy of *Who's Who*. Furtively she turned to GUDE, Jerry. Born nineteen forty-two, only child of Elphick and Mary Gude, educated at Winchester and King's College, Cambridge. That meant he was forty-five.

'I have never, EVER,' shouted Gude, 'let anyone down.'

Brayne's lips moved soundlessly.

'Although,' said Gude, 'God knows I have been let down many, MANY times myself. I have been endlessly disappointed by humanity.' Gude stopped speaking and stared ahead of him, as if in a trance.

Florence skimmed over Gude's literary achievements. 'Married, first, Lady Arabella Tempest (div); second, . . . ' Florence stared at the page. He had been married three times. Was he divorced now? She hurriedly consulted the book again. Yes, he was.

'Well,' said Brayne. 'Thank you so much for the piece.'

'When are you going to run it?' said Gude.

'I'll have to see what it's worth,' said Brayne absently.

'What it's worth?' said Gude. 'You got my play completely and utterly WRONG.'

'Naturally that's your opinion – '

'It's not an opinion. It's a FACT.'

Quintin Plugge wandered into the office. 'Ah, Jerry,' he said. 'Good to see you, old boy. Hear the play was a great success.'

'Apparently it's a matter of opinion,' said Gude fiercely.

'Never mind,' said Brayne, pacifically. 'Leave the piece with me and I'll give it a look.'

'Never mind?' Jerry Gude shouted. 'Just don't tell me to never mind. OK.'

In reply, Brayne walked over to the bookcase and began to thumb through the yellowing piles of newspapers. 'Have you found what you're looking for?' he said to Florence.

With a wild cry of anger, Gude suddenly turned and threw himself upon Brayne, grabbing him round the neck and bending his head back towards him.

Brayne cried out in pain. Gude released him abruptly and he fell on the floor. Gude turned and delivered a savage kick to Brayne's groin, which caused him to convulse in agony. Florence screamed as Brayne rolled towards her feet. In the distance she could hear the wail of a police siren which seemed to be approaching. Gude knelt on the floor and was just about to seize Brayne by the throat, when Plugge bravely intervened, hurling his fragile body upon Gude and, by sheer force of his own momentum, knocking him sideways against the floor.

'All right, Jerry,' Plugge gasped. 'Calm down, old chap.'

'Let me kill him,' Gude shouted, struggling to his feet. 'Let me finish him off.'

'Steady on, Jerry.'

By this time, Brayne was on his feet, too, advancing upon Gude with menace. He came towards him with fists clenched and was about to swing his right arm up under Gude's chin, when Florence caught Brayne a shattering blow on the side of his head with the *Who's Who*, which sent him spinning into the corner of the wall.

'Don't hit him,' she screamed.

'Steady on,' cried Plugge again. 'My dear Brayne, are you all right?'

Brayne moaned quietly against the wall. Gude breathed deeply, looking wildly round the room. He went over to Brayne's desk, where he stood motionless, resting either hand on the brown leather top.

'I have never EVER,' he shouted, 'met such a complete and utter PRICK as you are.' He gazed at Brayne, now hunched in a crouched position on the floor. 'I am an artist, and don't you ever, EVER speak like that to me again.'

Gude took a deep breath, preparing to continue his flow of

invective, but there was a sudden pause. Leaning forward, Gude's eyes took on a strange expression of intensity, while his face turned dramatically pale.

'I am,' said Gude, 'I am – ' but he was unable to finish his sentence as he leaned forward and expelled a copious stream of vomit over Brayne's desk.

Florence gave a cry of horror, as Gude's body heaved and jerked until he had voided himself of his unsavoury load. Plugge looked round the room in confusion. 'Oh, really,' he said. 'This is just too awful. I'll have to get Marigold to clear it up.'

He walked towards the door, just as a policeman, wearing a peaked cap and gloves, strode in at a brisk pace. 'Nine-nine-nine call, sir,' he said. 'What's the emergency?'

'Emergency, officer?' said Plugge. 'I can't imagine.'

'Girl downstairs dialled us,' said the policeman. On the floor Brayne groaned loudly.

'She has a tendency to hysteria,' said Plugge.

Florence went over to Jerry. 'Are you all right?' she said.

The policeman regarded the shaking form of Gude. 'Is he an intruder?'

'No,' said Florence.

'Yes,' said Plugge. 'He has forced his way into the office and attacked my poor colleague down there on the floor.'

The officer regarded Brayne with concern. 'Has there been an assault, sir?'

'I don't want to make anything of it,' said Brayne, staggering to his feet. 'There's nothing going on now.'

'A break-in, sir?'

'Look,' said Plugge. 'If you could possibly take him away with you so we could clean up the office, we'll say no more about the whole thing.'

'Right you are,' said the policeman. 'Of course, we couldn't put him in the car like that. I'll radio for a van.'

'Thank you so much,' said Plugge.

The policeman propelled the now quiescent Gude out through the door. As he passed Florence he gazed at her – it seemed to her –

in silent entreaty. 'Where are you taking him?' she said to the officer.

'Somewhere he can have a nice rest, miss,' he said. 'Don't you worry about him. He's an old friend of the Force.'

Gude was removed from the room. Florence became aware of Brayne staring at her with a hostile expression. 'Can you explain yourself, Florence?' he said. 'First, you come here with that reprobate and interrupt my morning. Second, you hit me heavily on the head. Have you gone mad?'

'Of course not. He's much older than you. You might have killed him. I'm sorry about your head. Is there a bruise?'

He regarded her coldly. 'I think I'd like to be left alone.'

'But Alexander – '

Plugge took her arm. 'Shall we go and have some coffee? Marigold will clear up all this mess.'

'Are you coming, Alexander.'

Brayne turned away. 'Thank you, Florence, but I would prefer to take an aspirin and sit quietly. Just go away, please, and leave me alone.'

'Come along,' said Plugge. 'It's best to leave him for a little while.'

'Jerry been in?' Vernon Corner took up his usual seat at the corner of the bar and ordered a large whisky. Behind him Maurice Earish and Gerard Bunsen were having an intense conversation.

'Should have been in,' said Galen Bone. 'Hasn't turned up. Fucking late. He's probably lying in some gutter.'

'He's been a bit under the weather since his play,' said Corner.

'It got good reviews. He's fucking lucky.'

'A bad one from the *Commentator*. He's taken it to heart.'

'Well, what's one out of many?'

'Jerry's a perfectionist,' said Corner. 'He wanted them all to be good.'

'And so these amazing monuments to public travel are being desecrated,' Bunsen was saying, 'in an attempt to modernise the Underground stations. The great work of Prykke, Pryce and others is simply being vandalised by bureaucrats who know no better.' He sighed deeply. 'I think I'll just go and look at my bicycle.' He went nervously to the window.

'Is it all right?' said Earish.

'Yes. I wanted to bring it inside, but that landlord person wouldn't let me.'

'Shall we order some lunch? Galen what can you bring us?'

'I told him it was priceless. He told me to fuck off.'

'Steak and kidney, chicken pie, cod and chips.'

'Steak and kidney.'

'Same here.'

Bone slammed a pile of knives and forks on the table.

'Can I have some too,' said Lucinda Harpie-Kerr, coming in in a great gust of perfume.

'What?'

'Steak and kidney.'

'If you want. You should go on a diet. You're getting too fat.'

'Only my stomach. Hello boys,' she said to Earish and Corner.

'Do you know Lucinda Harpie-Kerr,' Earish said, introducing Bunsen. He shuddered in distaste.

'Pleased to meet you,' she said, coughing loudly. She took off her fur coat and flung it onto a chair. Several strands of animal hair were left adhering to her face.

Bone slammed plates of steak and kidney pie on the table.

'Tomato sauce please,' said Lucinda Harpie-Kerr.

'You're fucking joking.'

'No, I'm not.'

'You can't eat steak and kidney with tomato sauce.'

'Why not?'

'Because I say so.'

'They've got brown sauce.'

'So what?'

'So why can't I have tomato sauce?'

'Because,' said Bone slowly, 'you're twice as fat and three times as ugly.'

Angrily, Lucinda Harpie-Kerr got up from the table and strode off in search of the sauce bottle.

'What an abrasive person the landlord is,' said Bunsen, eating pie.

At the Normandie tea room, Quintin Plugge and Florence Barge gazed at each other over a tray of coffee.

'What an unfortunate incident,' said Plugge.

'I've never seen a fight before,' said Florence in excitement. 'I thought you were very brave to stop them, before they drew blood.'

'Gude's notorious for his temper. Do you know him well?'

'I don't know him at all. I keep meeting him by accident.'

'Of course, I don't believe there are such things as accidents.' Plugge's eyes glinted behind his spectacles. 'No, I believe that all these events are preordained. We meet who we are destined to meet. Our fate is ineluctable.'

'You mean I'm fated to meet Jerry Gude?' Florence considered the idea with interest. Then she said: 'I'm surprised Jerry knocked Alexander down so easily. After all he's a much older man.'

'Yes, but he's had a lot of experience in fighting. Alexander isn't very warlike.'

'No,' said Florence.

'But he's terribly clever,' said Plugge. 'We all admire him tremendously.'

'Do you?'

'Yes. You probably wonder what I'm doing working at a small magazine like the *Commentator*. At my age it probably seems rather pathetic to you.'

'No, no.'

'It gives me time,' said Plugge, 'to concentrate on my life's work. You see' – his eyes gleamed gently behind his spectacles – 'something happened to me when I was in my thirties, which completely changed the course of my life. I hope I'm not boring you?'

'No.'

'Well,' said Plugge, leaning forward. 'It happened one day

when I was wandering around in one of those awful new shopping precincts in Brickmanstead, which is the nearest town to where I live. You know how they've ruined the centres of these old market towns with new developments, well I was – '

'It's so hard to make a living as a freelance,' Earish was saying. 'You know, rates have hardly gone up at all during the last three years. You see all these journalists on salaries – with their cars and expenses and free meals – they just live off their expenses and bank their salaries, you know. Whereas the freelance writer – '

'My dear, I know,' said Bunsen. 'Talent and financial reward only rarely go hand in hand.'

'Well, don't assume that I'm all that well off,' said Lucinda.

'You've got a big salary and a company car,' said Earish enviously.

'Well, I have expensive tastes. And I have to maintain my ex-husband,' she said, laughing loudly. 'I give Jerry an allowance, you know. And I collect all his laundry once a week in a bag.'

'That's pretty impressive,' said Earish. 'Would you like to do mine too?'

'Hello,' said Pauline, coming into the pub with a thin young man. Earish and Corner nodded silently.

'We're talking about money,' said Earish. 'That's why we're all so depressed.'

'Are you fucking eating or not?' said Bone, appearing suddenly from behind the bar. 'Because I'm closing the kitchen in five minutes.'

Pauline eyed the food on Earish's plate. 'I'll have some of that,' she said, indicating the mess of pastry and meat. 'What about you, Norman?'

Her companion regarded the food in horror. 'No,' he said in a soft voice, as though it was contaminated.

'Cheer up,' said Lucinda Harpie-Kerr, looking at him hungrily. 'You look as if you could do with building up.'

The man regarded her with a fearful expression. His face was skeletally thin and his hair cut in a uniform length of a quarter of an inch over his entire head. He wore a navy blue T-shirt and black trousers and jacket, which hung stiffly on his thin body.

'I'm Lucinda,' said Lucinda Harpie-Kerr, extending a hand. The man took it doubtfully, as if the long red nails were dangerous.

'This is a friend of mine, Norman Crisp,' said Pauline. 'We were just looking for somewhere to have a drink, so we came in here.'

'Terrible mistake,' said Corner.

Bone banged down another plate of food.

'This is the best fucking food you'll get in London,' he shouted. 'And very good value, considering the price.'

'That's the trouble,' said Lucinda. She smiled fiercely at Norman Crisp. 'So, Norman, what do you do?'

Crisp regarded her fearfully. 'He's one of the government's casualty figures, at present,' said Pauline. 'Unemployed, but hopeful of a career in the media.'

'Oh really,' said Lucinda Harpie-Kerr. She tapped Crisp lightly on the arm. 'London is a wicked city. Don't let yourself get led astray.' She laughed at some length.

'And suddenly I knew with blinding certitude that I had been shown something that would change the rest of my life.'

Florence nodded politely.

'It was, of course, a curious place to experience such a revelation. But the Divine manifests itself in all kinds of places and to all kinds of people. That was one of the first things I realised. There are no intellectual shortcuts to the truth. Insight has nothing to do with intellect. It was a humbling discovery. The first thing I did was to go down on my knees and acknowledge that something extraordinary and terrifying had happened to me. Of course, no one took any notice. In these sorts of places it is a common enough sight to see all kinds of disturbed people in all sorts of unhappy situations. Ever since then, I have felt that my main work in life is to convert this experience into written form. That is why I do my regular pieces for the magazine just to guarantee a modest income. But – perhaps I'm boring you.'

'No, no,' said Florence. 'Should we go and see if Alexander has recovered?'

'Yes. Let me just outline the nature of this book. See if it makes any sense to you.' Relentlessly Plugge ordered more coffee.

'How's the programme coming along?' said Corner.

'Jerry's coming in to record his script tomorrow,' said Pauline. 'We're all very excited about it.'

'Is he really?' Earish laid aside his knife and fork.

'Then we start the interviews.'

'I'm looking forward to mine,' said Lucinda Harpie-Kerr. 'I'm quite nervous about it. I've never been on the television before.'

Norman Crisp leaned forward suddenly. 'You shouldn't worry,' he said softly. 'There's nothing to it, really. You just act natural. Be yourself.'

'Perhaps you'd like a drink with me sometime, lovey,' said Lucinda nudging Norman Crisp fiercely. 'You can tell me all about your television career.'

He looked at her in horror. Bone appeared abruptly again. 'Anyone here own a bike?' he shouted. 'Horrible old rusty thing?'

Bunsen leapt nervously to his feet. 'Absolutely,' he cried. 'Yes, actually it's mine.'

'Bad luck,' said Bone pleasantly. 'Some geezer in a lorry just backed into it. You won't ride that no more, I can tell you.'

· CHAPTER · VII ·

'I have a really interesting job for you this morning, my darling,' said Mrs Crisp. 'It comes up regularly, but I try to save it for my best girls.' She smiled and nodded at Florence, dropping cigarette ash with a delicate, scattering movement, over her handbag.

'That's lovely, Mrs Crisp. What is it?'

'Fruit pies. Individual. Apple, apple and blackberry, apple and raspberry. And – a new line – apple and gooseberry.'

'Delicious.'

'Individually wrapped and designed for the single person. For the older person, perhaps,' said Mrs Crisp indulgently, 'living alone on a frugal diet, who would enjoy a wholesome treat.'

'Are they wholesome?' said Florence. 'I should have thought that the pastry would have a very high fat content, and what about all that sugar?'

'Nice healthy sugar,' said Mrs Crisp. 'We don't eat enough of it these days.' She smiled and her blackened teeth emphasised the point. 'But you needn't worry about that, Florence. All you have to do is to sell 'em. Persuade people that one of these nice fruit pies is just what they want for their tea.'

'I'll do it, Mrs Crisp.' Florence looked curiously at a green plastic bag which Mrs Crisp had laid invitingly on the table in front of her. 'Is that – '

'It's a lovely costume this time,' said Mrs Crisp. 'The ideas they come up with. I think it's marvellous – I really do.'

Florence looked apprehensive.

'You'll look lovely dear,' said Mrs Crisp forcefully. 'No one will miss you. Those pies will sell like hot cakes.' Mrs Crisp laughed with a creaking, rustling effort of her lungs.

Florence opened the plastic bag. A short bright green tunic emerged, decorated with a white stripe at the neck and the hem. A white apron accompanied it, decorated with darker green apple motifs.

'Wait till you see the hat,' said Mrs Crisp. 'They've really gone to town on that.'

'My god – ' said Florence, unwrapping a vivid green hat in the shape of half an apple, with a huge stalk and leaf rising triumphantly out of the crown. 'I can't possibly wear this, Mrs Crisp.'

'It's very fetching. After all, you don't want to look tasteful, do you? You want something that will really catch people's eye. Something nice and loud. I think it suits you.'

'It's gross,' said Florence. 'I just can't do it.'

'Here's your list of stores. They want you to start at D'Arblays this morning.'

'Oh what horrible shops,' said Florence, reading the list. 'I never go in them. I can't bear D'Arblays, it's always empty. Like a tomb.'

'Well, you've no choice about that dear,' said Mrs Crisp. 'You can always pop out for a drink, if you feel your strength draining away.'

Florence picked up the tunic in disgust.

'If you don't want to do it,' said Mrs Crisp, 'I've got girls who'd jump at this job.'

'No, no, Mrs Crisp. I'll have a go.'

'That's the spirit, Florence.'

Quickly she changed into the livid costume.

'On with the job then.'

'Goodbye, Mrs Crisp.'

'Don't forget your hat,' said Mrs Crisp, waving it at Florence by the stalk.

'Thanks.'

Florence decided to take a bus to Marble Arch, then walk through Hyde Park to D'Arblays department store. A watery sun shone ineffectually through the yellowish cloud, but its appearance was enough to induce people – office workers, tourists, the melancholy unemployed – to offer up their bodies to its warmth. As Florence walked along the path, they lay on all sides of her, still wrapped in their coats, as though decimated by an act of war or simply abandoning the struggle to persevere through their dreary, monotonous days. With legs splayed apart and mouths slightly open, middle-aged men lay motionless. Women too, with arms pressed tightly over their eyes, lay hoping for warmth and solace from the shallow, miserly rays.

Picking her way through the bodies, Florence walked on, carrying her hat. As she turned right to go towards Knightsbridge a figure came up to her and said, 'Do you have any idea where something called Channel Six is?'

Florence stopped and considered Jerry Gude. He was wearing National Health spectacles and a thin leather jacket. 'Christ,' he said,' I can't find my way round London any more.'

'Well,' said Florence. 'It's you again.'

'Yes, it's me,' said Gude. Then he said, 'I know your face.'

'We can't keep on meeting like this,' said Florence. 'You have a very bad memory indeed.'

'Why are you dressed up like that?' said Gude. 'I've never seen anything so ridiculous in my life.'

'These are my working clothes,' she said.

'Work?' said Gude. 'What possible work can entail dressing up like that?'

'Fruit pies.'

'What?'

'I'm selling them.'

'Pies?'

'Individual ones.'

'How original,' said Gude. 'What's that you're carrying?'

'My hat,' said Florence. 'It's part of the costume.'

'Put it on.'

'No, I couldn't.'

'You must,' said Gude.

'No.'

'You really must put on the hat.'

Florence took the hat from under her arm and set it on her head. Its stem rose triumphantly. The leaves stood erect and proud.

Gude stepped back with simulated admiration. 'I've never seen anything quite like it,' he said in wonder. 'The effect is breathtaking.'

'The pies are apple, you see,' said Florence. 'Well, of course you get the point.'

'It's not exactly subtle,' said Gude.

They walked for a little way in silence along the path.

'I can't find where I'm supposed to be going,' said Gude helplessly. 'Will you come and help me.'

'No, I have to be at the shop by ten.'

They walked on a little further. Gude ran a hand through his hair. 'It's just the name I've forgotten,' he said. 'I'm sorry, I've got an awful memory. I can't remember very much at all these days. Sometimes I can't remember where I live or what I had for lunch.'

'Here's D'Arblays,' said Florence.

Gude leaned against the entrance doors.

'I must go and sell the pies.'

'I still don't know where I'm going,' said Gude staring down the pavement.

'Ask a policeman,' said Florence, swiftly going inside the shop.

'Your stand is over there,' said the manager regarding her without interest. 'Your stocks are there in two cardboard cartons. Do you think you'll need any more?'

'How many are in the cartons?'

'Two hundred and fifty in each.'

'That should be enough.'

'OK.'

Florence put the apple hat on her head.

The manager stared at her. 'Do they give you that, afterwards?'

'What?'

'That outfit. Can you keep it?'

'Good heavens no. What possible use would it be. I should

hardly go round wearing it in the street.'

'Might come in useful,' said the manager. 'You could wear it to a party.'

'I have to give it back.'

'Pity.'

Florence set up her display stall by the entrance to the shop in a position where she could accost customers as they were queuing for the checkout. Her table was draped with a bright green cloth made of simulated grass. On top of the grass she put a paper plate, containing varieties of the apple pies.

The shop was disappointingly empty. Florence stood expectantly at her table, smiling at the cashier who was reading a magazine at her till. She looked curiously round at the shelves of better quality groceries – capers, gentlemen's relish, bottled ginger and Bath Olivers – and smelled the strong, rather nauseating smells of smoked bacon and cold meats at the delicatessen counter opposite her stall. Behind the counter a bored youth, wearing a white hat and coat, was busily scratching a boil on his neck. After some time he coughed moistly over the meat and turned his attention to a pimple inside his right nostril. The wall tiles of the Food Hall shone with the lustre of years. On each wall colourful landscapes evoked the living creatures which had happily sacrificed themselves to satisfy the appetites of D'Arblays customers. Rich brown cows grazed on lush, emerald grass; pliant fish surged through impossibly blue waters and prize-winning vegetables pushed up triumphant leaves through glowing brown soil. The hall was like a museum of provision, frozen into stillness. Still no one came in. Florence regarded the cartons of pies, awaiting their first sampler. She tried a slice of the apple and blackberry. It tasted unremarkable, certainly nothing like the exaggerated claims its makers made for it. She ate another slice. The pastry was poor and rather heavy. She ate the rest of the pie. The cashier eyed her.

Meeting her look of rebuke, Florence emerged from her counter and offered her a pie. She accepted silently and without surprise. The acned butcher eyed her too.

'Would you care for a pie?' she said, her voice ringing out in the empty shop.

'All right,' he said. 'I don't mind.'

Florence passed a pie over the counter. Silently he took it and pressed a large segment into his mouth. Crumbs fell at random over the cooked tongue. He chewed slowly and laboriously.

'What do you think of it?' said Florence.

'All right.'

'Oh, good.'

A customer entered the emptiness of the shop. Nervously Florence retreated to her stall. A young woman, well dressed and tall, with long blonde hair, was moving slowly through the shelves of cocktail biscuits with an air of purpose. She picked up several tins of biscuits and stared hard at them, putting them down as if they displeased her. She wore a dress and jacket which were well cut and expensive. She put a tin of biscuits down, then picked it up again and strode towards the checkout. A moment later Florence heard her voice, loud and confident, ringing through the food hall.

'Do you have any anchovies at all?'

'Dunno,' said the girl. 'If they're not on the shelf . . .'

'Naturally they're not. Or I wouldn't have asked.'

'We 'aven't got 'em then.'

'Could you check,' said the woman challengingly.

'Er . . .'

'If it's not too much trouble.'

The girl shouted across the shop, ' 'Ave we got any anchovies?'

An unseen voice shouted back. 'No.'

The girl said, 'No, we 'aven't.'

'Yes,' said Amanda Plugge loudly. 'I've got the message. So kind of you to take all this trouble.' She pulled the biscuits out of her basket and banged them down loudly on the cash desk. 'You can put these back on the shelf yourself,' she said. 'I've no intention of buying them now.' As she was about to leave Florence stepped out from behind her stall and said: 'I wonder if you would like to try one of these delicious individual fruit pies?'

'What?' shouted Amanda Plugge in irritation.

'They're a new line. Just the thing for supper on a tray.'

Amanda Plugge stopped and stared at Florence. She stood with her legs planted slightly apart. 'After the amazing rudeness of the staff in this shop,' she said, 'I have no intention of coming here ever again, let alone buying a fruit pie.'

'Oh – '

'I have to catch my train. I can't waste any more time in here.' She strode out in a gust of indignation. The trace of expensive perfume lingered behind her. The cashier surveyed her without emotion.

'Is it always as quiet as this?' said Florence.

'Yeah.'

'Must be rather boring for you?'

'Yeah.'

The conversation faltered. There was a long silence. Two middle-aged men came into the shop and each took a wire basket. They bought a random selection of provisions including a tin of instant rice pudding.

'Would you like to try one of these individual fruit pies?' said Florence, smiling vivaciously.

'Oh, no, I never eat things like that,' said one of the men. His companion laughed. 'He won't touch anything with apple in it, dear. It's the one thing he just won't eat.'

'That's right,' said his friend. 'It's the one thing I just can't manage.'

'Perhaps you'd like to try one,' Florence said to his companion. 'What about a free sample?'

'Oh, if you like,' said the man and put a segment of apple and raspberry into his mouth.

'It's all right,' he said to his friend. 'It's all right, you know.'

Florence held the packet invitingly before him. 'How about one for supper tonight.'

'No, I don't think so, thank you,' he said smiling. 'Thanks ever so, but no.'

They left the food hall, with a friendly wave.

Florence stared at her undiminished stocks of pies. The doors opened again and Jerry Gude came into the shop. He moved purposefully through the shelves until he found Florence sitting amid her stocks, reading a copy of the *Daily Mirror* which the butcher had lent her.

'Oh, hello,' said Florence in surprise. 'Haven't you found it yet?'

'No,' said Gude. 'How many have you sold?'

'None at all. Would you like a slice?'

'No,' said Gude.

'They don't look very good, do they?'

'No. How many have you got there?'

'About five hundred.'

'I'll buy them,' he said.

'Buy what?'

'I'll buy the pies.'

'How many?'

'All of them,' said Gude. 'How much?'

Florence stared at him. 'Don't be ridiculous,' she said. 'There are five hundred pies here. Just buy one.'

'No, I want them all.'

'You don't.'

'I do.'

'What will you do with them?'

'Eat them all, if necessary,' said Gude.

Florence laughed in admiration.

'My pies, please,' said Gude.

'That will be two hundred and fifty pounds exactly,' said Florence. 'You must be completely mad.'

Gude took out his cheque book and wrote out the amount with a flourish.

'How will you carry them?' said Florence, indicating the cartons piled behind the stall. 'Do you want a taxi?'

Gude shrugged. 'No,' he said.

'Well, we can't just leave them here.'

Gude went over to the cashier. 'Get me the manager,' he said. The girl rang a bell on her till.

'Yes,' said the manager, appearing after several minutes. 'Can I help you?' He looked at Gude suspiciously.

'I want these delivering,' said Gude, indicating the pies.

'He's just bought them all,' Florence said breathlessly.

'What, all of them?' said the manager.

'Yes,' she said, handing over the cheque.

The manager stared at Gude. 'What is the address, sir?'

'Dog and Biscuit, Turkey Street, W1,' said Gude.

'Deliveries on Thursday.'

'Morning or afternoon?'

'Can't say, I'm sorry.'

'Now,' said Gude, 'come and help me find this bloody TV company. You can take the whole week off work.'

'It was,' said Lady Arabella Spring-Greene, 'an unusual marriage. How can I describe it? It didn't last very long, you know.'

Pauline nodded and waited sympathetically.

'He was,' said Arabella, 'not what you would think of as an ideal husband.'

Pauline, clutching her briefcase, looked around the drawing room of Arabella's London house. It was long and airy, with cream walls, and green and white curtains exploded in a cloud of swirling fabric at either side of the room. Bookcases extended on either side of the marble fireplace, and patterned Turkish rugs covered the polished wooden floor. Flowers spilled from jugs and bowls – lilies, roses and a mass of jasmine. At the furthest window a tangled mat of creeper hung down, casting a green shade. After a suitable pause, Arabella led Pauline up the first flight of stairs into a room with a balcony which overlooked the garden. Here the light was soft and rosy, for the walls were covered in pink silk fabric and a vast, white sofa was scattered with a profusion of tiny cushions, each made from a different shade of rose fabric. The furniture was dark – a bookcase, a bureau and an antique desk heaped with piles of paper. On one corner a circular table was covered with a white lace cloth and cluttered with a collection of photographs. An oval mirror above the fireplace reflected the soft light of the room in which Arabella's skin glowed and burned with the delicacy of a peach.

She stood at the door for several minutes, waiting for Pauline to take in the exceptional qualities of the room, then observing that she was writing nothing invited her to sit on the sofa.

'Would you like tea, or coffee?' Arabella said. 'Or something . . .'

'Don't bother,' said Pauline. 'Let's talk about Jerry Gude.'

'Where would you like to start?' said Arabella, wandering over to the window and staring out into the garden.

'What was he like when you first met him?' Pauline said. 'Could you give us some idea about the qualities that first made you realise he was – well, a talented writer.'

'Talented?' said Arabella. 'I've always thought of him as a genius. I know he hasn't done much – but it's all there inside of him, all that potential. Have you talked to him yet? As soon as you talk to him you'll see what I mean.'

'He's due to start recording his script this morning,' said Pauline.

'Ah,' said Arabella. The bowl of pot pourri on the round table gave a heady fragrance to the room.

'It's all so long ago,' she said, and looked down at the long, sloping terrace.

'How did you first meet him?' said Pauline, as the wheels of the tape recorder spun silently in front of her.

Arabella sighed. 'So long ago. Almost a different life. A different generation. It's hard to explain how things were then. Jerry was – well, he was a very exciting person in those days.'

'In what way?'

'He didn't recognise – how can I say it – the frontiers of experience. Everything was a possibility to him. It was exciting to be in his company. For him, fantasies were there to be achieved, rather than simply entertained as fantasies. He went further than most of us – further than any of us.'

Pauline made notes with her biro.

'I'm going to smoke,' said Arabella. 'Do you . . .?'

'No thanks,' said Pauline.

To her surprise, Arabella reached into the centre of the pot-pourri jar and took out a small lace-trimmed pouch from which she extracted a coil of grass-like substance and a packet of cigarette papers. Pauline watched with interest as she expertly rolled a perfect cylinder and lit it with a slim lapis lazuli lighter.

After a few moments the heady smell of cannabis began to fill the room. Arabella closed her eyes and inhaled deeply.

'It was a good time,' she said. 'It all seemed possible in those days. The dream was going to become a reality.' She paused and took another deep breath of smoke.

'What dream?' said Pauline.

'What?'

'What dream?'

'I suppose you don't remember the Sixties,' said Arabella, looking at Pauline critically. It was hard to determine just how old she was.

'Before my time.'

'Ah. Well, the dream of a better world. Of changing society. Of young people just doing what they wanted to do, you know. Just saying to the previous generation, Look, we're going to do our own thing now.'

Pauline nodded.

Arabella walked round the room. 'Have you ever read *Be Cool*?' she said.

Pauline nodded. 'Naturally, as research for the programme,' she said. 'It's very important since it's the only work of prose Gude has ever written. Of course, its use as autobiography is limited, since he was only – what, twenty-six?'

'Twenty-four,' said Arabella.

'Twenty-four when he wrote it.'

'It changed the lives of a lot of people,' said Arabella. 'It was an incredibly important statement.' She went to the bookcase beside the fireplace, and drew out a battered copy of a garishly coloured paperback book. 'Here it is,' she said, turning over the pages. There was a thick layer of dust along the top of its yellowing leaves.

'I haven't read it recently. Not for quite a few years.' She turned the pages slowly.

'I was only nineteen when I first met Jerry Gude. I went to a party at Cambridge with my brother, and Jerry was there, reading poetry all night. He was very involved in poetry in those days – though he never published his poems. They were amazingly good. Everyone thought he'd go on to be a great poet, you know.' She continued to turn the pages of the book. "The revolution is now," she read. "People will turn each other on . . . . Don't trust philosophy. Nothing matters except the truth of a rock and roll lyric." There was a short silence. 'Of course,' said Arabella, 'you have to take it in its context. These days it sounds rather simplistic, doesn't it?'

'Possibly,' said Pauline.

'But the message is essentially true,' said Arabella. She looked through the book again. 'Of course, it only had a relatively small circulation. If Jerry had gone to America he'd really have taken off. But in England, somehow, things happen on a smaller scale. Here's another good bit: "Some of the hairiest people I know are bald." Isn't it amusing?'

'Yes,' said Pauline.

She picked up the book and read the back cover. "Danger," said a large pink sign. "Read this book aloud. Sing it. Love it. Study it. Eat. Digest. Excrete."

'Of course,' said Arabella, 'Jerry was for me a mind-blowing experience.' She laughed softly with dilated pupils. 'We really had a freaky time together. Jerry was a very charismatic person in those days. We had two really wild years when he went on lecture tours reading his stuff aloud throughout the country. He wrote some rock lyrics, too, you probably know about?'

'Yes,' said Pauline.

'And he gave the most incredible reading of his sonnets in Hyde Park. He wore a white dress and there were fantastic scenes with all the young people freaking out and kissing each other on the grass.'

'Was that before he joined the BBC?' said Pauline.

'Oh, yes,' said Arabella. 'That happened after we'd split up.'

'Tell me about your wedding.'

'It was really amazing. It was a total experience. I remember Jerry wore black boots, one of those silk, psychedelic scarves and a top hat. I wore a long white dress and I drew little flowers in lovely pastel colours on my face. Look, I'll show you a photograph.'

Pauline examined the wedding couple. Lady Arabella stood in bare feet with a necklace of bells round her neck, her hair flying in a golden haze around her head, decorated with leaves, flowers and spangled moons.

'Can you see the flowers?' she said.

Pauline looked closely at the photograph. Sure enough, she could see the floral artwork on her cheeks. Jerry Gude's teeth flashed in a grimace at the camera, although his eyes were invisible, masked by the impenetrable reflection from his glasses, which shone like two silver mirrors into the camera. In one corner of the photograph, at an oblique angle, a shouting face and shoulders had intruded into the group, clearly some associate of the wedding couple. Behind the couple stood an arrangement of guests, attired in conventional morning dress in sharp contrast to the bride and groom. They seemed uneasy, some trying to smile at the horror of the shouting face, some pretending not to notice that anything unusual was happening. The men stood stiffly, eyes straight ahead, their wives clutched handbags and regarded the camera with the conventional polite expressions of guests.

'Amazing,' said Arabella. 'People talked about that wedding for years. We had this incredible reception at my parents' country house, then we all went to the Beezer Club and had a party. It was such a good party. Of course, Jerry wasn't all that well known in those days. Not to the press. They thought it was much more funny that he was marrying me. The headlines all said things like "Peer's daughter in hippy marriage." The press absolutely adored the whole thing. I got very friendly with them. There were one or two who spent days standing outside my flat trying to get pictures of me and Jerry. Of course, nowadays, no one would be particularly interested. It was the first time a hippy had married into society. There were pictures all over *Vogue*.'

Pauline nodded. 'I'll just check the tape recorder,' she said, peering into the machine.

'Are you going to put all this into the programme?'

'As much as possible. It's only thirty minutes long.'

'Yes.'

'Of course, your marriage wasn't particularly long, was it?'

Arabella exhaled marijuana thoughtfully. 'No. It was good for a while, but we began to experience some hang-ups after a few months. It was partly the problem of money. Jerry didn't have any at all. So he spent mine, which was fine by me, but he didn't like it after a bit. And there was the problem of his book – '

'*Be Cool*?'

'Yes. He put a big sign on the front of the book, saying "Steal this. Take it away with you. Shoplifting is an act of reality." I think a lot of people took his advice. At any rate he didn't make any money out of it at all.' She went over to the table and handed Pauline a photograph of Gude. 'This is Jerry marching on the American Embassy in Grosvenor Square,' she said. Pauline looked at the wild, furious figure, wearing a donkey jacket, holding up a banner which said: 'US Fascist Imperialism KILLS.'

On either side stood two more angry figures, both wearing donkey jackets, their hair flowing in matted curls over their shoulders.

'Those two are Quintin Plugge and Aldous Watmough,' said Arabella. 'In those days they were very close to Jerry. Of course, they've changed a lot since.'

'Yes.'

'That was a great march. All our friends were on it.'

'Yes.'

'We stopped the war,' said Arabella. 'At least you have to give us credit for that.' She yawned decorously. 'It seems a long time ago. I married Ralph Spring-Greene soon after that. And – so on.' She spread her arms wide and let them drop to her sides.

'Did you – ?'

'Jerry was magnetic,' Arabella said, her eyes drooping as she sat back on the sofa. 'He's aged a lot since then. He's had quite a hard life. I think he drinks quite a lot these days.'

'Yes.'

'You're talking to all his wives, are you?'

'Yes. Everyone has agreed to cooperate with the programme.'

'At least I have first go.'

'Yes.'

'I'm surprised Amanda Plugge agreed to talk to you. I think there's rather a lot of bitterness there. There was quite a bit of hostility over the divorce. She had quite a lot of money, you know, and Jerry didn't behave very well. I had quite a lot of money as well, but it never mattered very much. So I gave him my flat in Holland Park and kept this house. It was all OK. No heavy scenes. Just one of those things that didn't work out.'

'Well, that's been very interesting,' said Pauline. 'I'll get in touch.'

The telephone rang.

Pauline began to pack up her equipment.

'Yes, he's an old friend of mine,' said Arabella, vaguely into the telephone. 'Oh, I've known him for years. I'm delighted about his new appointment.' Pauline packed up her tape-recorder.

'Who are you?' Arabella said. 'Oh, have we? I don't remember . . . Oh yes, at my party. You wrote a very nice paragraph, didn't you, about *The Englishwoman's WC*. Yes, how are you?'

Pauline busied herself packing up her notebook and pencils.

'Well, I've known him for years,' said Arabella. 'Oh, twenty years at least. Why do you want to know about all that? I can't think anyone's interested in it at all. Well, you'll have to come round here if you want – any afternoon I'm usually at home. Tomorrow is all right.'

She put the phone down looking puzzled.

There was a short pause. Arabella said, 'I don't see why the *Reporter* should ring me up about Evelyn Fragment, do you? A young man called Horlick wanted to know how long I'd known him. Do you think they're going to write a piece about it?'

'I should watch what you say,' said Pauline. 'Horlick is a thoroughly disreputable person. He's a gossip columnist.'

'Oh God,' said Arabella.

'Say, "No comment" next time.'

'What can they want?' Arabella's face assumed a red flush and then went white.

'So kind of you to spare the time,' said Pauline.

'Oh – that's all right. Look, I've invited this Horlick person round tomorrow afternoon. What do you think I should do?'

'Just be careful what you say.'

'Yes, yes, I will.'

'He's a very unreliable person.'

'I seem to remember he's just a boy,' said Arabella, looking puzzled. 'He sounded rather sweet. I adore the young, don't you? They keep one in touch with the world, otherwise one can become quite middle-aged. Perhaps I'm confusing him with someone else. I only met him for a moment.'

'Oh he's quite young,' said Pauline.

'Quite good-looking, wasn't he?'

'If you like that sort of thing . . .'

'Well . . .'

'Many thanks,' said Pauline, striding down the hall.

As she left she saw Arabella standing by the open door, with its gleaming stained glass lights, staring out into the drive, her face perplexed and anxious.

Pauline wondered what Horlick was up to. She opened a packet of Fruity Chews and ate them with concentration.

· CHAPTER · VIII ·

After ten minutes wandering round Knightsbridge Florence Barge and Jerry Gude came to a halt. Various directions given to them by passers-by turned out to be unreliable.

'Where is this fucking studio?' said Gude, screwing up his eyes in the bright morning sun. 'Why does everyone I ask turn out to be a foreigner or a moron?'

They stood in silence. Then Gude said, 'I'm pissed off with all this. Let's go and have breakfast.' He took Florence's hand and led her up the steps of the Green Park Hotel, whose dining room commanded a prospect across the park. Inside, they sat at a table in the sun. 'Champagne,' said Gude. 'We'll have a champagne breakfast. Bacon and eggs for me, and for my companion?'

The waiter eyed Florence's costume, perplexed.

'Kippers,' said Florence promptly.

They faced each other across the table. 'So, you're a Barge,' said Gude thoughtfully. 'Sweet little rich girl. Tell me, Miss Barge, are you seriously into real life yet, or are you just playing at it?'

His eyes turned a deeper blue as he stared at her.

'What's wrong with having fun?'

'Is it all a game, or have you realised yet that this is a one-way ticket? You're never coming back this way again. I mean,' said Gude, as the champagne arrived. 'Are you wasting your youth?' He poured her a glass. 'Pissing about in the streets dressed like an apple. Is it all just for a laugh, Florence? Visiting your boring boyfriend. Do you really want to see him every week? Ask yourself.

Have you discovered yet, Florence, that sex is the only serious thing in life?'

Florence pushed the kipper round the plate. She found Gude both alarming and fascinating. She thought of all his previous wives. Had he asked them the same question?

'What do you really think of me?' said Gude, draining his glass.

'I like you,' she said daringly. 'And I think you're very rude.'

'Drawing-room manners, Florence,' said Gude, 'ceased to interest me many years ago.'

'What's wrong with being polite?'

'Meaningless ritual,' said Gude. 'Be yourself. Discover who you really are. It can't be done if we all sit around like maiden ladies at a tea-party. Take yourself, Florence. Do you know who you really are?'

The question sounded exciting.

'Don't you want to get rid of all your emotional baggage, your hang-ups, your class-ridden preconceptions, and push out the frontiers?'

'Yes, I do!' she said bravely. 'Have you pushed out your frontiers, Jerry?'

'To the brink and back,' said Gude, refilling his glass. 'The going up is worth the coming down – at least it was to my generation. All the young want these days is possessions. Money. Security. Things. Money is a drug, Florence,' he went on. 'You can get hooked on it. Does money motivate you?'

'No,' said Florence truthfully. Relieved of the burden of mortgage payments, she rarely gave it much thought.

'Good,' said Gude breathing softly. 'If money motivates you you're not an artist.'

'Are you an artist,' she asked Gude. The champagne sparkled in her glass.

'Yes,' said Gude. 'And you can be too, Florence, if you decide to grow up,' said Gude. 'Discover yourself. Discover sex.'

Their eyes met over the bacon and kippers. Gude sat back at the table and lit a cigarette. 'What are you frightened of?' he said.

Florence thought of Alexander. She had certainly not discovered much about herself with him.

'I'll teach you how to be an artist,' said Gude. Absently he picked up her champagne glass and emptied it. 'I'll teach you all about yourself in five minutes,' he said, smiling at her hungrily. 'I'll just go and book a room.'

Florence felt as though she was advancing rapidly towards the brink of a precipice. At the last moment her courage failed her. 'What about your programme?' she said quickly. 'You'll be late for Channel Six.'

'Bloody hell,' said Gude, remembering his appointment. He asked for the bill. 'You've lost an opportunity, Florence Barge. It may never come your way again.'

They stood up. 'Look,' said Gude, 'you don't happen to have your cheque book on you, do you? I used my last cheque buying all those fucking pies.'

'I'll pay,' said Florence, writing out the amount. She felt she had failed a test. Suddenly she wished she had kept quiet about the interview.

The sun streamed through the lobby as they stood looking out through the glass doors into the Knightsbridge traffic. 'This is what it's about, Florence,' said Gude, putting his arm on her neck and turning her towards him. 'This is what it's really like.' She took a breath of surprise and found Gude's lips on hers. He tasted of champagne and tobacco. His body was hard and thin. He was intoxicating. After a few minutes, Gude spun her out into the street. She followed him, dazzled by the sunlight and champagne.

'Someone in reception to see you, Charlie.'

'He's two hours late,' said Enever in annoyance. 'Show him up.'

Downstairs in Channel Six, Gude was holding Florence's hand.

'Come in and give me inspiration.'

'I can't in this costume.'

'What's your phone number?' said Gude. 'Have dinner with me.'

'You'll never remember,' said Florence.

'Don't be mean,' said Gude. 'Don't give me a hard time. Be nice.' He kissed her hand.

Florence gave him her number. Gude wrote it down on his shirt cuff. 'I'll call you,' he said.

They waved as the lift doors closed upon Gude. Florence went back to the flat in a state of turmoil.

'I want you,' Enever said, 'to forget about the studio and everyone here. I want you to talk to that camera as if it was the most important person in your life.'

'Like my last wife?' said Gude. He sat at a small table in the studio surrounded by bright lights. He looked from side to side in some confusion, staring at the production team who were busy adjusting light and sound levels on the opposite side of the table.

'Where is the camera?' said Gude. 'This takes me back to my days at the BBC. Of course, things were somewhat more primitive in those days.'

'This is the camera,' said Enever. 'It will be fixed on you throughout.'

Gude stared into the lens. His eyes bulged slightly.

'Do you have your script?' said Enever.

'Script?'

'Look, there's no need to worry about anything. The words will appear up here in front of you,' – Enever waved his hand at the tele-prompter – 'and all you have to do is read them.'

Gude stared at the screen silently.

'Show him how it works,' said Enever.

A technician made an adjustment and a stream of words moved swiftly across the screen. Gude read with difficulty – 'life . . . drink . . . one too many'. 'Christ,' he said. 'It will have to go slower than that. I can't read the words from here. Who wrote them, anyway?'

'You did, Jerry,' said Enever. 'They're your own words.'

'I've never seen them before,' said Gude, beginning to sweat. 'Look, I'll have to have a cigarette.'

Nervously he scrabbled at a packet of Gauloises.

'I like that,' said Enever. 'I like that a lot. Look, let's use that image. It makes him look scared. I think it might add an air of drama to the programme.'

'OK,' said Pauline, who had come into the room a few minutes earlier.

'Oh, hello,' said Enever. 'How did you get on?'

'Very well,' said Pauline. 'She's a natural for television.'

'Which wife have you been talking to?' said Gude, from behind the table. 'The lacerate-him-with-kindness-and-regrets one, or the boil-him-in-tar one, or the good-old-Jerry version?'

'The former,' said Pauline.

'I can keep the fags?' said Gude.

'Keeps the fags,' said Enever.

'Anti-smoking lobby?' said Pauline. 'Might be a black mark?'

'Bugger them,' said Enever.

Gude clutched his packet, fearing that they might be taken away from him.

'It can only add to the verisimilitude of the portrait we are trying to paint. After all, he's supposed to look as if he smokes forty a day.'

'Sixty,' said Gude.

'No one is pretending that he is a healthy and – ' Enever hesitated – 'wholly fit person.'

'Least of all me,' said Gude.

'The point of the programme is to emphasise the toll life has taken on his person.'

'A heavy one,' said Gude. He drew on his cigarette. His hand was shaking visibly.

'Right. Let's just try a read-through,' said Enever. 'Just sit at the table, Jerry, yes, that's right, put your head on your hands if you like, and repeat the words as they come across the screen. OK. Off you go.'

'Now?'

'If you like.'

There was a silence, during which Gude remained silent and immobile.

'In your own time,' said Enever. 'Whenever you're ready.'

Gude looked in desperation towards the screen. 'I've always believed in living dangerously,' he said slowly, 'that's why I married three women who'd like to kill me today . . .'

He stared at Enever in dismay.

'Christ,' he said, 'I can't say this stuff.'

'Jerry, my old mate,' said Enever, 'you wrote it.'

'I cannot believe,' said Gude slowly, 'that my pen ever gave expression to sentiments such as these.'

'Well, it's too late to start changing very much. You can alter the odd line if you like.'

'I'm not going to change anything,' said Gude raising his voice slightly. 'I'm a professional. I don't let anyone down. I'll say whatever is on the fucking card. I'll say I'm a child molester and a flasher, if you like. By all means. All I'm saying is that I didn't write it.'

'OK then,' said Enever. 'You just say the words as they come up. Whoever wrote them. Off we go.'

'Ready?' said Gude.

'Yes. All right.

'I have turned to most things over the years to sustain me through this obstacle course we call life – women, words, alcohol – but what I would most like now is a stiff gin and orange.' He stopped and looked at Enever.

'Is that in the script?'

'No, I've just said it.'

'What do you mean?'

'Obviously,' said Gude, 'I would like a drink. Lots of ice, freshly squeezed orange. Nothing out of a can. I mean that I'm not going on with this fucking rubbish, unless someone gives me a drink.'

'Can you get him a drink, Pauline?' said Enever.

Gude stared across his table at her.

'There might be a problem,' said Pauline. 'They lock up the alcohol in the studios; they're only allowed to have it in the hospitality suite.'

Enever looked at his watch. 'Look, we're wasting time,' he said. 'Can't you get him a drink in here?'

Gude lifted his head and looked uneasily round the room.

'Well, it isn't allowed,' said Pauline. 'I'm just making the point. I'll see what I can do.' She left the room.

Enever looked at Jerry.

'I don't suppose you could just wait a bit, could you?' he said. 'Or make do with something like coffee?'

With dignity, Gude rose to his feet. 'I'm going to have a drink,' he said, 'before I read another of those fucking words. It's up to you. Either I stay and have one here, or I'm going to get one in the pub.'

'Just hang on a bit,' said Enever.

Pauline came back with a tray and glasses. 'I'm supposed to sign for this but there was no one there so I just took it.'

'OK,' said Enever. 'Problem solved.'

He looked at Pauline. 'No need to mention any more about it,' he said. 'Forget the whole thing. Shall I pour you one, Jerry?' Gude nodded silently, stretching out his hand to take the drink. He clutched the glass.

'As a matter of fact,' Enever said suddenly, 'I've had a good idea. I think we'll have the gin bottle on the table. Yes, we'll include it in the film. Cigarettes on the left, bottle on the right.' Gude drained his glass. 'We'll actually watch him drinking. We'll get him to pour out the gin and actually drink while he's reading the script. That's brilliant,' Enever told himself. 'I've never seen that done before.'

Pauline made a noise of objection.

'Keep your mouth shut, you stupid cow,' said Gude, reassured by his first glass. 'Let him do what he wants. It's his job.' Pauline stared at him and adjusted her glasses.

She walked over to Gude's table.

'Don't speak to me like that again,' she said, 'or that bottle and those fags will go just like that. Immediately.' She snapped her fingers in Gude's face.

'Just like my second wife,' he said. 'Venom running through her veins. OK, OK. If it's all right with you, madam, I'll have another glass.'

'He's looking a bit shiny,' said Enever. 'Could you just take off that bit of glare.'

A make-up girl advanced towards Gude with a sponge and a pot of powder. He ducked nervously.

'You're not going to make me look like some film star, are you?' he said. 'Don't overdo the glamour or women will be falling before me in the street. I can't afford to disappoint them all.'

'Right,' said Enever. 'Let's get back to the script, Jerry.'

'Why did I ever agree to do this?' said Gude. 'OK, roll the words again.'

There was a short silence.

'Over to you, Jerry,' said Enever.

Gude coughed at length. 'Sorry,' he said. 'Just a bit nervous still.'

'Right, take your time.'

'OK.'

'Last week I had a drink with a woman who confessed that she owned a hundred and fifty pairs of knickers . . .'

He stopped again.

'What's the matter, Jerry?'

'I can't believe I ever wrote that. Why aren't there any jokes in the script?'

'What do you want to say instead?'

'I'll talk about my wives, shall I?'

'Whatever you like, Jerry.'

Some time later the bottle of gin was almost empty. Gude had relaxed perceptibly. He leaned forward across the table and spoke out loudly to the listening world. 'There's nothing wrong with women until you marry one of them. I've been married three times, and I'm still confused. What do women want? Just blood? Or money too?' He paused and took a long drag at his cigarette. 'Is anyone still out there?' he shouted from behind the table. Enever was sitting gazing at Gude with a kind of fascinated horror.

'Yes, we're all out here, Jerry,' he said. 'We're all still here. Do you think you need quite so many pauses in between the words?'

'Pauses?'

'Yes. It might be better to just say the words a little bit quicker. Just at your normal talking pace.'

'I'm not putting in any pauses,' said Gude looking bewildered. 'This is the way I always talk.'

'Ah. Right Jerry,' said Enever. 'On you go.'

Pauline brought some coffee over. 'Absolute disaster,' she said. 'Unless you can get him going, no one will watch.'

'It's the way he is,' said Enever. 'People will be interested to see the way he is now.'

'Well, it has a certain macabre fascination. Like seeing a corpse exhumed.'

'Do you think he was always like this?'

'Arabella Spring-Greene describes him as magnetic and charismatic.'

'Well.'

'Of course that was some time ago. He's taken a lot of drink and drugs since then.'

'It's amazing he's still alive really. People will be surprised that he's survived.'

'Is he still alive?'

'Apparently,' said Enever.

'Look, he's saying something again.'

'My first wife believed in romance,' Gude was saying slowly. 'I've always been a romantic. I believed once that women were gentle, affectionate creatures, the weaker sex. I . . .'

'We could get someone in quickly to brighten up the script for him.'

'He couldn't possibly learn anything else in time.'

Gude said some more words from his script. Then he stopped. He looked at Enever and laughed.

'Shall we call it a day here?' said Enever. There was a note of weariness in his voice. The recording had not been a success. 'We'll have to try and film it on another day.'

Pauline looked at the clock. 'It's only twelve,' she said. 'We're booked for another two hours. We could easily get the whole thing finished this morning.'

'He can't . . .,' Enever started to say.

'If you go into another day, you're adding thousands to the budget. Look, he's got familiar with this script. You needn't use much of it. Just have his wives talking in the middle of it. And the voice-overs from his friends.'

'I know,' said Enever. 'But – '

Gude shouted to him from behind the table.

'It's not quite the way I planned to do this,' said Enever, looking pained. 'It's in his own interests to make a good impression, don't you think, rather than shouting and raving like this.'

'There is NOTHING,' shouted Gude, 'NOTHING I hate MORE, than the sight of women with fat BUMS wearing jeans.'

'He's ranting,' said Enever. 'What are we going to do? There's no way we can control him, even if he does record the rest of the script.'

'Let's give him some more booze,' said Pauline. 'That might quieten him down again. He's probably just going through a manic phase, which could well be followed by depression and torpor.'

'Yes, I'm talking to YOU, you fat cow. YOU, yes YOU.' Gude stood up with difficulty and pointed at Pauline.

'Oh God,' said Enever.

'You are a supercilious, condescending, patronising BITCH.'

'Don't worry,' said Pauline, 'I can handle it.'

'Cheers Jerry,' she said, thrusting another drink into his hand.

'Cheers, you fat slag,' said Gude, emptying his glass in one go.

'Do you think you could read the words again?' said Enever. 'We'll try and record it this time, shall we?'

'I am a professional,' said Gude, sitting down at the table again and gripping its edges. 'I have never, EVER, let anyone down.'

'OK, start the words again.'

'My nanny,' said Gude slowly and carefully, 'taught me all about sex when I was exactly seven-and-a-half years old . . .'

Florence and Marigold sat together in the kitchen sharing a bottle of white wine.

'I can't believe you've met that awful man again,' said Marigold. 'Why do you keep walking into him like this?'

'He was looking for Channel Six,' said Florence. 'Just wandering around the streets in a daze. He bought all the pies. We had champagne together.'

Marigold refilled their glasses.

'I can't understand why you even spoke to him. I thought he was the most offensive man I've ever met. What's got into you? Do you find him attractive?'

'No, of course not,' said Florence crossly. 'He's a very interesting person. He has a lot of very original ideas. I've never met anyone quite like him before. He's had three wives.'

'Three?'

'Yes, I looked him up in *Who's Who*.'

'Quite a Bluebeard,' said Marigold scornfully. 'Be careful, Florence. He'll be after you next.'

'Nonsense,' said Florence, sounding pleased.

'Anyway, what do you talk about?' said Marigold.

'Well, about life, and self-discovery, and . . . sex.'

'Sex,' said Marigold. 'How predictable.'

'Well, at least it makes a change from Alexander.'

'I told you he was a pompous creep.'

'You have a point,' said Florence. 'He is a bit of a bore, isn't he?'

Marigold poured some more wine. 'I shouldn't be drinking this,' she said. 'I'm on a diet.'

'How are you getting on with Julian?'

'Not very well. He's really rather dim, you know.'

'Those awful spats.'

'And that braying voice.'

'Nevertheless, he is my only hope,' said Marigold, 'unless I get my best-seller finished.'

'How is it going?'

'Badly. The plot's no good. I've run out of ideas. I could put your horrible friend in the book.'

'Jerry's written a book. He was telling me about it this morning.'

'What sort of a book? A novel?'

'No, an autobiography. *Be Cool.*'

'Sounds crap,' said Marigold.

'It's out of print,' said Florence. 'I'm going to order it from the library.'

· CHAPTER · IX ·

The story led the Man of the World column. Accompanied by an out-of-date photograph of Lady Arabella and an unflattering representation of Evelyn Fragment, the headline declared: 'Free-love Frolic for Family Man'. Remaining paragraphs outlined the exuberant activities of Lady Arabella and Fragment in the days of their youth when they had attended the Blackthorn Rock Festival amid scenes of nakedness and euphoria and Fragment had decorated Lady Arabella's unclothed breasts with gold and silver paint. The story, Watmough thought, as he read the Diary thoughtfully, was remarkably accurate. For once, Horlick had got his facts right. Guiltily, Watmough tried to remember exactly how much he had told him. Surely, just a vague hint, nothing more than that. He read the story again. It was uncompromising in its emphasis on the difficulties of Fragment's remaining in the Cabinet. Quite justifiable, thought Watmough. It was undeniably true that a certain irony attended Fragment's appointment. Nevertheless Watmough frowned as he turned to the rest of the papers. His morning, customarily untroubled, was clouded by the story, for as it happened he was lunching Fragment at the Roastbeef Club that very day.

'Cheers,' said Watmough an hour later, greeting the doorman of the Roastbeef. 'Good to see you, Sam.' Watmough steered his way through the gloomy portals of the club just before twelve. The day was brilliant, but there was a sharpness in the air which indicated cold weather moving in from the east. Climbing the stairs, Watmough saw with affection the heavy Corinthian columns, the noble winding staircase, and, beyond, the reassuringly solid oak doors that led to the sombre recesses of the dining room. Watmough went to the members' bar, where red plush chairs were arranged around a blazing coal fire. All was reassurance, solidity and continuance. Here Watmough began his day, surrounded by geniality and warmth. Here he assumed his place in a world where the great and the good contended to buy him drinks. Here he felt at his most radical, a spirit of revolution and freedom, safely outspoken at the conservative heart of things.

'Watmough!' He turned to see Norris Pleasant striding towards him over the worn turkey carpet.

'Pleasant!' said Watmough without enthusiasm.

They exchanged compliments on each other's appearance in a wary manner.

'Your usual, Mr Watmough?' said the Irish barman.

'Indeed, Liam,' said Watmough. 'And for you, Norris – what will you have?'

'I'll take an arak, Aldous.'

'Certainly,' said Watmough. 'Liam, an arak for my companion. What is it?'

'It is full of health-giving properties. I advise you to have one too.'

'No fancy stuff for me,' said Watmough, seizing the substantial pink gin which Liam put reverently on his table.

'Well, cheers.'

'Cheers.'

They drank in silence.

'Rare to find you in here,' said Watmough. 'You're looking pretty fit, Pleasant. Fit and prosperous I dare say.'

Pleasant did not deny it.

There was another silence.

'Any new books in the pipeline? God, that drink looks awful, Pleasant. It's all yellow. Are you sure it's doing you good?'

'My new book comes out this week, Aldous. That's why you find me here. Yes, the drink is excellent. It contains a great many trace elements not found elsewhere in these quantities.'

Watmough stared at him enviously.

'A new book this week? Sequel to the others?'

'Naturally, it takes the subject further. But I also advance along an exciting new direction.'

'Oh.'

'Yes, a successor to *Joy in the Evening* – with which you may be familiar.'

'No, I'm not, Norris.'

'It was a book intended to help those in the sunset of their emotional lives,' said Pleasant perfunctorily. 'You might benefit from it, Aldous. However, my new work advances the bold and – if you like – startling idea that we give up sex completely. A period of voluntary chastity for everyone.'

Watmough stared at him.

Pleasant smiled back confidently, keen to display the famously perfect teeth. Around his eyes his skin was suspiciously taut. Watmough wondered if he had had a facelift. The hairline was good and the hair still luxuriant; perhaps he had had a hair transplant too.

'I take a new line, you see Aldous. I give it up for good.'

'You mean you don't – any more?'

'No.'

'I see,' said Watmough thoughtfully. 'Will that idea catch on?'

Pleasant smiled back at him. 'Oh the book will be a best-seller, Aldous,' he said. 'There's no doubt of that. Whatever I write is a best-seller, whatever it's called.'

'Fortunate,' said Watmough.

'I go on writing,' said Pleasant, 'not to satisfy my material wants, but to explore the frontiers of the psychology of sex. To push them back, to find out the precise nature of the most powerful impulse we know, Aldous.'

'Yes, quite.'

'Of course, work occupies only a proportion of my life. Travelling also takes up a great deal of my time. Then there are my television appearances. I'm on the Marius Grope show next week.'

'How much time do you spend in Ravello?' said Watmough.

'Oh, just four to six months. I travel around quite a bit. Italy is such a stimulating place. And Merrily likes to keep me active.'

'Merrily?'

'A young friend of mine,' said Pleasant.

'Ah.'

'I don't think you've met her, Aldous.'

Watmough thought for a moment. 'Do you mean that pretty little girl with red hair? Sat on my knee at Arabella's Gold and Silver Ball two years ago?'

'No, that wasn't Merrily. I had another friend then,' said Pleasant vaguely. 'Young girls want their freedom after a while. They want to move on, they want a little independence and excitement. Who can blame them? In a purely physical sense I'm old enough to be their – what?'

'Grandfather.'

'Let's say uncle.' Pleasant simpered, creasing his dark, mahogany skin. 'But these girls – I adore them all, Aldous. They bring their youth, their vivacity, their charming naivety. I offer a little luxury, a little tenderness, a little experience.'

How disgusting, thought Watmough. Here was Pleasant bragging away like a dirty old man. How ridiculous he looked, with his pale suit and leather handbag, looking like a proper Dago. 'I thought you said you'd given all that up, anyway?' he said peevishly.

Pleasant smiled at him again. 'In the book, in the book. I don't apply the philosophy too rigorously to my own private life.'

Watmough stared moodily into his pink gin. After all, he himself was quite a young man, he thought. The same age as Pleasant, although he did not cover himself with disgusting lotions and his skin did not look like cured plastic.

'Another drink?' said Pleasant. 'It would be my pleasure.'

He ordered a pink gin and a second arak.

'Minitz is confident that this new book will break all records,' he said smugly. 'We have great hopes for it. There will be signings, chat shows, interviews.' Pleasant drained his arak. 'Naturally I am expecting a full-scale attack from the *Commentator*. I hear that

Brayne is planning to devote half the magazine to annihilating my work.'

'Do you see much of Alexander these days?'

'Not a great deal. There was a recent unfortunate incident over lunch.'

'Yes, I heard you'd made an appearance,' said Watmough. 'Sorry I missed you. Bit slow over the stickies!'

'Alexander was not amused.'

'No. He's a bit on the serious side, isn't he?' said Watmough. 'Old before his years. Pity you two can't patch things up.'

'He has attempted to write me out of his life completely.'

'A rum business,' said Watmough.

'One I am resigned to. He despises everything I believe in.'

'Oh come, that sounds a little extreme.'

'He is young,' said Pleasant. 'He will give in at the end. There is a great deal of money involved.' Pleasant yawned, discreetly hiding his mouth behind his hand. 'I apologise, Aldous. A combination of jet lag and the quality of the water I am forced to drink in my hotel. There is, too, the wearying round of the celebrity circus. One feels the pressure, but one can't let Minitz down. He's done so much for this book.'

'Do you see yourself as a television star, Norris?'

'I am an advertisement for the book in a literal sense. People look at me and judge by my appearance how I have profited by the regime I advocate. But I think I'm in pretty good shape, Aldous, for a man of my years. How old do you think I look?'

'I don't know Norris. How old are you?'

'No, no, tell me how old you think I look.'

'Well, Norris, you're forty-five aren't you? Weren't you at Cambridge at the same time as I – '

'Never mind all that, Aldous. Just tell me how old you think I look, assuming you had never met me. At a guess. As a member of the public, watching me on television.'

'Forty-five.'

'I am commonly taken for under forty,' said Pleasant. 'You yourself Aldous, look well over fifty. I am physically fit, healthy and I have the body of a much younger man. I can . . .'

'I don't think that's quite true, Norris,' said Watmough thoughtfully. 'I think I look quite young for my age. Certainly not over fifty. Nowhere near.'

'Just look at yourself,' said Pleasant. 'Physically you're in terrible shape. You've taken no pride in your body, Aldous. You've let it deteriorate badly.'

Watmough considered his body. He scarcely gave it any thought at all. It was functional, rarely letting him down, giving little need for maintenance. It occupied rather more space than it used to; his stomach, particularly, had swelled comfortably to accommodate the substantial quantities of drink and food it daily incorporated. But surely, not to such a degree as to be noticeably unpleasing. 'Well, Norris, you may be right,' Watmough said uneasily. 'But there's nothing I can do about it. After all – '

Pleasant interrupted him, his eyes gleaming with the intensity of a prophet. 'But there is, Aldous,' he said softly. 'You can start now. Take some exercise. A little mild jogging round the park. Nothing too strenuous, nothing too demanding. Drink only white wine and – '

'Ha! Give up the hard stuff,' shouted Watmough. 'Oh, no, Pleasant, you can't start cheating the proletariat of their liquor.'

'Vitamins are the key to your problem,' Pleasant continued, undeterred. 'Your body has exhausted its natural reserves of essential minerals, leaving your skin poisoned and your system choked and sluggish with toxic deposits. You need a supplement – selenium and Vitamin E, I'd say, then a measured programme of zinc additives . . .'

He spoke on for several minutes.

'. . . nitrium and extract of seaweed, Vitamin K compound and ginseng,' Pleasant continued. 'Aromatherapy and cell rejuvenation . . .'

Watmough stared into his empty glass. He wondered if Minitz would launch his own book with such enthusiasm. Not, of course, that he wanted to sit in a shop window signing books. Not, of course, that many people would want to buy it.

'. . . purely on external appearance,' said Pleasant. 'I might have a different diagnosis after a full physical check. For example, Aldous, are you suffering from any small but irritating complaints. Varicose veins, piles, for example. Any prostate trouble, yet?'

'Don't talk balls,' said Watmough in irritation. 'I'm as fit as you are. I'm doing a book, in fact, Norris,' he said, determined to change the subject. 'For your own publisher.'

'Minitz?'

'Yes.'

'Morton is trying to develop a wider range of titles this year. He is determined to – as he puts it – go places among intellectual circles.'

Watmough smiled a little. 'Yes? Of course, he didn't seem to have a very sound background knowledge of Westminster or the British political system, but he did say he was particularly keen to develop the area of modern biography. He said . . .'

'Morton is a man of wide interests.'

'Yes. Are you lunching here, Norris?' said Watmough, hoping that he would not be obliged to invite him to join his own table.

'I am,' said Pleasant. 'I'm doing an interview with someone from the *Reporter*. A writer called Horlick. Is he familiar to you?'

'Er – I know the name,' said Watmough, frowning.

'A star writer, I understand.'

'I wouldn't say that – ' Watmough stopped as Evelyn Fragment came into the bar with a hunted expression. 'Aldous,' he said, with a low exclamation.

'Evelyn, old friend,' said Watmough.

The diary story hung, unmentioned, in the air.

They shook hands.

'An excellent column on Sunday,' said Fragment slowly, with a grave expression. 'Though I wonder if you're exactly right about the influence of interest rates on the competitive position of our small businesses.'

'Always open to correction,' said Watmough.

'Well,' said Fragment. He looked enquiringly at Pleasant, who had got up from his armchair and was examining a calf-covered, gold-edged diary.

'Oh. Norris Pleasant, Evelyn Fragment,' said Watmough, introducing them. They shook hands.

'A real pleasure,' said Pleasant fulsomely.

'Indeed,' said Fragment, looking a little way beyond his head.

'Excuse us, Norris,' said Watmough, 'we must go and get our grub. My guest likes to pretend he is a busy man.'

Fragment sighed. He looked tired, Watmough noticed, and his skin had a chalky consistency.

'Go right ahead,' said Pleasant. 'I look forward to seeing you in Ravello, Aldous.'

Fragment and Watmough walked through into the dining room, where the gloom of the dark-panelled walls enveloped them and the reassuring scents of cooking calmed their spirits.

'Odd sort of chap,' said Fragment.

'Pleasant? Old friend from Cambridge days. One of the filthy rich now.'

'Do I know the name?'

'Yes, he's written a lot of books about sex. Sort of manuals.'

'*Joy in the Morning*,' said Fragment with surprising promptness.

'That's it. He's written a good deal more since then. Another one just coming out. Quite a production line.'

'What about?'

'Giving it up.'

'Do us all good,' said Fragment, laughing with forced humour.

There was a silence, while the diary story seemed a possible subject for conversation. The moment passed.

'Ha! Ha!' said Watmough. 'You're right, Evelyn.' The remark fell lamely in the air. They sat at a table prized for its discretion, situated in an alcove between the high window and the long central table where the more convivial lunched in a long row. Here Fragment and Watmough had taken lunch for many years. A bottle of wine was placed reassuringly on the table in front of them. Watmough regarded it with affection. 'The woodcock, I think,' he said. 'Same for you Fragment? The game is usually pretty good here.'

'Whatever you're ordering,' said Fragment vaguely.

'The woodcock for two,' said Watmough, ordering. 'So, old friend, how are things?' he said, affecting jollity.

Fragment regarded him with an abstract, worried expression. 'Well, Aldous, things are very – ' he stopped and stared into the interior of the room where a line of men with red faces were shouting and waving their arms at each other in cheerful conversation. 'Things are – Do you know, Aldous, I've just come from a meeting at the Home Office where there was the most lovely little girl taking notes. She was sitting there with her knees crossed and the sun from the window shone just across her hair which looked quite golden. What a lovely little girl she was.'

The two men sat in silence while Fragment indulged his romantic reverie.

'Do you know, Aldous,' he went on. 'I thought how nice it would be if she was sitting on my knee.'

Watmough listened in sympathetic silence.

'She was such a pretty little girl. Couldn't have been more than nineteen, and you could tell she was awfully clever.'

'She sounds charming, Evelyn.'

'She was. Quite lovely.'

'Yes.'

There was a silence. The diary paragraph festered in the air.

Watmough wondered if Fragment would ever get round to mentioning the subject.

Pleasant passed at a slight distance from the table, waving and smiling. In his wake, Horlick moved clumsily, clutching his notebook and knocking over a chair.

'Is that person an American?'

'No, he just looks rather unreal.'

'Yes.'

'He spends his time having all sorts of treatment to his skin. He thinks it makes him look younger. But I don't think he looks all that younger than me, eh?'

'He looks well preserved.'

'If you like that sort of thing. I think it's repellent. His face doesn't look as if its covered with skin, but a layer of – what? – plastic or polythene.'

Fragment leaned forward. 'Do women like it? Does he live an – active life?' His face darkened slightly and his forehead creased in a frown of concentration.

'He gives it all up in his book, but in practice he still has a pretty busy time. Or so he says.'

Fragment sat back and considered this information.

'Anyway,' said Watmough, deciding he would finally bring the story out into the open. 'What's bothering you? Some difficulty with . . .?'

Fragment turned abruptly from his study of Pleasant. 'Yes, Aldous,' he said. 'The thing is, I'm being forced by the leader to spearhead this family life campaign and I can see no end of trouble ahead. These moral crusades are all very well, but they have a nasty habit of backfiring and going off all over your face.'

'Yes, as I wrote the other week, Evelyn, it's a desperate grab for popularity. All this stuff about moral regeneration is nonsense. I advised you in my column to have nothing to do with it.'

'I'd no choice, Aldous. You must see that I had to take the job.'

'A desperate, populist measure designed to grab votes in the short term. But it won't work. In the end the people don't like that sort of thing.'

'They don't like things like video nasties, Aldous. There's a lot of groundswell about that. Our own poll shows that they want us to take a lead in banning them.'

'Take no notice of opinion polls. It is only the mad and dangerous who answer them, and half of them don't tell the truth. The lunatic fringe. Take no notice. Carry on as usual. Leave sex alone – that's my advice, Evelyn.'

After a moment Watmough realised that his advice had been unfortunate. He coughed uncomfortably. Fragment stared at him. Watmough cleared his throat. 'Look, Evelyn – '

'I can't,' said Fragment, ploughing on. 'I'm launching a Task Force next week. Clean up the streets. Clean up the country. I've got a speech in the House today launching the Family comes First campaign.'

'Bloody hell,' said Watmough, probing the woodcock with his knife. 'Do you like these things quite so underdone, Evelyn?' A spurt of blood shot out across Watmough's plate as he attempted to saw off one of the legs of the tiny bird.

'Mine's the same,' said Fragment, peering into his bird. A tide of blood had soaked his mashed potatoes, colouring them crimson.

'The game is usually excellent here. Look, I'm sorry. Shall we send them back?'

'Oh, don't bother,' said Fragment. 'I'm not particularly hungry as it happens.' He toyed with a slice of breast.

'I'll see what I can manage to chew,' said Watmough half-heartedly. 'I realise you're in a – in a hurry. Seems such a pity to go without lunch, though.'

They looked across the room at the table where Pleasant and Horlick were conducting their interview. They saw Horlick's head moving up and down as he nodded while Pleasant spoke. He was writing rather slowly. They saw Pleasant pause and drum his fingers on the table, while Horlick's pen crawled across the page. At intervals Horlick would laugh – a loud, searing noise which grated on Watmough's ears but appeared to bring some satisfaction to Pleasant.

'What are they talking about?'

'His latest book.'

'Who is he talking to?'

'No idea,' said Watmough hastily. 'Some magazine writer, I think. Looks a pretty seedy bloke.'

'If it's anyone from the *Reporter*,' said Fragment darkly, 'I've a good mind to go over and – Look, Aldous,' he said, his voice trembling with emotion. 'I don't know if you've read Man of the World this morning, but there's the most appalling story about – '

'Gutter stuff,' said Watmough hastily. 'Yes I did see it, old friend. You have my sympathy.'

The subject was out in the open at last. They both breathed a sigh of relief.

'Laughably inaccurate, of course,' said Fragment.

'Typical media smear,' said Watmough.

'One feels wild with fury. Of course, I shall demand an apology . . . This sort of thing, though quite untrue, is of course not particularly helpful for me at the moment.'

Watmough nodded sympathetically. 'Another bottle?'

'If you can run to it,' said Fragment.

'One doesn't go very far these days,' said Watmough.

Some time later, when the dining room was almost empty of its lunchers, and the last of the discreet conversations had run its course, Fragment and Watmough rose to take a liqueur by the fire in the lobby. There was no sign of Horlick and Pleasant, who had apparently finished the interview or were continuing it elsewhere.

'Just deny everything,' said Watmough, rather incoherently, 'and things will die down.' Two bottles of claret and the prospect of a glass of Beaumes de Venise had entirely washed away the stirrings of guilt which had disturbed him throughout the lunch.

'If I find the bastard who gave them the tip-off,' said Fragment darkly, 'I shall bloody well kill him with my bare hands.'

Watmough nodded comfortably. Indeed, at that moment he felt that his connection with the story was so remote as to free him entirely from any responsibility.

'It puts me in an appalling difficulty,' said Fragment. 'Particularly in the light of my speech this afternoon. There's bound to be a lot of press interest. I should think they'll send all their gossip hounds down to the Commons. I hope you might write a conciliatory piece about this for the *Commentator*, Aldous. You know, along the lines of vicious hounding . . . right to privacy . . . standards of the gutter press, that sort of thing.'

'I'll have a go, Evelyn. No guarantee that they'll take it, of course. Young Brayne is a bit of a prude in these matters.'

'I thought he was terrifically pompous,' said Fragment. 'I wished I'd never gone to the lunch. All they did was fish around for bits of smut.'

'I'll do what I can,' said Watmough.

'You may be interested to know,' said Fragment, lowering his voice, 'that our friend in the Treasury is considering increasing the Premium Bond top prize.'

'Is that so?'

'An article which aired that particular theory would worry that department no end. Yes, it would really put the cat among the pigeons. Shake them up no end.'

'Point taken. Thanks, old friend.'

'Don't mention it.'

They sat back, each conscious of having done his duty and delivered what was expected of him. Watmough said, 'Isn't that Maurice Earish over there? You know him don't you, Evelyn?'

'Yes,' said Fragment unenthusiastically. 'He wrote a rather poor profile of me for the *Guardian*. I don't like the cut of his jib altogether much.'

They advanced towards the door.

'Hello, comrade,' said Watmough, as they passed the familiar figure which sat on an upright couch near the front entrance.

The figure did not move. As they came nearer it became clear that Earish, although wholly upright, was no longer receptive to his surroundings. His head, while remaining vertical, leaned slightly against the head of the bench, while his hands were folded neatly in his lap. His face was a little flushed and his mouth slightly open. 'Maurice seems to have had a good lunch,' said Watmough.

'I never thought he was much of a fellow,' said Fragment. 'His profile was very superficial. He called me insubstantial with a tendency to banality. Typical Leftist cant.'

'No, he's completely gone,' said Watmough. 'Quite beyond us.'

'Hmm,' said Fragment distantly. 'Well, Aldous, thank you for my lunch. I am only sorry the circumstances were not happier.'

'A pleasure, Evelyn. Best of luck with your speech.'

Fragment sighed and nervously moistened his lips. 'I'm not going to pretend I'm looking forward to it,' he said, 'but as you know, Aldous – '

Watmough looked out through the lobby, hoping that Fragment was not going to begin once again on the importance of family life – 'I'm not a funker. If I've said I'll do something, then I jolly well pull all the stops out and take it on with – '

At this point, Earish gave a convulsive shudder and emitted a loud noise, like a bark or shout of alarm. They stopped and regarded him apprehensively, but his disturbance was momentary and he rapidly resumed his state of relaxation. The only change in his appearance was a shift of position which resulted in the lower half of his body slumping further down the bench, still in a rigid position, so that his knees were now only a foot or so from the floor.

As Earish's body slid down the bench, so the afternoon edition of the *London Evening Mail* which had previously been folded beneath his hands slipped from his knee and fell onto the floor. Without thinking, Watmough stooped and picked it up. He read the front page then stopped suddenly and tried unsuccessfully to reinsert the newspaper under Earish's folded hands.

Seeing his fumbled haste, Fragment seized the paper. 'My God!' he shouted. 'It's on the front page. God, it's got onto the evening paper now.' Watmough opened his mouth, but while he was weighing up the appropriate response, Fragment spread out the front page and read the words: 'CLEAN-UP MINISTER IN NAKED DRUGS FROLIC'. The headline was accompanied by a large picture of Fragment captured in a moment of indignation from his recent Soho walkabout. Fragment stared at the page, then turned to Watmough. He sought for words. He pointed silently to the paper. His face flushed a dark, deep purple.

'Who is giving them all this stuff?' he said. He made several jabbing motions at the paper, then he said, 'It is the finish. It is the finish.'

'Rubbish,' said Watmough in a feeble attempt at outrage. 'This is a mere follow-up of the diary story. It will all die down. Just carry on as usual.'

Fragment waved the paper above his head. 'I am going to take them for every penny they've got,' he shouted, causing the doorman to look up in surprise. 'No one is going to write this sort of filth with impunity. I'm going to the highest powers in the land, I shall – '

'Don't get – '

'By God, there will be blood in the corridors of Westminster,' shouted Fragment, rushing out into the street, where his driver – who had already read the *Evening Mail* – stared straight ahead with the stony face of tact. The door slammed shut and Fragment was borne away from the Roastbeef at high speed. Watmough thought the walk to the Commons might do him good and set off down Whitehall towards the distant flags and the shining turrets of the Houses of Parliament. Behind at the Roastbeef, Earish emitted another noise of alarm and sank slowly from his bench onto the floor.

· CHAPTER · X ·

'He was a monster,' said Amanda Plugge, quietly. 'He still is. He is an egomaniacal, greedy, reckless, totally self-pitying, utterly contemptible shit. He uses people and then throws them away. Everyone is manipulated to do exactly what he wants. And when he no longer has any use for them – they're screwed up like a piece of paper and dropped into the wastepaper basket.'

Pauline sat back and nodded in a sympathetic manner. It was no good, she thought, to let Amanda Plugge carry on like this in too frank and emotional a manner. They couldn't possibly use stuff like this. Besides, she was becoming too agitated to remember anything really useful. 'Could we go back to your first impression of Jerry? Where did you first meet him?'

Amanda laughed bitterly. 'I was working in London. I was a secretary in those days, working for Napier and Wright. They're a very smart firm of lawyers.'

'I'm familiar with them,' said Pauline.

'Anyway,' said Amanda, 'I used to sit in reception and entertain the important clients while they were waiting to be seen. One day a man almost fell through the door, breathing alcohol all over the place and shouting the most incomprehensible abuse about a woman who – naturally – turned out to be his ex-wife. I mean Arabella Spring-Greene, of course. And there was Jerry, shouting and stamping all over the office, complaining that she was forcing him out of his house without a penny to his name.'

'How interesting,' said Pauline.

'It was an unusual introduction,' said Amanda coldly. 'But in those days Jerry gave off a sort of charm, a sort of charisma. Rather than being appalled by him, as I would be now, I thought he was rather fascinating. I suppose I'd never met anyone like him before in my life.'

'Had you seen his play at the time?'

'No, I never went much to the theatre. He started his television programme while we were married, which did nothing to help our relationship. Particularly after he said – that word on the screen. He became a celebrity overnight in a very vulgar way. It wasn't true, by the way, about his being turned out of his house by Arabella. I happen to know that she was very generous to him. She gave him her Holland Park flat and a very substantial cash sum. But it's typical of him to twist everything to suit himself.'

Pauline nodded and peered into the revolving wheels of the tape recorder.

Upstairs, Quintin Plugge was writing his weekly *Commentator* column on a sheet of white lined paper. His handwriting, small and sloping, made a mark like the trail of an insect. 'Yet now, wherever one goes,' he wrote, 'one is confronted by the ultimate horror of the plastic marmalade pot, a container which is as aesthetically unappealing as it is difficult to open.'

Plugge stared at the words he had written. They covered three lines. He knew from experience that there were eighteen more lines to fill.

He sighed and looked out of the window. The rain fell steadily in the November morning mist, a cold insistent curtain which obscured the garden. Moisture dripped from leaves, from branches, from the conservatory roof. He wondered what it would be like to be abroad at that moment, drinking coffee in the Piazza della Signoria in Florence, or perhaps at Fiesole, looking down over the Arno and the great, marvellous city. He sighed, and stared at the paper again.

'These pots are difficult to open,' he repeated, 'and contain, when one has penetrated the inner plastic jar, a mere smear of marmalade, certainly not enough for two pieces of toast.' He imagined breakfasting on croissants, coffee and fresh orange juice in some Italian lakeside hotel, at Como perhaps, sitting on a balcony, overlooking the lake where poor D. H. Lawrence had spent two summers and Keats had travelled. Surely not Keats. He considered the question. Wordsworth, he thought, and just possibly Shelley. Milton? No, almost certainly not. What was the Greek for breakfast, he wondered. One of those annoying, unimportant words that one could never remember. What did the ancients eat for breakfast? He thought of Homer. But all he could remember was the word for slaughtering a hundred oxen and something about the smell of roast meat. An unattractive thought for this damp English morning. He stared at his pen and unscrewed the top to check his ink supplies. Yes, there was enough ink there. It welled gently from his nib and made a blot on the paper. 'Damn,' said Plugge. He wiped it carefully with his handkerchief and resumed his column.

'So no sooner has one struggled to open the plastic container, than it is necessary to open yet another. Why, oh why, do hotels persist with the belief that anyone prefers plastic to a good old-fashioned jar of thick-cut Oxford marmalade? As ever, the arguments are economic. Hotels will tell us, I suppose, that it is cheaper to provide the little plastic pots. But I wonder. Wouldn't they attract more visitors if they simply put the traditional old-fashioned jars on the table, with a little silver spoon' – after a moment's thought he crossed out the word 'silver' – 'and allowed us to eat marmalade as we do in our own homes, from an old-fashioned jar?'

He saw that he had used the phrase 'old-fashioned' three times in his previous paragraph. He yawned and stared at the rain. What was the Greek for breakfast? It was no good, he would have to look it up. Eagerly he leapt up from his paper and turned to the glass-fronted bookcase on one side of the chimney. He took out his old, battered copy of Liddell & Scott's Greek Lexicon and turned the wafer thin, browning pages with care. Something to do with morning? Or meal? What was meal anyway?

Absorbed he looked up at the clock, to discover that nearly forty minutes had elapsed. It was nearly lunchtime. He considered the piece of paper on his desk. Not enough yet. Hastily he took up his pen again.

'Walking down Long Acre to lunch at Agnellis,' he wrote, 'I was amazed and appalled to see the number of people eating in the streets. Have young people completely abandoned the civilised custom of eating in restaurants? I was rudely jostled by a young man whose vivid clothing and plaited black hair proclaimed him to be a member of what is known, I believe, as the Rastafarian persuasion; he was moving at high speed, being transported on roller skates, and his progress was erratic – so much so that I was nearly knocked off my feet. As it was, his right hand, which clutched a parcel of food, collided with my shoulder, leaving a smear of tomato ketchup down my sleeve; this apparently had dripped from his bun composed of noxious foul-smelling relishes covering a synthetic circle of meat.'

Plugge sighed. Five more lines to go before the sheet was filled. That, and another half page would do. He looked at the clock. The time advanced alarmingly. He heard the nanny coming up the stairs and he prayed that she would not stop, put her head round the door and ask him how it was going. The footsteps continued.

'I suppose it is too much to ask,' he continued, 'that persons do not eat in public. But everywhere I look now, people seem to be eating food in the street. It is demoralising, and as for the litter, the streets are highly disagreeable for pedestrians. How unattractive the human face looks when it is crammed with food. It is almost as if . . .' He laid down his pen and stared out into the garden again.

A sharp repetitive banging noise made him stop and look up at the ceiling. The noise was overhead. It must be the baby. He wondered what was happening. Plugge gazed vacantly at the ceiling. The banging stopped, then began again. Plugge tapped his fingers on the desk. The banging stopped.

Downstairs in the study, Amanda smiled at Pauline in a gesture of exaggerated tolerance. 'I'm sorry,' she said. 'All this noise. I suppose one just has to get used to it. Do you have children yourself?'

'No,' said Pauline.

'Well,' said Amanda. 'Quintin and I started rather late. It is frightfully disruptive. More than one would have believed. You see, I've tried to set this little business up. I've opened a small antiques shop, but it is so difficult to spend the time I need on it. And Quintin works at home so much, it's almost impossible to get him out from under my feet.' She assumed a worried expression. 'Just a minute,' she said, 'I must remind him he's taking the baby to a birthday party at two. Would you excuse me just a minute.'

' – as if we are endorsing the values of the take-away society in a happy acceptance of instant gratification.'

That would do. The banging started again. Far in the distance, Plugge could hear footsteps coming up the stairs. Amanda was advancing. People told him, Plugge thought gloomily, how lucky he was to work at home.

He turned to the next sheet of paper. One more paragraph. 'Turning on the radio the other day,' he wrote, ' – I mean the Third Programme, of course; does anyone listen to the Home Service any more? – I was struck by – '

His wife put her head round the door. 'My God, haven't you finished yet?' she said, continuing without waiting for a reply. 'Don't forget you're taking Giles to the Cartons this afternoon. He has to leave by two. Don't be late.'

'I won't forget. I just have to get this finished.'

'Good heavens,' said Amanda sighing loudly. 'If I had half your time I could have written a whole novel by now. Just sitting there at the desk all morning, gazing into the garden. What actually do you do all the time? I wonder how you'd manage if you had to keep up with my routine. I must say, I never have time to sit there staring into the garden, wondering what will be for supper. It must be marvellous to live such an incredibly selfish life.'

'Must get on,' said Plugge. 'Do you mind if I just finish this before the sermon begins?'

'Oh, quite. Just because someone is – for once – paying some attention to me.'

'What?'

'I know it's hard for you to accept that anyone could possibly be interested in my opinion, but there's no need for you to sulk just because I have a researcher with a tape recorder in there, rather than you.'

'Well, it would be inappropriate for me to be there. I don't know Jerry very well. Not as well as you, certainly.'

'Of course,' said Amanda smiling in a sarcastic manner. 'You don't want me ever to mention Jerry's name again, do you? You won't accept the fact that I ever knew him, let alone lived with him for seven years. You just want to sweep it all away – '

'No, I don't – '

' – under the carpet in your usual style, just pretending that the past never happened. Well, I envy you. I wish I could deal with life's problems like that, just turning away and pretending that nothing ever disturbed the surface of my calm little pond. I wish – '

Plugge sighed while his wife continued in a similar vein for several minutes.

'Isn't the researcher waiting for you?' he said eventually.

'Yes.'

'I'll just finish this then, shall I?'

'So selfish,' said his wife and slammed the door.

'So sorry,' she said, returning to the drawing room where Pauline was sitting impassively on the sofa.

'How would you describe Jerry's character?' Pauline said. 'Was he, for example, generous, or mean, gregarious, solitary, that sort of thing?'

'Oh well,' said Amanda, her mouth twisting into a smile. 'He was incredibly generous all the time with other people's money. Never his own. I was lucky enough to have a small private income which I inherited. Jerry, of course, regarded this as his own – his own personal fund. I was never consulted about what he spent, or when he spent it. Jerry was always very fond of giving away other people's money. He was very hospitable, very generous when it didn't cost him anything. I remember one occasion when he invited fifty people back to our house for an impromptu supper party. He dialled up some restaurant for take-away meals and plied them all with drink. He thought it was amusing. Of course, it was quite amusing at the time. But none of those people were his friends. None. Not really. Not one of them ever invited us back, for example; they were all just scroungers, like Jerry.'

'So you would say that he enjoyed spontaneity.'

'Yes. Parties, dinners, drinks, it all had to be done on the spur of the moment. He had no concept of an ordered life. But of course it was the drinking that was too much for me in the end. All those rows and rows of bottles. And the dreadful mornings after the parties. This isn't very edifying stuff for your programme really.'

'It's essential background information,' said Pauline.

'I don't suppose you'll be able to put any of this in.'

'I personally stopped listening to any music composed after eighteen fifty several years ago, and there is nothing on my record shelves which might be described as "modern". I have often thought it is a waste of time to try and pretend to enjoy music which no one likes, and no one can listen to, even though they are told it is smart and clever. Why, oh why, can't we all admit that Britten and Tippett are masters of cacophony and that we all prefer Mozart? Then no one would ever again have to sit through a concert of barbaric, ugly, sounds pretending he was enjoying his evening because it was the right thing to do.'

With relief Plugge put down his pen. He had reached the end of the second half of his sheet. He took out an envelope and addressed it to Brayne at the *Commentator*. How hard it was to make a diary really interesting. He wondered if people had more eventful lives than he did. He supposed so. His own existence sounded unutterably dull when he wrote about it. For a moment, gloom overwhelmed him. Then he remembered that his life had been given special meaning by his vision in the shopping precinct. Dullness was a small price to pay for divine revelation.

'Seen Jerry today?' said Maurice Earish coming into the Dog and Biscuit. Vernon Corner waved in recognition. 'How do, my old mate. He'll be in any minute now. Can I get you one?'

'That's very civil of you.'

'Gin and French?'

'If you can run to it.'

'Cheers.'

'Mind you,' said Corner. 'It was a rough old night.'

'Was it?'

'Yes, quite a bit of excitement in here. That chap from the *Reporter* was in bragging about his scoop. That story about Fragment. I'm afraid our friend did not take to him at all.'

'You mean Jerry?'

'Yes.'

'Bit of a row?'

'Not half.'

'What about?' said Earish. His expression changed. 'What happened?'

'Well, our friend was in here after rather a tiring day in the television studio. This programme has got him rather overwrought and he doesn't like the producer, some smart-arse whizz-kid who's somebody's son and who has a lot of ideas about what he wants Jerry to say.'

'Oh God,' said Earish. 'The BBC – what is happening to the programmes there? I switched on last night after supper – '

'Well, he was shouting quite a bit about this young whizz kid,' said Corner, 'and Galen didn't help by – '

' – and I found myself watching a lot of women talking in the most repulsive, clinical detail about the menopause. Yes, we were spared nothing of the symptoms. Bleeding, hot flushes, emotional instability . . .'

' – shouting that Jerry was a lazy fucker who hadn't done anything for the last ten years and that no one was interested in him anyway – '

' – I just couldn't believe it. This sort of thing coming from the BBC. Why do we need to know about it, especially just after supper? It's like sex education – '

' – so, of course, Jerry started shouting back – '

' – which is thrust onto children of six and seven these days. Yes, they're taught all about condoms and the Pill and Aids and of course, because they know about it, they all want to go off and do it. It's the schools that are to blame. Would you want your children taught about it? Of course, you haven't any, but if you had, you wouldn't want them to come home talking about contraceptive jelly would you? And you don't want to have to watch it after supper.'

' – and so he was pretty excited by the time Horlick came in.'

'Horlick?' said Earish. 'He's a peculiar chap, isn't he? What do you make of him?'

'I'd watch your back with him,' said Corner promptly. 'He was full of himself about his big story.'

'The Fragment affair?'

'Yes. Bragging away to anyone who'd listen. So Jerry comes up to him and gives him a long speech about sex and revolution and free love – '

'His favourite topic,' said Earish sourly.

'And he shouts at Horlick to leave Fragment's private life alone. Then we get a lot more stuff about Jerry's sex life. Not what you'd want your mother to hear. Old Jerry seemed to take it all personally. Claimed he was striking a blow for tolerance. It was a real old set to.'

'What's the latest on the Fragment affair?'

'There's more stuff today in the *Reporter* all about Lady Arabella and the wild parties her set used to go to. The implication is that Fragment used to be pretty keen on exotic substances in those days and took not a few with the gracious lady.'

'Good heavens.'

'There's a page about sex communes, and another page about the terrible consequences of free love.'

'Who's written that?'

'Norris Pleasant.'

'The sex guru?'

'That's your man. Mind you, he's taking a different line these days.'

'What's that?'

'Pair-bonding, old son. Partners for life. No more putting it about with the fairer sex.'

'That's quite a change of heart.'

'Better still, he suggests we all give it up.'

'I've been doing that for years,' said Earish bleakly.

'My friend,' said Corner, 'you're in a perfect position to merge your vibrant personality with another vibrant personality and become one vibrancy with the woman of your choice.' He laughed loudly.

'You're very well informed about it all.'

'*Prankster* is doing a big number on the book. It could put us out of business.'

'Poor old Fragment.'

'There is the matter of the breasts,' said Corner. 'He does not deny that he painted them. Daubed, more like.'

'Breasts?' said Bone, emerging with disconcerting suddenness from behind the bar. 'Bloody disgusting, isn't it? I mean, there he is standing up in the House of Commons telling us all how to behave, while he was having a positive fucking orgy.' Bone's voice rose in a crescendo of excitement. 'Smearing women's breasts with paint, wasn't he? Like a fucking animal.'

'A lot of people were doing it at the time,' said Corner.

'Were they?' said Earish wistfully. 'I must say, I never did.'

'Did you never freak out on the grass, my friend?'

'No.'

'Did you never turn-on and drop out?' said Corner, wheezing with laughter.

'No. I never knew any women at all until I was twenty-three. I went to a public school, you know. It's incredible, isn't it,' Earish went on, 'to think of him prancing about naked in the middle of a field surrounded by a crowd of dope fiends.'

'What's going to happen then?' said Bone, sitting down abruptly. 'Is he going to resign then? A drink anyone?' Absently he took their orders. 'No, it's on me. A pleasure.'

'Probably,' said Earish.

'I wouldn't be too sure,' said Corner.

'I think his career is finished. The party are very squeamish about this sort of thing. How can he clear his name? No one's denying the story, are they?'

Corner looked at his watch. 'Jerry should be in soon.'

At that moment the door of the pub swung open and Jerry Gude came in, followed by a straggle of people carrying electrical equipment, television lights and cameras. 'Sorry about all this,' he said, with a negligent wave of the hand. 'Just another scene in the programme. They want to film a typical day in my life. They've been filming me frying bacon, blowing my nose, and I had to deter them from following me into the bog. This is the next scene.' Corner and Earish stared at him in amazement. 'All right if they all come in, Galen?' said Gude.

'My pleasure,' said Bone, springing into action behind the bar. 'Your colleagues are at liberty to capture the atmosphere of this famous pub if they so wish.' Bone spun excitedly to and fro, shouting at his staff and waving his arms in the air.

'This is the famous Dog and Biscuit,' said Gude, 'where we sit by the lavatories and waste the best days of our lives. Make yourselves at home.' The troupe of technicians came in and almost filled the interior. Charlie Enever came in and started telling them where to put the cameras.

'That's the prick who's making the film,' said Gude. Silently Corner handed him a drink.

'How's the programme coming along, Jerry boy?' said Corner.

'Well, it's high comedy,' said Gude languidly. 'They're recording me everywhere I go, getting into bed, making a cup of tea, going to the lavatory. They're interviewing my wives. That's the most sadistic aspect of the whole thing. Not only did I have to endure the agony of being married to them, but now I have to listen to them rehearsing their lists of grievances against me all over again.'

'Are they going to be on the programme?' said Earish.

'Extracts,' said Gude. 'The most blood-curdling bits.'

'Drinks on the house,' shouted Bone. 'Whatever you like.'

'Get a good shot of him,' Gude told Enever, 'or he'll change his mind.'

Bone ran down the length of the bar. 'I'm on sparkling form today,' he cried loudly. 'You're seeing me at the height of my powers. I'm incandescent. I'm immortal.'

'Calm down, Galen,' said Corner. 'All this will end in tears.'

'You're right,' said Bone, 'I'm one of those maniacs – what do you call them?'

'Manic depressives?'

'You're right. I'm up one minute and the next – ' Bone's hand swooped in a descriptive curve '– the next I'm down. In the depths. Depressed.'

'Seize the moment,' said Jerry. 'Let the good times roll, Galen.'

The cameramen set up their lights. 'Let's have a party here, good people,' said Jerry Gude excitedly, swallowing another drink. 'Let's all do our bit for the programme.'

A little later there was quite a crowd at the Dog and Biscuit. At its centre Jerry Gude wheeled and spun, telling anecdotes, slipping from his stool to the floor. The lights of the cameras cast the pub into a dazzling radiance, the lights glittering on the row of bottles and sparkling on the small lamps that were attached to the walls. A cameraman moved round the sides of the room, training his camera on the centre where Jerry was now shouting, now dropping his voice to a theatrical whisper. Enever crouched by the bar and gave directions. From time to time, Bone would emerge from the bar and dramatically deliver a short speech. As people passed by in the street, they looked inside in curiosity, drawn by the noise and the shouting. Regulars were soon battling to get through the door, pushing aside the cameramen in their haste to get to the bar.

'Look at them all trying to get in,' said Earish, who was squashed into the corner by the lavatory door. 'What insatiable desire to be on television.'

'Well, everyone does it now,' said Corner. 'Even the Royals want to go on the box.'

'Well, I don't,' said Earish. 'I was just having a quiet drink when all this madness started. I'd get out if I could but I can't make my way to the door through this scrum.'

A group of girls, clearly tourists, were gazing at Gude in admiration, impressed by his apparent celebrity. 'He's lost none of his popularity,' said Corner. 'Amazing how women like a bit of fame.'

'Odd that Gude's never had any children, don't you think?' said Earish. 'What with all these wives and girlfriends. Do you think there's something, well – you know . . .'

'He's always denied it,' said Corner, 'but the general feeling is that women are safe with him.'

'You mean?'

'Fires blanks, old mate.'

'Oh.'

'Of course, no one has actually proved it – '

Earish was silent for a few minutes. Then he said, 'What I can't understand is how he does it. I just wish someone would explain to me how he gets away with it. What is the secret of his success with all these women?'

Corner sighed, not because the secret of Jerry Gude's success did not interest him, but because he had conducted this conversation with so many people before on so many different occasions.

'There's been a message for you,' said Marigold, scowling at Florence Barge. 'I nearly put the phone down, he was so bloody rude.'

'Was it Jerry?'

'He was so drunk I could hardly tell who it was. He spoke very slowly and all his words were slurred. That didn't stop him telling me I was a stuck-up, supercilious bitch.'

'What did he want?' said Florence eagerly. In spite of herself she smiled at Marigold.

'I can't understand why you find this shit so attractive.'

'People – women,' said Florence, 'women don't understand him. He's had a terribly hard time. I know he doesn't make a very good impression. I thought he was awful at first. But he's really very sensitive.'

Marigold scowled at her again. 'Well, the next time he rings, he's going to get an earful,' she said. 'You're so impressionable, Flo. Can't you see that he just uses women and then chucks them away.'

Florence glared at her angrily. 'He actually likes women very much.'

'Find out the hard way,' said Marigold. 'I'm in a very bad temper. I've put on six pounds this week. It's working at that bloody *Commentator*, cooking all those pies and puddings. I can't help tasting them. All they think about there is food.'

'Jerry hardly seems to eat,' said Florence. 'He's terribly thin and uncared for. He's asked me to have dinner with him.'

'Dinner?'

'Yes.'

'Are you going?'

'Yes. Why not?'

'You must be mad.'

'His book is really strange. It's all about taking drugs, and being yourself, and sex.'

'All that Sixties stuff,' said Marigold with disdain. 'That's terribly old hat.'

'I think it's fascinating,' said Florence defensively.

Marigold looked at her. 'Florence, you mustn't be so impressionable. No one believes in that any more. Ask the brilliant Alexander.'

'Oh, he doesn't believe it. But he doesn't like sex anyway.'

There was a short constrained silence.

Florence switched on the radio. 'In a statement today,' a voice announced, 'the Bishop of Brigg condemned what he called the totally unjustifiable campaign to smear the reputation of the Minister for the Family, Evelyn Fragment. Referring to a series of items appearing in the gossip column of a daily newspaper, the Bishop said: "It is not for any of us today to offer moral judgements about the private life of a public figure." The Bishop went on to say that the modern tendency to condemn sexual liberty and freedom was a trend that he personally regretted. "Sex can be a way to God," the Bishop said, "We are too ready to condemn it out of hand these days." '

Florence switched off the radio impatiently. 'I'm sick of hearing about Evelyn Fragment,' she said. 'Alexander goes on about him all the time.' She switched on the television. 'How's Julian?'

'I've discovered that he owns a lot of property in Worcestershire,' said Marigold. 'He's seriously rich. I wonder if the idea of marriage has entered his head.'

'Do you want to marry him?'

'Why not? I don't think he'll ever ask me. Do you think, if I went away to India or somewhere, he'd realise how much I meant to him, and ask for my hand when I came home?'

'No,' said Florence.

'Neither do I.'

'How's the novel?'

'I can't think what to do with my heroine.'

'Imagine if it's a best-seller. It will make you millions.'

A burst of applause came from the television set. A man in a roll-neck sweater said: 'And now, will you welcome please, my final guest this evening, whose books have made him a welcome friend in all our homes.'

'It's the Marius Grope show,' said Marigold.

'Would you welcome Norris Pleasant.' Another burst of applause rang out from the delighted audience.

'Who is he?' said Florence.

'He does all those sex books,' said Marigold. 'You know, *Joy in the Morning, Joy in the Afternoon* – I didn't know he was still going.'

They watched as Pleasant bared his teeth at the audience and sat back on the studio sofa.

'How extraordinary,' said Florence, suddenly. 'Look at his face. He looks just like Alexander.'

Marigold stared as Pleasant said: 'Only through the new demands of intimacy and fidelity can we discover what true sexuality is all about.'

'Strikingly similar,' said Marigold. 'Apart from his skin. I wonder how he gets it to go that horrible colour.'

'There's an uncanny resemblance,' said Florence. 'They could be related.'

'Perhaps they are,' said Marigold giggling.

'Don't be ridiculous,' said Florence.

The telephone rang again.

'Must be your drunk,' said Marigold.

'Hello?' said Florence, seizing the phone.

'Who the hell is that?' said an angry voice at the end of the line. It was hard to distinguish the words. 'Hello?' said Gude loudly. 'Is that you, you stuck-up bitch? Look, just take a fucking message will you?'

'Jerry? This is Florence speaking.'

'Oh,' said Gude. 'Christ, it's you.'

There was a moment's silence, while he breathed heavily down the phone. In the distance Florence could hear the sound of coins showering from a fruit machine and the sound of laughter and shouted conversation.

'Look,' Gude's voice came again down the phone, even more slowly than before. 'Look, I'm sorry . . . I just wanted to say, thank you . . . thank you for saving my life . . .'

There was another silence. 'Are you there, Jerry?' said Florence. 'Some fat bitch answered it before,' he came on again. 'Wouldn't take a fucking message.' After a short pause she heard the unmistakable sound of Gude weeping into the telephone. In the distance someone shouted: 'It's one pound sixty and don't fucking argue with me.' There was a loud crashing noise as if a chair or stool had fallen over.

'Oh God,' said Gude, crying into the telephone. 'God, I'm washed up. I haven't made anyone happy in the last twenty years.'

'Jerry? Do you want me to – '

Another crash came from very close to her ear. Jerry's voice did not return. 'Hello?' said Florence anxiously. 'Jerry, are you still there?'

She was about to hang up when a different, strange voice said into the phone: 'Hello miss?'

'Hello?'

'This is a friend of Jerry's speaking. He's not – he's not very well at the moment. All right? He can't speak to you just now. Not just at the moment.'

'Is he all right?'

'No problem,' the voice said. Then it said, 'What?' in response to something shouted in the distance.

'Hello?' said Florence, but the telephone suddenly went dead.

Later that evening, the West End Central police force were alerted to a disturbance in the street ouside the Dog and Biscuit. Officers sent round to investigate the complaint came upon a group of people standing outside a Chinese restaurant, watching with an impassive curiosity. The crowd remained motionless in a semi-circle, arranged around the outside of the restaurant. In front, a number of Chinese people were shouting loudly. Their voices were high and angry as they pointed and waved, unable to make themselves understood. At the door, two of them were holding Gude by the arms, and shouting fiercely at him. He was struggling and occasionally kicking out with his feet as he attempted to free himself.

'He kicked the car, officer,' said Bone on the pavement. 'He's been under a lot of stress. It was nothing personal. He didn't mean to do it.'

The Chinese shouted and pointed to a Mercedes which bore the marks of Gude's boot.

'It's the first he's kicked for a long time,' said Bone. Corner and Earish stood among the silent crowd.

'We'll have to take him away,' said the policeman. 'Familiar face, aren't you? Back to your old tricks again?' They each laid a hand on his shoulder and put him into the police car.

'Did he kick it hard?' said Earish.

'It belongs to the Chinese Driving School,' said Corner thoughtfully. 'I expect that was the trouble.'

· CHAPTER · XI ·

'Arabella, I must know what your position on this matter is before I can issue a statement.'

Arabella Spring-Greene stood unsteadily by the bookcase of her study, her eyes heavily ringed with last night's make-up which she had neglected to remove.

'Evelyn, I'm not used to getting up so early,' she said hoarsely. 'Can I get you some coffee?'

Fragment turned from the fireplace and carefully positioned his profile against the morning light which flooded softly through the thin lace curtain.

'I am sorry to come to you so early, Arabella, but I must know exactly who is giving this information to Horlick.'

Lady Arabella coughed at some length and reached for a cigarette from her ivory box on the table.

After she had drawn a few breathfuls of smoke into her lungs she said, 'It's bloody, Evelyn. Really these people are awful shits.' She coughed again.

Fragment drank his coffee slowly. Then he put his cup down. 'It's more than bloody, Arabella,' he said slowly. 'It could be final.' He turned to her with a look of pained indignation, waiting for her reply. After a few moments, it became clear that she was not going to say anything, but was sitting hunched on the sofa staring at the wall. 'It could be final,' Fragment repeated, a little more firmly.

'What?' said Arabella huskily.

'My position is unimaginably grave.'

'Because of this ridiculous story.'

'Naturally my whole political credibility is at stake.'

'Well, won't it just blow over? After all, it was years ago. Who cares about that sort of thing these days?'

'Well, people do care,' said Fragment. 'That was the whole point of my speech in the Commons. That is the whole point of my appointment as Family Minister. People do care. I care. And . . . the point is, Arabella, I must put an unpleasant question to you directly and I hope you will understand the reasons I am forced to do this. As far as I am aware not one of my family or associates has spoken to any representative of the press. Some of the information was so detailed and personal that only . . . Well, in fine, I must put it to you directly: Did you tell Horlick yourself?'

'Oh, Horlick. He's a silly boy,' said Arabella.

'Did you tell him?'

'No. No, I don't think so. I don't remember telling him. I suppose I might have done.'

'Arabella, please concentrate.'

'Oh God, Evelyn, I am concentrating.'

'Just think. Is there any occasion on which you might have told him?'

'Well Evelyn, there are lots of occasions aren't there? He was at my publishing party. Perhaps you told him yourself there.'

'Don't be ridiculous. Did you tell him?'

'I can't remember.'

'Try.'

'I can't see why it matters. It was twenty years ago, Evelyn. And it was hardly a secret at the time.'

'I ask because if you had told him, I would have had to ask also whether you mentioned anything about our – that we were still friends with each other.'

Arabella stared at him and lit another cigarette.

'He didn't say anything about that in the story.'

'No, but the implication was that we had enjoyed a – a romantic association. I am gravely worried that Horlick plans a sequel to the original piece, pursuing this line of enquiry. Indicating, I mean, that we are still enjoying a romantic friendship.'

'Not very often,' said Arabella.

'What?'

'Only rarely, these days. Anyway, I thought your wife knew all about it.'

Fragment frowned. 'She does know. We have an understanding, Arabella, which is that my wife, a splendid woman in so many ways as you know, accepts a certain amount of, well, flexibility in my life. She is perfectly prepared to keep up her end and carry out her excellent support work at home, on condition that we preserve the status quo. In other words, she is not prepared to see my name appearing in the gossip columns. That is not in the deal at all.'

'A very understanding woman,' said Arabella.

'She is a remarkable person,' said Fragment dutifully.

'Yes.'

Fragment coughed and observed a moment's silence. Then he said. 'Arabella, if I am to sue Horlick and the paper, I must have your assurance that you have not told him anything. That you will confirm my statement.'

Arabella said nothing.

'Tell me the truth,' said Fragment. 'What have you told this disreputable and cheapskate hack?'

Arabella said, 'I think he's rather sweet.'

'Who?'

'Horlick.'

'Sweet?'

'Yes.'

'You amaze me, Arabella. What can you be thinking of?'

Arabella regarded him with annoyance.

'If you really want the truth, Evelyn, he is a sweet, thoughtful boy and he is an absolutely fantastic lover. I don't know what I told him. I probably told him you were a complete bore and prig and self-obsessed careerist. Who cares what you did twenty years ago? I don't. He was a sweet, loving boy and I'm terribly fond of him. I'm going to give a party for him next month.'

'God Almighty,' said Fragment. 'Arabella, this conversation

formally terminates our relationship. I cannot express the distress this revelation has caused me. Horlick! One more trophy to add to your list of young men. Horlick! A reptile. A slug. One of the lowest forms of life. What has happened to your sense of discrimination?'

'You're being awfully silly,' said Arabella, coughing again.

'You have ruined my career.'

Arabella yawned.

'Have you no feelings?'

'It's so early in the morning.'

Fragment stared coldly at her. 'I can't believe that you are at all concerned about this matter,' he said. 'You are calmly sitting here making the most disgusting and revolting confession and you seem to show no compunction for what you have done.'

'I think you're over-reacting to the situation.'

Fragment stared at her again.

'Have you any idea what you're saying?'

Arabella half shut her eyes.

'My career is at stake, and you seem to think I'm overdoing it. There seems to be no way of making you realise what you have done.'

'I've just had a little fun,' said Arabella. 'Now I'm going back to sleep.'

'Goodbye,' said Fragment, rising swiftly to his feet. 'This is the end of everything. I must formally thank you for the years of our association which I hope has been to our mutual benefit.'

'Evelyn you are the most pompous prig,' said Arabella. 'Just fuck off for good, would you.'

The flat was filled with flowers. Roses, carnations, lilies overflowed from tables and windowsills. In the hall, buckets stood in a line containing still unwrapped bunches. Vermilion, crimson, ruby and white mingled their colours in the failing December light. Perfume flooded the air. Jerry Gude had bought up the entire contents of a florist's shop.

Marigold was bending over the sink, crushing the stems of a bunch of white carnations. Florence was looking in vain for more vases. 'Well,' Marigold said, putting her hands on her hips. 'They're not from Alexander. That's for sure.'

The flat was unfamiliar, strangely exotic with its cargo of fragrant petals. 'They're from Jerry,' said Florence, reading the note again.

They stared at each other.

'Clearly he goes in for the grand gesture,' said Marigold. 'Don't let yourself be taken in by it, Flo.'

'He must have bought everything in the shop,' said Florence. 'He must have spent hundreds. I've never known anyone buy a shopful of flowers.'

'He must have a guilty conscience.'

'What are you doing to the carnations?'

'Crushing the stems. It makes them last longer.'

'Do be careful,' said Florence, rushing over to the sink. 'One of the flowers has dropped off.'

'And what is Alexander going to say about all this?' said Marigold accusingly.

'He won't say anything,' said Florence firmly. 'I've no intention of telling him.'

'Off to Clapham as usual tonight?'

'It's Tuesday,' said Florence. Reluctantly she prepared for the visit to Brayne. Instead of her customary basket she took a D'Arblays plastic bag. Its contents were disappointing. Inside was a loaf of sliced white bread, a tin of baked beans and two individual fruit pie samples which had escaped Gude's purchase. Wearily Florence set off for the Underground.

'My dear Florence,' said Brayne opening his front door. 'Greetings. Come in from the cold and disclose the contents of your basket.'

Florence stepped inside. She regarded him coldly. How stout he was growing. His hips bulged slightly over the rim of his trouser waistband. He was wearing a fawn cashmere pullover which, she saw with distaste, was slightly stained with food.

He was nosing about in the plastic bag like a dog looking for food.

'Nothing very exciting in it tonight,' she said sharply. 'I've had a very busy day.'

'With your vouchers?'

'No. That was last week.'

'What were you doing today?' He sounded bored. Now he had the bag open.

'I filled in a lot of forms at the job centre. I claimed to be a fast and accurate typist.'

'What's this, Florence? What on earth have you brought for supper?' She saw Brayne's face droop and flush with displeasure.

'Beans,' she said. 'We'll have beans on toast. What's wrong with that.'

'Out of a can?' said Brayne, his voice rising with a squeal of dismay.

'Yes. Millions of people eat them every day.'

'Tinned beans?'

'Yes.'

He stared at her with his mouth open. He did not know what to say. 'And what are these?' said Brayne, digging into the bag again and bringing out two packets of fruit pies.

'What do you mean?'

'What are these objects?' He held them out at arm's length as though contact with them would contaminate him.

'Fruit pies, of course. What do you think they are?'

'They are disgusting.'

'Well, I've sold no less than five hundred of them this week,' said Florence, goaded into bravado.

'What?'

'I sold out of my entire stock.'

'How did you manage that? I should have thought you would be lucky to sell one of these repellent objects.'

'Sheer genius,' said Florence in irritation. 'Would you like me to heat up the beans?'

The meal was not enjoyable. They sat and made polite

conversation while Brayne sawed his way through the sliced toast and shovelled beans into his mouth with an expression of fastidious disgust.

'Is anything the matter, Florence?' he said after some minutes.

'No,' she said, crossly.

'Oh.'

'Are you enjoying the beans?'

'A surprising experience,' said Brayne. 'It is interesting to have an insight into how the working class regularly eat. The plebeian diet, as it were. I might write a column about it. No wonder they are all so dwarfish and malformed.'

Florence pushed her plate away.

'Aren't you having any?'

'No, I'm not hungry.'

'I'll finish off yours then, shall I?' said Brayne, leaning over and scooping the remains of her dinner onto his plate.

Later, he said: 'What do you think about this business over Evelyn Fragment?'

'I couldn't care less about politics,' said Florence.

'It's not about politics,' said Brayne impatiently. 'It's a question of morality. Clearly he is in an impossible position. The man must resign.'

'Why does he have to do anything?'

'He has to go,' said Brayne. 'I intend to write a leader to that effect.'

'I don't think he's done anything wrong.'

'You must see,' said Brayne in a patient voice, 'that his position has become ludicrous. He is speaking on behalf of the moral majority. He has painted a woman's breasts amid orgiastic scenes of drug-induced frenzy. Well, he can't have it both ways, can he?'

'Why not? It was all such a long time ago. Why should you hold the past against him? He might be quite different now. People do change, Alexander.'

'We are prisoners of the past, Florence. What happened, happened. We can never escape it.'

Florence served the apple pies.

'This is quite inedible,' said Brayne, taking a large bite.

'I don't like them much.'

'And yet you say someone bought the whole lot?'

'Yes. Five hundred pies.'

Brayne cleared his plate.

'Who was it?'

'Oh, just somebody who came in.'

'You mean that a perfect stranger just came in and bought your entire stock of pies?'

'Yes.'

'An odd tale,' said Brayne.

Florence kept a guilty silence.

'Do you want that pie?'

'No.'

'Well, you might as well leave it in the kitchen. I might finish it after I've done my work tonight. Sometimes it's hard work completing a chapter. I often feel rather hungry when I've finished.'

After they had finished supper, Brayne switched on his black and white television set. They watched as the flickering picture revealed a line of people sitting behind a table in front of an audience.

'It's A Matter of Opinion,' said Brayne. 'We'll just see if anyone interesting is on.'

He picked up a current affairs magazine and began to read it. Florence yawned. A man in a bow tie and velvet jacket was addressing the audience. 'Time to turn the clock back,' he was saying. 'The sexual revolution has come full circle. We are now facing the great challenge of intimacy, perhaps for life, with one – '

'Oh, look, it's Pleasant again,' said Florence in surprise. 'Alexander, do look. He was on the Marius Grope show the other day. He looks exactly like you.'

Brayne lowered his magazine. 'Hmm?' he said vaguely.

'He could be your double. Just a bit older. Have you got a famous relative?'

'. . . the ideal of high monogamy,' Pleasant went on, 'is the deepest challenge of all, as I explain in my new book. Perhaps we could hear how the audience feel about this exciting new concept.'

Brayne stared at the television set. Then he flushed deep red, jumped up from his chair and turned the programme off.

'Alexander!' said Florence in annoyance. 'I was watching it.'

'A lot of rubbish,' said Brayne, chewing his lips.

'I wanted you to see Pleasant. The similarity is amazing.'

'Don't be ridiculous, Florence,' said Brayne brusquely. 'Come away from the television. Would you like me to read to you from my latest chapter?'

Florence looked at her watch.

'Good,' said Brayne.

'I must go in a moment,' said Florence. 'I don't want to be late home tonight.'

'Feeling a little tired?' said Brayne, going to his desk. 'You mustn't let me keep you too long. I think you'll like this chapter. It's about moral absolutes.'

He began to read: 'It is to the Beatles that we must look for an explanation for the present generation's tragic sense of moral decay and degeneration. John, Paul, George, Ringo – for ten years those names, banal and innocent-sounding, dominated our culture so totally that the pop ethic they espoused became accepted and even admired as a normative standard. And what did it all amount to – the self-conceit, the proclamation that they were the philosophers of a new age? Absolving youth from the duties hitherto laid upon it, the Beatles cast their generation into a wilderness of self-admiration, assuring them that they were the centre of their own universe.

'I used to be mad at my school,'

Brayne declaimed,

'The teachers who taught me weren't cool.'

'Thus the generation of the cool was born, the people who were smarter and wiser than their teachers. Current educational standards, sadly, proved that they were not, after all, as clever as they thought.'

He stopped. 'What do you think of it so far?'

Florence yawned. 'I like the Beatles,' she said. 'Sergeant Pepper is one of my favourites.'

'Sergeant Pepper?' said Brayne looking puzzled. 'Who is he?'

'It's an album, of course.'

'Never heard of it,' said Brayne. 'You don't listen to the Beatles do you, Florence? Dear me, what a long way we have to go to improve your taste.'

'Why do you always sneer at what people like? The Beatles made a whole generation of young people free to be themselves. To discard the materialism of their parents, to find out where they were going.'

Brayne looked at her in astonishment. 'I didn't realise you were a thwarted hippie, Florence,' he said. 'Twenty years too late, I'm afraid.'

'Hippies burned their money,' she told him. 'Money is a drug. Possessions are a form of madness.'

Brayne's mouth dropped open.

'What's wrong with your mouth?' said Florence. 'Shut it, Alexander.'

'What can you have been reading, Florence?' he said, in exaggerated astonishment. 'How have these extraordinary sentiments found their way into your brain?'

'I can think for myself,' she said, getting up from the chair.

'No, you can't,' said Brayne immediately. 'I've never known you to think of anything for yourself. It's what I like about you, Florence,' he added hastily.

'Then don't waste your time talking to me,' said Florence advancing angrily into the hall. 'Find someone else who won't answer back, someone who will sit here, week after week, being bored to death by your longwinded, tedious and boring book.'

Brayne reached towards her and put his hands on either side of her shoulders.

'Florence, don't be so silly.' He bent towards her and tried to kiss her cheek. Furiously she pushed him hard in the chest and he spun backwards across the hall, banging heavily into a hatstand.

'Don't come any nearer,' Florence shouted, seizing an umbrella from the hatstand. 'I shall use this, Alexander. I shall hit you if you touch me.'

She waved the umbrella menacingly at him. Its handle was made in the shape of a bird's head with two glittering orange eyes and a sharp, pointed beak.

Brayne backed away nervously. 'Be careful with that umbrella,' he said. 'There's a nasty point at the end. Don't wave it about, Florence. Mind the pictures.'

Infuriated by the sight of his cowering figure, Florence brought the umbrella smartly down upon the back of his neck with a cracking blow. The beak made sharp contact with his neck. Brayne shrieked in pain. Florence threw the umbrella on top of him and ran out of the house, slamming the door behind her.

Left alone in the hall, Brayne bent his head towards the dado and tenderly probed the injured part of his neck. Craning his head round, he tried to inspect the bruise in the mirror. Florence must have gone mad. He fetched some ice from the refrigerator and sat mournfully with it applied to his neck until it began to melt and soaked his collar. He turned to his book. He was damned if he'd lose a night's work because of a silly girl's bad temper. He sat at the desk and spread his papers before him. Shock acted as a catalyst; inspiration possessed him so that he wrote fast and furiously, wielding his fountain pen with energy and speed. In his denunciation of the Fab Four he turned slightly red and began to breathe fast. Inside him hatred for the Beatles welled up like a spring, ready to overflow all over the page. 'And so,' he wrote furiously, 'we see the legacy of that widely admired coolness which has pervaded the whole of our education system, so that today the process of learning – a painful and difficult thing in itself – must be tricked up and decked out as fun, as amusing, as "cool". Indeed, we have come so far that we have now almost eliminated the painful business of memory, learning and mastery of texts.'

He sat up and wiped his forehead. The chapter was coming along excellently. And there was still God to tackle. Brayne – having momentarily discharged his abomination for the Beatles – considered his position on God. The Beatles had been at work here, too. For the Church, led by the appalling Bishop of Brigg, had also attempted to make itself 'cool', using modern, barbaric rites and introducing embraces and guitars into the services. Brayne sighed and went into the kitchen where he made himself cocoa. The individual fruit pie sat invitingly on a plate. He took it to his desk. The bruise on his neck throbbed painfully. What could explain Florence's behaviour?

Flushed from her attack on Brayne, Florence caught her train with a sense of triumph. The thought of his astonished face as the umbrella descended caused her to laugh out loud in the compartment. A man opposite looked quickly at her then nervously raised the evening paper to cover his face. On the front page she saw a large picture of Evelyn Fragment looking out in anguish. She thought he looked a rather slimy sort of person. When she got home the flat was in darkness. Marigold must be out trying to urge Jasper towards marriage. A great wave of mingled scents from Gude's flowers assailed her. She went into the kitchen and stared out into the darkness through the kitchen window. Down below, the chiropodist's flat was softly lit. She saw through the thin net curtains that two figures were moving about in the dim, soft light. Clearly, a late night consultation. Florence put the kettle on.

Brayne finished his cocoa. He turned the radio onto the World Service. A disc jockey was announcing the order of the Top Twenty for the benefit of listeners abroad. The World Service! thought Brayne. What was happening to the BBC? He went over to his desk and made a note on his large notepad. It would be a good subject for an article, he thought. He might ask poor old Maurice Earish to do it. He was always raving about the BBC. He adjusted the radio to Today in Parliament. His eyes roamed the bookshelves. In one corner he pulled out a copy of *Be Cool* by Jerry

Gude. Angrily Brayne slammed it onto his desk. Opening it at random he read: 'Hippies burn money. Money is a drug. Possessions are a form of madness.' Brayne stared at the page. Here were Florence's very words staring up at him. She had been reading Jerry Gude. She had memorised his naive, pitiful ramblings. Brayne took a quick breath as he remembered their curious arrival together at the *Commentator* on that dreadful day when Gude had rushed at him like a madman. Could it be that Florence had fallen victim to Gude, that notorious philanderer and drunk? Brayne ground his teeth in fury.

The kettle boiled. Florence looked down again at the scene in the chiropodist's flat. There were two people in the consulting room. Some attention was being paid to parts of the body which were obviously not the feet. Two figures rolled and squirmed on the consulting couch. Florence looked more closely. One of the figures suddenly sat up and wandered over to the window. Impulsively he pulled open the curtains and stood looking up into the night sky. His face, Florence saw, was familiar. It was the face of Evelyn Fragment. He stood at the open window for some minutes looking out. Then he returned to the couch. Again the bodies were interlocked and intertwined.

'Order, Order,' said the speaker. Brayne paced up and down his sitting room entertaining horrible thoughts of Florence in Gude's lecherous embrace. Out of the night, Fragment's voice spoke out in defence of his Family bill. 'For the most important question, for our people and our country, is what sort of a generation will follow us. Our young must step behind us; they are the providers of tomorrow. They will defend our people, clothe our poor, feed our hungry and take us into the next millennium. All depends on them. What kind of legacy will they inherit from us? Is it too much to ask us to strike a blow for decency which – ' There were loud heckles and baying laughter which for a moment drowned Fragment's wobbling, strained voice.

'Order,' said the Speaker. 'Order, order.'

'A blow for decency for which future generations will respect us. The tide has turned,' Fragment shouted. 'We are leading the fight towards a brighter, purer tomorrow.'

· CHAPTER · XII ·

'I was wondering when you'd get round to me,' said Lucinda Harpie-Kerr in a loud voice. 'I suppose I'm last on the list.'

Pauline nodded. 'As his most recent wife,' she said. 'I'm working in strict chronological order.'

'What did you say your name was?'

'Pauline.'

'Well, Pauline, you won't be able to broadcast a word of what I have to say. It'll turn your libel lawyers white with fear. It'll kill them,' said Lucinda Harpie-Kerr in satisfaction.

There was a grinding noise as she clashed the gears of her Alfa Süd vigorously. The car shot forward down the narrow Chelsea street, closely missing a line of parked cars on the nearside.

Pauline nodded and smiled. She was not easily discouraged by bravado. The confessions of Norman Crisp had been far worse, she was sure, than anything Lucinda could produce.

'Anyway,' said Lucinda Harpie-Kerr, 'you'll get all the dirt from me. All the truth the others daren't tell. All the facts. The relationship will be laid bare.'

'That's great,' said Pauline.

'Oh yes,' said Lucinda, 'I shall hold nothing back.' The car lurched and swerved round a corner as she thrust her foot hard on the accelerator. Pauline gripped her notebook tightly.

'Now,' said Lucinda. 'Can you read a map, Pauline? We have to go to a tiny little place called Aston Bywater. It's somewhere in Oxfordshire, I think. God knows where. Do you think you could navigate for me, lovey?'

Pauline nodded and peered into the glove compartment where she found a pile of road maps, creased, torn and incorrectly folded.

'I'll just get the tape recorder going,' she said. 'You just talk whenever you feel you can. I don't want to upset your concentration.'

'Darling, I've been driving since I was sixteen,' shouted Lucinda. 'I can do it with my eyes closed if necessary. Hold tight. Sorry. Right, off we go. Early days with Jerry? You want to hear all about that?' She ground the gears. Pauline winced.

'I suppose you want me to tell you how brilliant he was,' she said. 'Well, lovey, I think I got the dregs. By the time he got round to me he was far from his original sparkling self. His first wife was quite different from me, by the way. I suppose you've talked to her? She represented Jerry's rise in society. She knew how to hold her knife and fork all right. She was aristocratic. She pulled him up by his bootstrings. For all that stuff about being a hippy and rebel, he's fearfully snobbish, you know. He's a terrible name-dropper, as you've probably discovered.'

The car swung out through west London and began its approach to the M4 at tremendous speed. Cars to the right pulled out in alarm as Lucinda rushed down the slip road. She entered the motorway at seventy miles an hour. 'Sorry I've got to put my foot down a bit,' she said, seeing Pauline flinch. 'You don't mind if we get on a bit do you? Or I'm going to be late for the interview.'

'Who are you going to see?'

'Man with thirteen wives,' said Lucinda promptly. 'Belongs to some strange religious sect, I think.'

'You're writing a piece about him?'

'Yes, village Romeo stuff. We're doing a big special on him this Sunday. The interesting thing about him is that he has no arms and legs, so naturally our readers will be interested to know – '

'Yes, quite,' said Pauline.

'We've got a photographer coming to do some family shots . . .'

'Yes.'

'Worth a try, anyhow, Pauline?' said Lucinda, laughing throatily.

The car shot out suddenly into the fast lane and launched itself into a sudden burst of acceleration. Pauline looked at the speed indicator. The needle was over a hundred.

After a short pause, Lucinda went on.

'Now, what did Arabella Spring-Greene see in Jerry, is what you want to know. What did we all see in him? I've often asked myself that question.'

'Coach!' said Pauline sharply.

'What?'

'Coach ahead.'

They were approaching the rear of a labouring coach at a rapid pace.

'Damn!' Lucinda Harpie-Kerr braked abruptly. She paused three feet short of the coach and looked over her left shoulder. Swerving suddenly to the left, she shot past it on the middle lane, veering wildly to the right again when she had passed it. They left a fanfare of horns behind them.

'These bloody buses shouldn't be on the motorway at all,' she said, 'let alone going down the fast lane. It wasn't doing anywhere near seventy. Well, I suppose Jerry offered excitement. It certainly wasn't the money that attracted me. I must say, my salary got him through some difficult moments. I suppose he had a lot of money once. There wasn't any sign of it when I knew him, however.'

Pauline nodded, her eyes fastened on the road.

'It's a funny thing,' said Lucinda, 'but he always liked blondes. I think that was the reason we got married, really. You know, I turned up at his flat in Holland Park to interview him. That was how we met. And a few drinks later there were Jerry and I all over the rug – the magic carpet was what he used to call it.' She laughed loudly. 'I told you this would be unfit for family viewing. Anyway, perhaps it was the hair that did it. Of course,' she added, 'to be strictly truthful with you, I give it a little help these days. But I was once a very natural blonde.'

Pauline smiled and nodded. No one, she thought, could possibly imagine that dreadful yellow hair could be anything other than artificial.

'Keep your eyes open for exit six,' said Lucinda as they rushed past the airport. 'God, I love the sound of those big jets taking off, don't you?' She bent her head in Pauline's direction. 'Can you see one, lovey? We should be just under the flight path now.'

Pauline gripped her tape recorder. The Alfa swung from side to side down the middle lane. 'Damn Mercedes drivers,' shouted Lucinda, as a car flashed past them, hooting loudly. She wound the window down and shouted abuse into the rushing air. 'No planes?'

'No – '

'Look, there's a big one, Air Jamaica!' shouted Lucinda excitedly. 'Don't you just wish you were up there in the sky, heading for the Bahamas?' She began to sing: 'Trains and boats and planes . . . ' in a low, rusty voice.

'Exit six is coming up next,' said Pauline.

'Thank you, lovey,' said Lucinda. 'We're picking a friend of mine up there. He's been doing a temporary job in Slough.'

The engine roared and throbbed.

'Do you want to know what he was like in bed?' said Lucinda. 'Don't be shy. You only have to ask. Well, my dear, I don't know if you've had much experience of the stronger sex, but – frankly, Jerry was prone to extreme fatigue by the time I got round to him. He was tired very often. You see what I mean. Too tired . . . You take my meaning.'

Pauline nodded.

'I don't know if you've had much experience of life,' said Lucinda. 'I hope you don't mind me talking frankly to you like this, woman to woman, but you don't look to me like the sort of girl that has much success with men. No offence, darling, but I'm right aren't I? You don't mind plain speaking? I've always gone in for it myself. So, Pauline, you probably won't know quite what I'm referring to when I tell you about Jerry's nightly performance.'

'I doubt if we could include it in the programme,' said Pauline stonily.

'Well this is just for reference, darling,' said Lucinda Harpie-Kerr. 'Between you and me. Strictly off the record, but . . .'

Watmough was standing in a crowd of journalists in the Blushing Grape wine bar just behind Fleet Street. It was so crowded that no one could sit down or change his position once he had secured space by the bar. Instead, everyone remained motionless, pressed up against each other, holding their glasses up under their noses.

'I hear Fragment is making a statement this afternoon,' said Earish. 'Is that right, Watmough?'

'I heard he was going to see the PM.'

'He's decided to go,' said Julian Jasper with authority. 'Everyone is talking about it at the House. This claret's pretty rough, Watmough. What possessed you to order it?'

'Good enough for us workers,' said Watmough. 'There's no chance Fragment will jack it in. No chance.'

'Another glass?'

'Thanks, I will.'

'It's a fairly tame misdemeanour,' said Earish.

'Just a bit of smearing and screwing,' said Watmough. 'Most of us have done a lot worse.'

'That's not the point,' said Jasper quickly. 'The party regarded him as a good egg. Now he's let them down. A bit unsound, is the verdict. It's effectively ruined his chances of going any higher, anyway. Otherwise he might have been in line for the top job, you know, one day . . .'

'What, Number Ten?' said Earish.

'Just possible,' said Watmough. 'One of the coming men.'

'Not any more,' said Jasper.

'What a shabby business,' said Earish remotely, 'as if any of us cares what he did in his wild and misspent youth.'

'It isn't so much that anybody cares now,' said Jasper, 'it's just a matter of political credibility.'

'For some periods he would do no work at all,' said Lucinda Harpie-Kerr. 'In fact, his day was frequently one of total leisure. I would get home from work and find he hadn't got out of bed all day. Amazing isn't it, darling? He would spend the whole day lying in the sheets, I suppose. I never knew how he passed the time. When I came in he'd be sprawled there in his dressing gown, clutching a gin and orange and staring at the ceiling.'

'Really?'

'Yes. Sometimes he'd suggest I got into bed with him. Don't blush, Pauline, I'll spare you the details. More often I didn't, though. After a while it wasn't really very inviting, you know, to see him lying there after I'd been putting in a hard day's work. Frankly it was a real turn-off. After a while, darling, it got on my nerves. I mean, I like a man who's a real man. That's natural, isn't it? I think most women feel like me. Jerry didn't behave like a man at all, he just let himself go.'

'Have you kept any of his letters, or diaries from the period?' said Pauline.

'Well, he didn't write very much. At least not to me. A diary? No, I don't think he kept one. Too much effort,' said Lucinda, peering ahead at the motorway signs. 'Yes. Here we go. Exit six.' The car abruptly pulled sharp left and swung off down the exit road. 'You know, Pauline, he wasn't that sort of writer. He didn't write very much. I suppose he wrote a lot once – before my time naturally, but I never saw him doing much . . .'

'Yes, I see.'

'It's so gloomy being part of someone else's past,' said Lucinda Harpie-Kerr. 'I suppose that's my only contribution to history. Had I known it at the time, of course, I could have made my contribution a little more colourful.'

'Cheers.'

'Of course, the theory is that Arabella shopped him herself,' said Jasper.

'Well, Horlick has been fed some pretty accurate stuff,' said Jasper shouting above the roar of conversation in the Blushing Grape. 'Who else would give him all that background?'

Watmough studied his glass guiltily.

'First story Horlick has ever got,' said Earish peevishly. 'Quite undeserved. He's virtually illiterate.'

'Good for him,' said Watmough.

'He's an awfully gauche person, you know. I suppose he'll win an award for all this.' Earish stared morosely at the throng of drinkers. 'I suppose one of the hardest things to endure about this profession,' he said, 'is the apparently unstoppable rise of the mediocre all the way to the top.'

'Careful!' shouted Pauline, holding onto her seat. Lucinda Harpie-Kerr's foot stabbed at the brake. The car screamed to a halt as a man with an earring leapt just in time to safety on the edge of the grass verge.

'Oh God,' said Pauline.

Lucinda wound down her window.

'Darling!' she shouted. 'Hop in. Bang on time. This is Pauline.'

'We've met,' said Norman Crisp, getting into the back seat.

'Oh, Norman,' said Pauline, still visibly shaken.

'You two know each other?'

'Yes.'

'Fantastic. Norman and I are making a weekend of this little outing. Are you getting out, Pauline? We're not there yet. This is the middle of the country, isn't it?'

'It's only the Slough ring road,' said Norman.

'I can get home by train,' said Pauline hastily. 'Thank you so much for the interview. Most interesting.'

'Darling, come and sit beside me in the front,' said Lucinda. 'Much more cosy. Goodbye Pauline. Now, which way is our village Romeo? Norman darling, can you read a map?'

The car shot forward down the main road. She saw Lucinda Harpie-Kerr's head nod and turn as she addressed her companion in the front seat. The car swerved violently and disappeared round a bend. Pauline watched the empty road for several minutes, then turned and began to walk in the direction of the railway station.

Horlick poked a piece of cold ham around on his plate and said: 'Tell me, how have you become a success?'

'Are you asking people for tips?' said Charlie Enever, leaning back in his chair in a dimly lit dining area of the Blushing Grape. This part of the wine bar had sawdust scattered all over the floor and was decorated with bunches of plastic hops and reproduction items of agricultural machinery. Horlick peered through the dim light at him.

'Ha, ha! No, of course not. Let me put it this way. Er, what are the qualities that have made you the success you are today? You know – brains, hard work, talent, opportunities . . . that sort of thing.'

Enever gazed at a rustic milk churn at the side of the table.

'I really can't say,' he murmured with studied indifference. 'I don't think I can answer that for you, can I?'

'I suppose not,' said Horlick. He filled his mouth with a piece of cold ham. 'You've been very successful, haven't you?'

'I'm sorry?' said Enever. 'I didn't quite catch that.'

'I said,' said Horlick indistinctly, 'that you've been very successful.' He looked at Enever with envy.

Enever shrugged. 'Depends what you mean by success. On whose terms? OK, I've made some films that some people have quite liked. . . . But – ' Enever opened his hands and shut them again in a gesture of fatalistic resignation.

'Hmm,' said Horlick. 'I say, I think my tape recorder's gone bust. Just a minute. I don't think the wheels are going round.'

Enever yawned.

'Yes. They've stopped. Oh bugger. Just a sec. God, I'm sorry about this,' said Horlick, dismantling his tape recorder on the table. 'Now, let's just see what's up with this little bit of modern technology.'

Enever sipped a little wine, while Horlick muttered to himself and flicked switches on the tape recorder. 'That should do it,' he said. 'I've put some new batteries in. Just a second.' He held the tape recorder to his mouth and said in a low, sonorous voice: 'Testing, testing, one two three four five six seven. All good children go to heaven.'

He put the tape recorder back on the table and pressed a switch.

'GO TO HEAVEN,' said Horlick's voice at a surprisingly loud

volume. Several people at nearby tables turned to stare at him. 'Just a bit loud,' said Horlick. He made an adjustment. This time his voice sang out high and shrill, at soprano pitch.

'Just speeded up a little,' said Horlick. 'Nothing to worry about.'

'Ah,' said Enever.

'OK, off we go again,' said Horlick. 'Sorry about that. I suppose you're used to technology and all that with your job.'

Enever ignored him.

'So you were saying,' Horlick said vaguely. 'Now – what were you in fact going to say? Er . . . I say, how do you decide what films to make? Where do you get the ideas from?'

'Well,' said Enever. His eyes searched the wine bar beyond Horlick's head. 'It's hard to say, isn't it? Probably an idea one has had for some months suddenly crystallises . . .'

'Crystallises – Yup, I'm with you so far,' said Horlick nodding vigorously.

Enever gave up the attempt.

There was a prolonged silence.

'Perhaps you could describe your day,' said Horlick. 'Just to give the readers an idea of your timetable.'

'Well, I rise at six-thirty,' said Enever. 'I start straight away with some reading – the Russians at the moment, Turgenev, Tolstoy, in the original, of course. I never find translations satisfying, do you? Then, a little history over breakfast – Macaulay probably – then I'm in – '

'I say,' said Horlick, 'this is incredible. Just let me make sure I'm getting all this.'

He pushed the switch on the tape recorder. Enever's voice, high-pitched and unintelligible, screamed out over the tables. 'Bloody hell,' said Horlick. 'Just a minute.'

He pushed another switch. The voice, this time low and growling, spoke angrily in a primitive, mumbling roar.

'No,' said Horlick. 'Sorry I haven't got it at all. This bloody machine's no damn good. I'll just have to get my notebook out.' He dug into his jacket pocket and unearthed a bent and shabby leather covered notepad stuffed with bits of loose paper. 'Hang on while I find a pen.' He dug around further in his pocket and took out an old blunt pencil.

'Right,' said Horlick. 'We're in business. Now, what time did you say you got up? Six or seven?'

Enever stared at him. 'Actually, that was all a joke.'

Horlick opened his mouth, then shut it again.

'You know, it was supposed to be a parody of what everyone says when they're asked that question. Actually, I do what everyone else does in the morning. Get up. Have a piece of toast. Read a newspaper.'

'Oh, I see,' said Horlick. Then he laughed loudly. 'Yes, very good joke. I'll just write that down!'

Enever sighed. He looked at his watch. 'I'll have to go soon,' he said. 'I've got to edit a film tonight.'

'Ah,' said Horlick. 'What is that?'

'It's a profile of Jerry Gude,' said Enever.

'Oh, everyone's talking about that,' said Horlick.

'Oh.'

There was a silence.

'Anyway, I suppose I'd better ask you about yourself,' said Horlick. 'Er . . . where did you go to school, for example?'

'Look,' said Enever, 'I've just seen someone across there I must just have a word with. Would you mind? Best of luck with your book. Do let me know if you need any more information.'

'Well . . ' said Horlick, but Enever had risen hastily from his chair and gone swiftly across the room to the crowd at the bar, where he quickly disappeared within the mass of tightly pressed, rigid bodies. After some considerable struggle, he fought his way through the crush and made a swift exit through the fire escape. Horlick finished the remains of his ham and then he tapped on the table for a little while and read through the meagre contents of his notebook. After he had sat there for some time, he began to wonder if Enever was going to come back. After another ten minutes, he decided to order some pudding.

'Mr Horlick?' said the waitress, coming up to the table. 'Your office on the telephone. Could you telephone Morton Minitz urgently. He wants to speak to you at once.'

Horlick hummed a little tune. Then he got up and began the difficult journey to the phone box. He would assure Minitz that the book was going brilliantly well. He just needed a little more time to finish his researches . . .

· CHAPTER · XIII ·

'I've got something really special for you today, my darling.' Mrs Crisp blew out a long plume of smoke and smiled at Florence until her eyes crinkled almost out of sight. She went to her clothes rack and drew out a large plastic bag which apparently contained something white and bulky. She unwrapped it with pride.

'What is it?' said Florence in amazement as Mrs Crisp shook out a tumbling mass of nylon net with sequinned decorations.

'Gorgeous, isn't it dear?' said Mrs Crisp, her cigarette clamped between her teeth as she grimly shook out the folds of white nylon. 'Christmas fairy. Haven't they made a good job of it? Looks almost new to me.'

'Fairy?'

'It's a really good job at Mosiman's toy shop. You have to stand in the enchanted forest and wave the kids through to Father Christmas. They've even given you a wand.'

'Do I get wings?' said Florence.

Mrs Crisp rummaged in the bag. 'They're here,' she said, triumphantly pulling out a pair of plastic circles decorated with gold dust. 'And here's your wand.'

Florence examined it. 'It's just a stick covered with silver paper,' she said.

'Well, what do you expect, darling?' said Mrs Crisp. 'Not the real thing, surely, Florence.'

'What do I have to do?'

'You give out balloons with Mosiman's Toy Shop written on 'em. It's good money.'

'How long for?'

'Start next week until Christmas.'

Florence stared at the white net. 'No, I can't do it, Mrs Crisp,' she said.

'It's a lovely costume.'

'I don't like children.'

'It's not the kids you should worry about,' said Mrs Crisp darkly, 'it's their parents. Particularly the fathers. You get a lot of flak from them.'

'Oh God,' said Florence. 'It's no good. I'm just not up to the job any more.'

'Well, make your mind up. There's thousands would jump at it, if you don't want it.'

Florence put down the wand. She looked round at the dingy office with its paraffin stove burning in the corner and the dim electric light under the brown shade.

'You'll have to take me off your books, Mrs Crisp,' she said. 'I've got no future in promotions.'

'You haven't got the determination,' said Mrs Crisp. 'That's half the battle. If you're not prepared to stick this out, you'll never succeed at anything.'

'Perhaps I could do something completely different?'

'I should get married if I were you dear,' said Mrs Crisp. 'Find a rich man and settle down. Don't think I'd work if I didn't need to.'

'Doesn't Mr Crisp make enough to support you?'

'There is no Mr Crisp,' said Mrs Crisp darkly. 'The least said about him the better. And I've got my responsibilities. Life's been hard, although I'm not a moaner. I've never been one to complain. But what with Norman and all his troubles – '

'Norman?'

'Norman Crisp, my boy. He's not a bad boy whatever they say about him. He's had a few difficulties, Florence, but he's always been a good boy to his mother. I'm afraid he doesn't take to my new gentleman friend, which makes it all very difficult.'

'Who's your gentleman friend?'

'Got a bit of money behind him. Owns a very nice pub. Bought me lobster the first time he took me out. Bit of class about him. Norman can't stand the sight of him. But that's enough of my troubles, Florence. Do you want the job or not?'

'I'll do it,' said Florence, fired by the story of Mrs Crisp's vicissitudes.

'Pricy time, Christmas.'

'After all, it's only a job.'

'That's the spirit, dear.'

'Give me the costume.'

'Of course,' said Corner, 'he can't afford to pay his fine. After all, it isn't the first time he's kicked a car. The magistrates came down pretty heavy on him.'

'Are you sure?' said Earish. 'I know everyone is always saying how badly off he is, but I'd have thought he'd have some money. Everyone has just a bit of money, don't they?'

'Jerry hasn't got any.'

'Why not?' said Earish, his voice rising on a note of complaint. 'I haven't got any money either, come to that. No one feels sorry for me, do they?'

'Ah, well, you could have, couldn't you? If you worked harder.'

'I do work hard. No one wants any of my articles, that's all.'

'He's fucking broke,' said Galen Bone. 'He can't pay his bar bill, let alone any fucking fine. The other week a whole lot of fruit pies turned up here – disgusting, horrible packets they were. Jerry had gone fucking mad and bought five hundred. Of course, they came to take them away again at the end of the week. His fucking cheque had bounced, hadn't it.'

'We're having a collection,' said Corner. 'Everyone must do what they can. Dig deep, matey. It could be you in a few years time.'

'How much do you want?' said Earish reluctantly.

'How much can you spare?'

Earish rattled his hand around his pocket. He took out a fifty pence piece. 'Will this do?' he said.

Corner looked at him with reproach.

'You must be the meanest fucking man alive,' screamed Bone. 'You can't even buy a packet of crisps with fucking fifty pee.'

'I'm not well off, Galen,' Earish whined. 'I just can't afford it. Well, here's a pound. That's all I'm giving.'

Laboriously Corner wrote his name down on a long list.

'Lucinda's given him a bleeding cheque,' Bone shouted, 'for a hundred pounds.'

'Well, she's rich, isn't she? In fact, if you compare what Lucinda earns to what I earn, then she's been even meaner than I have. Anyway, what have you given?' he said to Corner.

'That is a matter for me and my conscience,' said Corner.

'Fucking pompous,' said Bone. 'He's given him a fiver. And he could afford a lot more.'

'Have you seen Lucinda recently?' said Earish.

'She's gone away for a long weekend with her new boyfriend,' said Corner. 'Haven't seen her since.'

'She seems very taken with him.'

'Personally I think he's one to watch. I don't like his manner one little bit.'

'He's fucking horrible,' said Bone. 'He's got mad staring eyes. He's fucking crazy. Next time he comes in I'm going to ban him, straight out.'

'Well, she was never much good at picking men.'

'No, look at poor old Jerry.'

'Hello, is that Pauline?'

'Speaking,' said Pauline, drinking scalding coffee from an enamel mug.

'Oh, this is Lucinda Harpie-Kerr speaking. How are you Pauline?'

'Well.'

Lucinda Harpie-Kerr was overcome by a prolonged burst of coughing which lasted for several minutes. 'Listen, Pauline dear,' she said, gasping for breath down the telephone. 'I just wanted to ask you something rather personal.'

'Go ahead.'

'You haven't seen Norman recently, have you darling?'

'Norman Crisp?'

'Yes.'

'No.'

'Oh, well, I thought as he was a friend of yours, you might just have run into him.'

'Haven't you seen him?'

'Not since the weekend. He was just a little bit odd, to tell you the truth. It didn't go too well.'

'Oh dear.'

'He seemed – well, do you know if he's ever been violent, Maureen? He doesn't seem very well balanced to me.'

'Well,' said Pauline, 'I think there's something I ought to tell you about Norman.'

'Don't tell me he's gay, Doreen,' said Lucinda Harpie-Kerr. 'I can't stand it. All the men I ever meet these days turn out to be gay.'

'I don't think he's gay,' said Pauline. 'I wouldn't know about that. It's just that he happens to be a murderer.'

High in his pink executive suite, Morton Minitz was standing with his arm lying heavily across Horlick's shoulders. Refreshed by a quantity of champagne, Horlick was gazing wildly round the room, his eyes bulging and unfocused.

'You'll take some caviar, Mr Horlick?' said Minitz, pumping him by the hand.

'Well, I've just had lunch,' said Horlick. 'Oh, if you insist . . .'

Minitz rang a bell by the fireplace. After a few minutes, a butler appeared. 'We'll take some caviar and another bottle of champagne,' said Minitz. The man disappeared.

'You may be wondering,' said Minitz, 'why I've asked you to come and see me, Mr Horlick.' The publisher smiled and his face split into deeply divided creases. Horlick opened his mouth to reply, but Minitz talked on.

'We have great hopes of you, Mr Horlick,' he said. 'Great hopes. I have already announced *Shooting Stars* in our spring catalogue, as a document of modern-day history. It will be a book that everyone will be talking about. You are making rapid and successful progress?'

'Well,' said Horlick, 'I've interviewed some hopeful candidates.'

'We look forward to publishing it under the Minitz imprint,' said Minitz slowly. 'Meanwhile, Mr Horlick, we have even greater hopes of you.'

Horlick stared at him expectantly.

'You are noted as one of the brightest young stars of your generation,' Minitz said. 'I understand your story about the Fragment scandal has left the rest of Fleet Street gasping.'

Horlick blushed with pleasure. 'Oh – well,' he said.

'I am planning to launch my own paper, Mr Horlick,' said Minitz. 'It will be my own weekly magazine. It is the most exciting project of my life. The crowning jewel in my empire. A magazine to provoke, stimulate and add to the quality of British life. A magazine which will be read by everyone who contributes to the intellectual life of our country.'

'Ah ha,' said Horlick.

The butler came back in, bearing a silver tray and a bottle of champagne.

'Put it there,' said Minitz. The man disappeared.

'Come and sit at the table, Mr Horlick,' said Minitz. 'You like caviar, don't you?'

'Well,' said Horlick, full of ham, 'yes, a bit.'

Minitz handed him a long-handled silver spoon. 'Dip into the bowl, Mr Horlick,' he ordered. 'Dip in.'

Obediently Horlick inserted the spoon into the silver dish and took out a mouthful of the dark, fishy eggs. Minitz leaned over and dipped his own spoon into the dish. 'Let us drink,' he said, 'to the jewel in my crown. And to the role I hope you will play in it.'

Their glasses clashed in the air.

'I want you to join my magazine, Mr Horlick,' said Minitz. 'I want to assemble the cream of British journalism to work for me, starting with you, Mr Horlick. I want you to join my organisation.'

Then Minitz named a salary that was so large that Horlick knocked over his drink in shock. The fizzing liquid flooded over the pink carpet. Minitz rang for the butler who came in again and began to clear up the spilled alcohol. When he had gone, Minitz walked over to the window which looked down nine floors to the heart of Soho spread out beneath them.

'You see that man,' he said quietly, indicating the disappearing butler. 'He is my personal butler. He will do anything that I say. If I opened this window and told him to jump, he would jump.'

There was a moment's silence. Horlick looked at Minitz with alarm. Minitz stood by the window looking down over the shining roofs and swirling traffic. His arm descended heavily on Horlick's shoulder. 'Mr Horlick,' he said softly in his ear. 'Mr Horlick, I want to make you a millionaire . . .'

'There can be no doubt,' wrote Brayne slowly, 'that Fragment has lived a life as full and flawed as that of other men. In normal circumstances we should say that it is no business of ours whether he has spent his youth amid wholesome pursuits or whether he has given way to the temptations of the carnal. But for a politician to pretend that what he does in his private life has no bearing on his public career, is naivety of the first order. We had high hopes of Evelyn Fragment. We wish him well. But we say that he must resign immediately. He has chosen to guide us towards a greater virtue in our moral behaviour. He must, therefore, be above all suspicion in his own. This clearly he cannot be. He must go now.'

Brayne laid down his fountain pan and studied his column. He read it twice, with satisfaction. In the room next door, he could hear Plugge clattering on the keys of his typewriter as he composed an account of Fragment's life. It was six-thirty. Marigold left the building, slamming the door loudly in a protest at the late hours she was forced to work. Brayne read through his piece once more. He thought he might make a few improvements. He began to write again. Plugge's typewriter banged out into the night.

As Brayne sat working on his leader, Florence was making her way to the Limace restaurant to meet Jerry Gude for dinner. Walking down Turkey Street she thought of Brayne with fury. He had not even apologised for being so rude to her. Since the incident with the umbrella there had been silence. She was not prepared to put up with him any more.

At the door of the Limace a man greeted her wearing large red spectacles and a loose grey suit. 'Jerry Gude's table,' she said confidently. The man regarded her with commiseration.

'He's here already,' he said.

Through the pillars in the lobby, the soft lights of the restaurant illuminated green plants, soft grey marbled walls and the starched white of the tablecloths. Her companion was already there, indeed he had taken his place at the table some time ago and now he gripped the tablecloth with both hands. At his feet a spoon sparkled in the light. An empty bottle of wine stood in front of him. A glass, now empty, lay on its side on the stiff white cloth. Gude's head, flushed and crimson, lay on the tablecloth beside a bowl of cold, congealed soup. His eyes were closed. The rest of the diners in the restaurant seemed unaware of his predicament; at any rate, they continued to eat and drink as if nothing upsetting had happened. Florence sat down in front of Gude and looked at him more closely. The bowl at his head, she saw now, did not contain soup but rather an assembly of mussels, some prised apart, some still clamped together, floating in a dark sea of cold liquor. Gude had been trying to deal with them when oblivion came upon him. The discarded mussels shells had not remained on the plate. Many of them were scattered over the tablecloth, and some, she saw, were lying in disorder around his shoes. She was uncertain what to do next.

The waiter hovered at her side.

'An aperitif?' he asked, ignoring her companion.

Florence ordered a glass of white wine. She stared at Gude's reddened face with emotion. His hair,. soiled by mussel juice, fell in curling tendrils over his hot forehead and coiled smoothly into the hollow of his neck. His cheek was covered by a light, grey bristle. Clearly he had not shaved before setting out to meet her. His eyelashes were long and dark – unlike his hair they had retained their youthful colour. His mouth was slightly open and his parted lips were pushed into a sneering grin upon the table.

The sight had repelled many women, but to Florence it was still untarnished by experience. Clearly Gude had been so overwrought at the prospect of meeting her again, he had simply drunk too much. Florence gazed at him undaunted.

'Pardon me, may I intrude?' Florence looked up with a start to see a dark and swarthy man standing at her side, smiling down at her. 'My name is Minitz,' he said. 'Morton Minitz. I could not help noticing your discomfort at the unfortunate predicament in which you find yourself.' Together they looked at Jerry Gude's motionless form.

'I – '

'Explanations are unnecessary,' said Minitz softly. 'My companions and I, whom you see at the next table, are familiar with Jerry – indeed we think he is a genius.' Florence looked across the room where she saw a group of people sitting at a round table, amid a great many wine bottles.

'Jerry is a little over-tired,' said Minitz.

'Yes, he's – '

'He's resting,' said Minitz slowly. 'He's feeling pretty happy now.'

They considered him silently.

'A great man, many people would say,' said Minitz, 'and I, let me assure you, am one of their number.'

'So am I.'

'He led the way forward for a generation of young and gifted people.'

On the white tablecloth Gude stirred briefly.

'Oh, is he waking up?' said Florence in agitation.

Minitz considered him. 'No, no,' he said. 'It seems that you have yet to begin your supper.'

'I haven't had anything,' said Florence, feeling ashamed, as though it was indecently gross and corporeal to discuss food over Gude's unconscious form. 'I only arrived here ten minutes ago. He was like that when I came in.'

Minitz shook his head softly in a gesture of sorrow. 'It would be an honour,' he said, 'if you would dine with us.'

'Oh, how sweet of you. But suppose he wakes up?'

'He won't,' said Minitz. 'I have called a car to take him home, courtesy of Minitz Publishing. He'll be just fine for the rest of the night.'

'I can't just abandon him . . .'

'Do you want to take him home yourself? No offence,' said Minitz, 'but I'm just spelling it out for you. Do you want that personal, though privileged responsibility? I mean, how well do you really know Jerry?'

Florence blushed. 'Not that well.'

Minitz smiled.

'He'll be better in the morning.'

'That's what all his girlfriends have thought,' said Minitz seriously. He placed his hands on the table. They were powerful and broad with stubby fingers. Several rings adorned them. 'My advice to you, although you have not asked for it, is never to think you can change his nature. You are not seeing Gude at his worst. You are seeing him as he really is. No one – not you, not the most perfect woman in the world, is ever going to change any of that. He has no better, he has no best. He simply is what he is.'

Florence frowned at her knife and fork.

'I can see you don't believe a single word I'm saying,' said Minitz, smiling. 'OK, you find it out the hard way. But you'll remember this conversation one day; and you'll know that every word I've said is the truth.'

There was a short silence.

'Just leave him here,' said Minitz. 'They've sent for a cab. He'll be fine.'

Reluctantly Florence got up from the table. As she did so, Gude raised his head and opened his eyes. He looked straight at her, with a piercing stare.

'Now, my friend,' said Minitz, 'we're going to take you home. You'll be back in bed, Jerry, in no time, and you can lie back, and take it easy.' It was uncertain whether Gude had heard him or not.

Fixing his eyes on Florence, he looked at her and his lips moved almost soundlessly.

'What?' said Florence. 'What did you say?'

'Marry me,' said Gude.

Then his head fell forward onto the tablecloth once more and the bowl of mussels tipped its remaining contents over the cloth.

'This,' said Minitz, 'is no scene for a lady. Let's get out of here. It will all be taken care of. My table is waiting. Allow me to escort you. Step carefully.'

Politely he took her arm and they went over to the circular table. Looking back she saw two waiters lift Jerry up by his arms and stagger to the door with him.

'They're used to him,' said Minitz. 'Believe me, it's not the first time it's happened. Let me pour you a drink.'

'How goes it, Quintin?' said Brayne, standing at the doorway of Plugge's small, cramped cubicle. 'Anywhere near finished yet?'

Plugge raised his head from his desk. His eyes were red-rimmed and running slightly. 'Almost there, Alexander,' he said vaguely. 'Just working on a passage about Fragment's contribution to the education debate. One must do him justice, you know, even though we are – as it were – sounding his death knell.'

Brayne smiled slightly. He felt like a god in his power to destroy a reputation. Fragment would never survive the crisis, he was sure of it. Downstairs in the empty building a noise like books falling heavily on the floor made him raise his head and listen. Surely Marigold had gone home long ago.

'Is that you, Marigold?' he shouted. In the silence his words hung in the empty air.

'Did you hear a noise, Plugge?' he said.

There was no reply. He looked at Plugge. His companion was gazing beyond him through the door with a strange expression which Brayne did not immediately recognise as fear. He turned quickly. Behind him the wild eyes of Norman Crisp gazed out into the office.

'He's got a knife,' said Plugge. 'Please dissuade him from using it.'

'I say, what can we do for you,' said Brayne, advancing towards

Crisp. Crisp waved a long butcher's knife in a threatening manner. 'Are you all right?' said Brayne.

'Go back,' said Crisp. 'I am prepared to resort to violence.'

'Who are you? What do you want?'

Crisp stared into the office. 'Until the world realises,' he shouted, 'none of us will be saved.'

'Saved from what?' said Brayne.

'From the fate that lies in store for all wicked men,' said Crisp loudly.

'Well, that's very interesting, but what can I do about it?' said Brayne crossly. 'I can't see how I can help you at the moment.'

'You must write about me in the magazine,' said Crisp.

'Why the *Commentator*? What could we do to save the world?'

'I don't know,' said Crisp. 'A man in a pub told me to get in touch with you. His name was Bunsen. He said that you would be interested in my words. He was a messenger from the angels.'

'Bloody Bunsen,' said Brayne. 'Now look here, it's quite late and Plugge and I were just finishing this issue. Why don't you put that knife away, and we'll have a chat about all this later on.'

'I shall keep the knife,' said Crisp, 'if it's all the same to you. I have also brought a small explosive device. I'll just put it here on the table.'

Brayne and Plugge stared at each other.

'Will it go off?' said Plugge. 'I rather feel I should ring my wife, you know, if I've got to stay here. She'll be frightfully cross if I'm late.'

'It is all in the hands of the Creator now,' said Crisp. 'We are staring eternity in the face.'

'Let's all sit down,' said Brayne in a less confident voice. 'Let's all sit down and have a chat about this.'

'This is Venetia,' said Minitz, introducing Florence to the blonde girl. 'And this is Norris Pleasant, the famous author of whom you may have heard.'

'She's far too young,' said Pleasant, smiling disagreeably. 'Pleasant is a great writer,' said Minitz in an unctuous manner.

'We have the honour of bringing out his latest book. And this is Mr Horlick' – Horlick nodded and winked – 'who has just joined our organisation as star writer of our new magazine.'

Minitz poured champagne into her glass.

'Do you have a boyfriend, Florence?' said Pleasant. His bronze face creased into grooves his permanent charm had etched in his skin.

Florence emptied her glass. 'No,' she said angrily, denying Brayne.

'Don't you go out with Alexander Brayne?' said Horlick leaning towards her.

'Not any more,' said Florence.

'Brayne,' said Pleasant. 'What a coincidence. What do you think of him?'

'We've had a row,' said Florence. Minitz refilled her glass. 'He's frightfully clever, but he doesn't like being contradicted.'

'But does he like sex?' said Pleasant

'I say!' said Horlick.

Florence emptied her second glass. 'I do not intend to mention him again,' she said. 'Is he a friend of yours?'

'No, not a friend,' said Pleasant. 'Though I've known him for many years. Longer than most people.'

'Have you?'

'Yes,' said Pleasant. 'I'm his father.'

'I have done wrong,' said Norman Crisp. He stopped talking and looked at the clock. His face was white and strained. 'I have done wrong and paid the penalty. But I have been given a chance to redeem the world. God has come to me and told me what I must do. I alone hold the fate of the world in my hands.'

'Has he really?' said Plugge. 'How frightfully interesting. What did he look like?'

'What?' said Crisp.

'When he came to you. When you had your moment of vision. You see the fascinating thing is – '

'Like a great ball of fire and flame. Like a great voice of power and earthquakes.'

'Amazing,' said Plugge, his eyes gleaming intensely behind his spectacles. 'You see I too have had a similar moment of revelation. The circumstances of my own case are different, however. I was in the Brickmanstead shopping precinct, when suddenly I was overwhelmed by a great and yet wholly personal presence.'

'What was your message?' said Crisp.

'Message? Well, I don't know if I was given a message as such – at least not in such forthright and uncompromising terms as your own – and yet I knew instantly – '

'Have you really got a bomb there?' said Brayne.

'Yes,' said Crisp. 'I learned how to make them when I was inside.'

'Look, if I could just phone my wife,' said Plugge, 'we could have the most fascinating conversation about this. You see, I'm writing a book – a great work, it will take me the whole of my life – on exactly this subject, the nature of divine revelation. I would be absolutely fascinated to probe more deeply into the nature of your own experience. Only my wife, Amanda, gets rather cross if I'm out later than expected. If I don't phone her she'll really go up the wall.'

'Stop talking,' Crisp suddenly shouted. 'Stop talking, both of you, and listen to me. There is very little time left for us all.'

After a while Florence Barge said: 'Why do you both have different names?'

'He took his late mother's name,' said Pleasant softly. 'He wanted no association with me.'

'He never mentioned you. He always told me his parents lived abroad.'

'We are like strangers to each other. He has developed an obsessive loathing of everything I stand for. Perhaps it was my fault. I sent him to one of those progressive schools where no one has to do any lessons.'

'Do you ever meet?' said Florence, marvelling at this hidden aspect of Brayne's life.

'From time to time, when we need to settle family affairs. I can't understand how I ever produced him.'

'Are you saved?' said Norman Crisp. He repeated the question.

'It's hard to say,' said Brayne. 'Yes, would be a little too confident. No, would be nakedly rude. I suppose, No, but I hope to be so, is the correct answer.'

Plugge stared at Crisp. 'I feel I am saved,' he said intensely. 'I feel it was for just such a purpose as this that I was restored to the faith in the shopping precinct.'

'I must take over control of all channels of communication,' said Crisp. 'I began with the television. I have some contacts in the popular press – a woman journalist has come under my control. I now intend to use the *Commentator* to spread my message.'

'Fine,' said Brayne, sensing a way out of their predicament. 'How much would you like? Could you get your message into half a page – or we could possibly allow you a whole one.'

'I intend to take over the whole of the magazine,' said Crisp firmly.

'A religious issue?' said Plugge. 'Yes, well, why not? It might work.'

'Take a pen and write,' said Crisp.

'Write what?'

'The word of God,' said Crisp firmly, 'the word of God as handed down to Norman Crisp.'

Brayne sighed. He looked at his watch. It was after eleven.

Horlick leaned towards Florence confidentially. 'I say,' he said, 'would you like to be in my book?'

'I'd adore it,' said Florence incoherently. Her glass had been refilled again. 'What's it called?'

'*Shooting Stars*.'

'I love the title.'

'It is rather original, isn't it? I'm rather pleased with it.'

'What is it about?'

'Oh, about people who are going to be famous in future. It's a collection of young and brilliant people. I'll put you in, shall I?'

'I haven't done anything yet,' said Florence. 'But I feel sure I'm going to be famous.'

'Doesn't matter,' said Horlick. 'I'll put you in the book, anyway.'

'Mr Horlick is a famous journalist,' said Minitz. 'He has exposed Evelyn Fragment for the hypocrite that he is.'

'I saw him the other night,' said Florence. 'Isn't he a creep? I hate his smarmy manner. He looks so sorry for himself.'

'Oh, you know him do you?' said Horlick with interest.

'I see him quite often. He visits the block of flats where I live,' said Florence. 'He always looks so depressed, although he goes away much more cheerful.'

'Aha,' said Horlick slowly. Then he said, 'Why does he visit your block of flats?'

'To see the chiropodist.'

Horlick nodded.

'She has the flat below.'

Horlick swayed towards her.

'Does he? How frightfully interesting.'

Florence drank some more champagne. She was flattered by Horlick's attention. Recklessly she went on.

'He's very friendly with his chiropodist.'

'Is he?' said Horlick. 'In what way?'

Florence drained her glass. 'I don't want you to mention this to anyone,' she said, conscious of Horlick's eagerness in her story. 'But he doesn't just get his feet done.'

'Not just his feet?'

'No, last week I saw him – well I saw him embracing the chiropodist.'

'My God,' said Horlick, hurriedly drawing out a notebook.

'So no one should feel sorry for him at all, should they?' said Florence indistinctly. 'You won't put all this in the paper will you? I'd feel terrible if you printed any of this.'

Horlick snapped his notebook shut. 'I wouldn't dream of putting it in the paper. I'm just making a note to include you in my book. I'm not writing anything about Fragment at all.'

'No. That would be very, very naughty.'

'I'm not that kind of journalist,' said Horlick seriously. 'I wouldn't dream of repeating things that people said to me at dinner parties.'

'No, I didn't think you were . . .'

'How often have you seen them there. . .?'

'Well, he's been in and out of the flat several times. But only once – you know.'

'Well,' said Horlick, 'Just give me your address, so that I can write to you and send you a sample chapter of my book. Just so that you can see if you want to be in it or not.'

Drunkenly, Florence supplied the necessary information.

Two hours later, Florence sat in the back of Morton Minitz's black Cadillac as it sped softly over the streets towards Clapham. 'I am honoured,' the publisher said, sitting beside her, 'to offer you a job in our organisation, Miss Barge. It will be my privilege to have you working for Minitz Enterprises.'

'I can't type,' said Florence carefully. The street outside seemed to rise and fall with disconcerting speed. 'I think it is only fair that I tell you that.'

'Typing is no obstacle to greatness,' said Minitz. 'Don't think of what you can't do, Miss Barge: concentrate on what you can do.' He smelt of cigars and lavender. Florence tried to focus on his short square fingers and his gold rings.

'You will play an invaluable role in launching my new magazine,' said Minitz. 'You will bring it style, taste and organisation.'

'What will I have to do?' said Florence.

'We'll talk about that later,' said Minitz. 'Is this where you wish to get out, Miss Barge?'

The car had stopped outside Brayne's house.

'Remember my words about Gude,' said Minitz. 'You don't believe me now, but you will understand one day.'

'I'll remember,' said Florence, walking unsteadily away from the kerb.

The car disappeared into the night. Florence stood in front of

Brayne's house, staring at the dark exterior. Fortified by champagne, she rang the doorbell. She was determined to announce that she would never speak to Brayne again. Impatiently she pressed the bell again.

The curtains were drawn, emitting no chink of light. Florence rang the doorbell again impatiently. There was no reply. She looked through the letter box, but the house appeared to be in darkness. How tiresome of him to have gone to bed. She rang for several minutes. There was no reply. She banged on the window. She went to the telephone box at the corner of the street and dialled his number. Still he did not answer. She left the phone off the hook in the box. Inside the house she could hear the bell ringing. She stepped into Brayne's front garden and hurled a handful of stones against the bedroom window. There was no sign of movement. Furiously she jammed the doorbell so that it rang constantly in a shrill, piercing note. In irritation she set off to look for a taxi. The streets were far too quiet. Florence had never walked on them so late. After a while she began to regret her decision to visit Brayne. It was unwise, surely, to expose herself to nocturnal risk. Perhaps there might be a bus. She looked down the empty street but saw only the glare of the orange lights and the fine oily sheen of light rain on the pavement. She walked on more quickly. Shadows danced menacingly on either side. A man was standing at the corner of the road. Slowly he turned and began to move towards her. Nervously she slowed her pace down. The man moved forward. She wondered whether to cross over to the other side of the street; perhaps this might provoke him into moving towards her. The euphoria induced by the champagne was evaporating quickly. She even thought warmly of Brayne. The man came nearer.

Florence gripped her handbag and decided she would have to make a run for it. In the light as he approached she saw that he was wearing well-polished, expensive-looking shoes. This reassured her. Certainly he was not a derelict, advancing towards her in drunken fury. Indeed, as he saw her, he too slackened his pace as if reluctant to approach her face to face.

Florence advanced. She lowered her gaze to the pavement. The man came nearer and nearer. Eventually he stopped perhaps a few yards away from her, and said in a clear voice: 'I wonder if you could possibly let me have a cigarette?'

Florence looked up and saw the weary, aristocratic face of Evelyn Fragment regarding her with a mournful expression. The corners of his mouth were pointing down and his eyes were heavy. He had a haggard appearance.

'I don't smoke. Would you like a peppermint?'

Fragment accepted graciously.

There was a short silence. 'A windy night,' said Fragment. 'Appalling weather, don't you think?'

'Quite unusually cold,' Florence responded politely, as if they were stuck in a lift together.

'It is.'

'Yes.'

They looked up and down the empty street. Fragment stepped first on one foot then on the other. 'Yes,' he said. Then he rubbed his hands together.

'Of course, it had been exceptionally mild until now.'

'Yes.'

They stood and smiled awkwardly at each other.

'Do you live round here?' said Fragment.

'No, I was just visiting someone.'

'Ah.'

Fragment regarded her with a sorrowful expression.

'May I escort you to a taxi?' he said. 'A person of your age should not be wandering the streets alone.'

'Thank you,' said Florence.

They walked silently down the streets. 'You have no idea who I am,' said Fragment, 'but I am undergoing a catastrophic change of fortune at this very moment. My world has been rocked to its very foundations. Moments such as these come once in a lifetime.'

Florence was unable to think of a suitable reply. They walked on in silence.

'I have cleared my desk,' said Fragment. 'My office is vacated.

All that talent and energy gone to waste . . . I was tipped for Number Ten, you know. I can say to you, with complete honesty, I would have been an excellent Prime Minister.'

There was no sign of a taxi as they walked the empty streets.

'I am so sorry,' said Florence.

'Why waste your sympathy?' said Fragment. 'No one else will feel the slightest bit sorry for me. My dear young woman, I mustn't unload my private worries onto you – is that an orange light I see in the distance?'

Florence saw the taxi approaching with relief.

'There is no need for anxiety on my part,' said Fragment. 'I am going to visit an old friend, Aldous Watmough, who burns the midnight oil pretty late. He is an old and trusted friend. I shall go and drink a great deal of his whisky.'

Fragment leaned forward and gently kissed Florence on the cheek. The taxi waited at the side of the road. 'What a waste it all is,' he said softly as he helped her into the cab.

'What a waste of so much genius.'

· CHAPTER · XIV ·

Enever and Pauline studied the morning paper. 'So he's gone,' said Pauline slowly. 'Fragment resigns. A grave embarrassment for the government.'

'Well, sex scandals have always been the Achilles heel of the party,' said Enever. 'Poor old sod. What a nation of hypocrites.'

'I never thought much of him.'

'Neither did I.'

'What have we got on the film?'

'All good stuff,' said Enever. 'I think this could be a prize winner. The performance of Gude himself is fantastic. He treads a perilous course. The air of danger – will he survive to the end of the programme? – gives us an unbelievable tension. The viewers will be on the edge of their seats.'

'We've pulled it off, then.'

'We should get an Oscar for this.'

In the Roastbeef Club, Watmough and Earish were sitting in the lobby, sunk gloomily into their armchairs. 'Poor old Fragment,' said Watmough. 'Poor bastard. They've got him by the balls. Another martyr to middle-class hypocrisy.'

'It's all over the papers,' said Earish. 'Personally I think he said too much. If he'd just sat it out, it would all have blown over. All that bleating about personal responsibility. He almost cried this morning.'

'Have you seen him this morning?'

'He was on breakfast television.'

'Good God. He was with me last night until four, drinking all my whisky. I wondered where he went after that.'

'I always watch it,' said Earish. 'It gives me a reason to get out of bed. I like the girl they have who does it. She reminds me of my nanny.'

Alerted by the unopened door, Marigold attempted to enter the *Commentator* building. After several moments, peering unsuccessfully through the letter box, she became aware that the shutters had been closed at a downstairs window and that the curtains were drawn upstairs. She put her face to the letter box and shouted loudly through it, 'Brayne! Open the door this minute. I'm not standing out here any longer.' After some time she decided that the circumstances were suspicious and went away to call the police.

Photographers sat politely outside Lady Arabella Spring-Greene's house in Kensington. They had been there since the early morning and occasionally one of them put a note through her letter box, inviting her, for a large sum of money, to give her exclusive story to them. Inside, Arabella stood at the window, staring out at them, her eyes bright with excitement. It reminded her of her wedding to Jerry Gude. They sat all over the lawn and some had climbed into trees, pointing cameras at the house. She moved around her room in a pink silk kaftan, wearing a necklace whose mirror-like pieces flashed and danced in the light. After a while, she drank some wine and took *Be Cool* from the bookcase. From time to time she went to the window and waved at the pressmen.

'I wonder where Brayne and Plugge can have got to,' said Earish. 'It's very unlike them to be late for a good lunch.'

'Let's start without them.'

'Might as well,' said Earish. 'I don't know if I can face all that turkey and stuffing today.'

'Best Christmas lunch in London. Can't you manage something?'

'I'd just rather have had it some other time.'

They wandered disconsolately into the dining room.

'And what do you want Father Christmas to bring you?' Florence spoke sternly to a small boy who was sitting yawning at her feet, waiting for his turn to enter Santa's magic grotto.

'A Vospur Two Thousand De Luxe,' he said.

'What's that?' said Florence.

The boy sighed wearily. 'It's a car. Your wand's coming undone.'

Florence attended to the peeling tinfoil.

'I've done this Santa twice before,' the child said. 'The free toys are worth two pounds. It's the best one.'

'Of course it is,' said Florence.

'Who are you supposed to be?'

'I am the magic fairy of the grotto.'

'They had a different one before. A fatter one.'

'I've been on a diet. It's your turn to go in now.'

Flashing blue lights surrounded the *Commentator* building, as a policeman with a loud hailer stood in the street and shouted: 'Come out now. Give yourself up. Come out and release your hostages.'

'They're putting up a telephone line,' said Horlick, standing in the middle of a crowd of reporters who had gone to write an account of the siege. 'Who's in there exactly?'

'Is there anything you want?' the policeman shouted into the empty square.

Moments later the figures of Brayne and Plugge appeared on the roof, clinging perilously to the balustrade. Their faces, white and distant, peered down over the square and the flashing lights. Brayne waved his arms in the air and appeared to be trying to speak. Plugge could be seen to turn his head this way and that, as if looking for means of escape. Brayne pointed behind him and shouted something. Minutes later, Norman Crisp appeared behind them, and with a gesture of exasperation, waved his arms at the police.

'Hello Norman,' the police negotiator shouted. 'How are you? We've got your mum down here. Do you want a word?'

Crisp stared down into the square where the squat figure of Mrs Crisp could be seen standing with her arms folded. Just behind her Galen Bone laid an arm protectively across her shoulders. 'Come down here Norman,' she shouted through the megaphone. 'Be a good boy, dear, and stop causing all this trouble for these nice young policemen.'

Galen Bone grabbed the megaphone out of her hand. 'Get down off the fucking roof,' he shouted loudly up at Crisp. 'We're all fucking freezing standing around down here. Bloody stupid idea to go up there in the first place. What's the fucking point of . . .' The police negotiator hastily snatched the megaphone away from him.

'Norman, would you like a cup of tea?' he shouted. But Crisp had withdrawn into the building. After a few minutes, the figures of Plugge and Brayne disappeared as a small detonation shook the building, causing the collapse of the roof and several floors. Mrs Crisp screamed and immediately the square became a scene of violent activity, as ambulances raced towards the building and police ran towards the rising dust.

The explosion was faintly audible in Mosiman's. Florence tried to fasten a drooping wing onto the back of her dress. 'Was that thunder?' said Santa's elf. 'Can you see the end of the queue yet?'

Florence stared out. 'Not yet.'

'Please can you tell me what Father Christmas will bring me this year,' a low voice said beside her ear. Florence looked down and saw Jerry Gude crouching at her knees. 'Put that fucking wand down,' said Gude, 'and let's go and get drunk together. I need cheering up, Florence. All this festivity and lights makes me very depressed.'

'Jerry!' she said. 'What are you doing here?'

'Christmas shopping.'

'Here you are, you little creeps,' said Gude, seizing the sack of presents and throwing its contents over the floor. The children, emboldened by his influence, dived wildly for presents.

'I owe you dinner,' said Gude. 'Let's get to know each other, Florence. Now, go and take off that stupid dress.'

'Oh God, this is dreadful,' said Watmough, staring at the tape machine in the lobby of the Roastbeef. 'They've had it. Gone. They're dead, Earish. Blown up apparently by some mindless terrorists.'

'I can't believe it. Who did it?'

'Some Arab sect, according to this.'

'Bastards,' said Earish.

'The building is completely destroyed.'

'I feel completely shattered by this news.'

'Do you think they could get us some brandy?'

'Double brandy, Galen,' said Earish some hours later. 'I've had a terrible shock.' He leaned heavily on the bar. 'What's happening to London. You can't go anywhere these days without being blown up by someone. It never used to be – '

'Shut up and stop fucking moaning,' said Bone, slamming the drink down on the counter. 'No one wants to listen to your boring problems. I've got worries of my own.'

Earish stared into the brandy glass. 'What's the matter, Galen?' he said in a slurred voice.

'Our friend Corner has absconded with Gude's collection money, that's all. He's run away with the fucking five hundred pounds he was supposed to pay his fine with. No longer at his address. I'll kill him,' screamed Bone, banging the top of the bar. 'I'll fucking murder him.'

'Keep calm, Galen,' said Earish, emptying his glass. 'Another brandy please.'

'How can I keep fucking calm when I've just seen some madman blow up some office in Bloomsbury? One minute, there he was. The next – Bang! It's a fucking shock to the system, I can tell you that. Mrs Crisp is very distressed about it all.'

'Who is Mrs Crisp?'

Galen put his hands on the table. 'She is shortly to do me the honour of becoming the second Mrs Bone. A charming woman. Common, but it's all I can expect to get at my age.' He glared round the bar again. 'That fucking Corner is banned for life. He won't get no more drinks here.'

'I never trusted him,' said Earish. 'He had a devious face. I suppose the temptation was too much for him. It might have been too much for me. I don't know how I'm going to live, now the *Commentator* has gone. I know it didn't pay much, but at least Brayne asked me to write now and again. I wonder who'll take my stuff now.'

'Who cares?' said Bone. 'Stop moaning. We've all got troubles.'

'Has Jerry been in today?'

'No. Try the nearest gutter,' shouted Bone furiously. 'Now shut up, or I'll fucking ban you too.'

Earish put his head on the counter and closed his eyes.

To the relief of Earish the *Commentator* did not perish with its editor in the Bloomsbury rubble, but rose again, phoenix-like, under the Minitz imprint. 'I hold the *Commentator* in great esteem,' Minitz told a press conference in his pink-carpeted suite two days after the explosion. 'My own magazine, which many of you have heard about, is on the threshold of production, with a talented, youthful and creative staff of the top writers in Fleet Street. It will be a privilege to take the name of that Bloomsbury paper. Gentlemen, and ladies, the Minitz *Commentator* has just been born. A great British tradition will go on.'

In Minitz House, Gerard Bunsen sat at his desk with his new telephone and secretary. No expense had been spared. As new editor of the *Commentator* he intended to launch the paper with a terrific bang. He began to write. 'What a tragedy it is to see the damage done to the once-priceless home of the *Commentator*. How appalling it is that this fine old building should have been destroyed almost beyond restoration by a mindless fanatical bomber. With a moment's thought, he could have placed his explosive device in a spot where it would have done far less damage, preserving, at the least, the outer structure of this irreplaceable house.'

Horlick, his star reporter, knocked on the door and burst in excitedly. 'I say, Bunsen,' he said, 'I've got the absolute scoop of the year for you. This is a really cracking yarn, I can promise you. Shit hot! Just the sort of thing to launch the mag.'

Bunsen looked up in irritation from his article.

'Yes?'

'Fragment!' shouted Horlick excitedly. 'I've got the best story on him so far.'

'What about him?'

'I can now exclusively reveal that he's been knocking off his chiropodist – once a week, at least – for months and months. Amazing isn't it? This is the big one, Bunsen. We've really got him now. This will absolutely force his resignation. We might even bring down the Government.'

'What are you talking about, you silly boy?' said Bunsen shrilly. 'Fragment has gone already.'

'Gone? Gone where? Fled the country? The bastard. That's just the sort of thing he would do.'

'He's resigned. He is no longer a minister of the Crown.'

'What?'

'He's resigned,' said Bunsen sighing.

'Christ. I don't believe it.'

'Don't you read the papers, dear?'

'Well, not very often, no,' said Horlick.

There was a short silence.

'So, you don't want the story then,' he said.

'Not awfully,' said Bunsen.

'Oh,' said Horlick. 'I'll go and try and find another story, shall I?'

'Why don't you do that,' said Bunsen.

'OK,' said Horlick and went out of the room.

Bunsen returned to his article. 'How many more of London's fine buildings,' he wrote, 'will be at risk from similar acts of mindless vandalism. The *Commentator* appeals to these terrorists to think of the priceless heritage they are so wickedly destroying. Why, oh why, can't they plant their bombs in some example of ghastly Sixties modernism, such as the National Theatre, where no one would mind if the entire building was blown up . . .'

'What's the time?' said Jerry Gude, opening his eyes suddenly. 'Christ it's dark. Is it time to go to bed again?' He was lying on the bed of his Holland Park flat in a profusion of crumpled sheets and strewn Sunday newspapers. For the last two days he had been teaching Florence Barge about self-discovery.

'It's nearly four. Almost dark. It's the shortest day of the year.'

'Get me a cigarette?' said Gude, coughing.

She handed him the packet of Gauloises.

'Read to me,' said Gude, stretching out comfortably on the bed. Florence picked up a paper. ' "MY WEEKEND WITH BOMBER," ' she read. ' "By Lucinda Harpie-Kerr." '

' "The young man was dark, good-looking and mysteriously self-possessed. We met as strangers in a crowded bar and ended up as more than just good friends. Little was I to know that twenty-four hours later he would kill two people and blow up a building. That night he was all smiles and tender, romantic thoughts." '

'Lucinda has really gone to town on this,' said Gude, stroking Florence's hair. 'Is it too painful to go on?'

'Poor Alexander,' said Florence. 'The last thing I did was throw stones at his window. I wish it had ended on a happy note.'

'Life's like that,' said Gude. 'I always wanted to leave my wives with pleasant memories, but they all ended up remembering the horrific parts. Read me some more.'

' "What was he like?" ' Florence read on. ' "The man now revealed to millions as an ice-cool determined fanatic? I can reveal that beneath the ruthless, calculating exterior there was a white-hot depth of fiery passion which would, within a few hours, erupt like a volcano and sweep me away on a tide of pounding romance . . ." '

'Completely over the top,' said Gude. 'Only Lucinda could manage such purple prose. Florence, you're taking it all very well.' He yawned and patted the bed. 'Come over here. I feel a tide of pounding romance coming on. It's time for another lesson in self-discovery, Florence.'

Later, Gude said, 'Go and get me a drink, Florence. I have to be pissed to sit through the programme. It's the most masochistic thing I've ever done.'

Florence turned on the television. 'Five minutes to go.'

She went into the kitchen and poured Gude a stiff gin and orange. The room was still cluttered with greasy plates, probably the same ones she had noticed on her first visit with the RIGHT-O vouchers. She stood amid the bacon and egg remains, surprised to find herself becoming almost a fixture in Jerry Gude's flat. The events of the last few days had been overwhelming. Poor Alexander had been blown up. Poor Plugge, too, had gone with him. And now she was lying on an unmade bed with Jerry Gude, fetching him drinks and lighting him cigarettes. A great deal had happened, and yet, Florence thought, nothing much seemed to have changed. She wondered if Jerry had overdone the importance of sex and self-discovery. He had talked about it a great deal. He had hinted at extraordinary results, he had encouraged high expectations. But so far, thought Florence, she hadn't discovered very much.

Music, soft and grave, came flooding into the kitchen. 'It's starting,' she heard Gude shout. 'I don't want to watch this. Am I crazy? Why did I get talked into doing it?' She took in his drink as he sat, propped up with pillows, watching the set eagerly. The title slowly filled the screen. 'Life at the Bottom', the words declared, quickly superseded by a close-up of Jerry Gude's face.

In her sitting room, Arabella Spring-Greene took a deep drag from her cigarette. The vegetable smell of cannabis filled the scented room, as she saw Gude stare sternly out towards his unseen audience, and begin to address them on the subject of his life. Arabella crept up to the television screen and knelt in front of it. As Gude spoke on tears welled in her eyes and fell slowly down her rose-blushed cheeks.

Surrounded by a mass of hand-written papers which she had been sorting out, Amanda Plugge stood in her late husband's study, staring at the screen. Her hands were tightly clenched, her body rigid. As Gude began to speak she dug her nails into the palms of her hands so that they made small incisions into the flesh. The flickering light played on her face. Gude's delivery was interrupted by a fit of coughing. Amanda stood still, staring into the tiny screen. Her face was stony.

In the Dog and Biscuit, Galen Bone sat with Earish and Lucinda Harpie-Kerr gazing up at the television set which was fixed to the wall. 'He looks fucking dreadful,' said Bone. 'Why didn't they give him some make-up?'

'Hush, lovey,' said Lucinda. 'I'm waiting for my first appearance. I had a facial and hair-do specially for this.'

On the screen Gude took a long drink of gin and orange.

'Cheers,' said Gude in his bedroom, emptying his glass. 'God knows why I did this, Florence. I must have been mad.' He grinned proudly at himself on the screen.

The camera cut away to Arabella Spring-Greene. 'Everything was a possibility to Jerry,' she told the audience softly. 'It was exciting to be in his company. He went further than most of us . . .'

Florence stared at her face, trying to see Jerry as he once was.

'Looks good for her age,' said Gude. 'She's worn well. I've been thinking, Florence, we might go for a holiday. Would you like Paris? If you could fork out for the tickets, and the hotel, I'll do the rest. I'm expecting a cheque at the end of the month.'

Amanda Plugge came on the screen. 'Parties, dinner, drinks,' she said, 'it all had to be done on the spur of the moment. He had no concept of an ordered life.' Her eyes, narrow and bitter, seemed to Florence to issue an unmistakeable warning.

'I bet she said far worse than that,' said Gude, blinking his eyes. 'Soured by the experience. I'm amazed she agreed to talk about me at all. Get me another drink, Florence. My strength is giving out.'

'Do you really want another?' she said, looking at the row of empty bottles in the corner of the room.

'You're beginning to sound like one of my ex-wives,' said Gude.

'You've only been here two days, and already you've got an edge of wifely concern in your voice. Don't nag, Florence. Get me a drink. Do it.'

Florence turned and went into the kitchen.

'I suppose Jerry offered excitement,' she heard Lucinda Harpie-Kerr announce. 'It certainly wasn't money that attracted me . . .'

As she poured Jerry's gin and orange, Florence considered the faces of Gude's three wives. Perhaps they had all made him drinks, too, and sat on his unmade bed. As she cut a slice of fresh orange she suddenly remembered the voice of Morton Minitz, firm and serious, at the Limace. 'Never think you can change his nature. You are seeing him as he really is.'

The camera came back to Gude, sitting behind his table, with the bottle and the packet of cigarettes. 'It's me again,' he shouted to Florence. 'Hurry up. You mustn't miss this bit.' The television image spoke. Gude laughed loudly at one of his own jokes.

In the kitchen, Florence stood quietly listening to fragments of the programme ' . . . spontaneity . . . a kind of charm,' she heard. ' . . . didn't last long . . .'

She went quietly into the hall and put on her coat. She looked for her handbag.

'Florence, what do you think?' said Gude, leaning back on his pillows. 'I like having a woman around. I feel I might just be ready to get married again. What about four wives? I've always believed in living dangerously.'

'I've always believed in living dangerously,' Gude announced to his unseen audience. Holding her breath, Florence stepped cautiously down the hall and opened the front door. A gust of icy air swept into the flat.

She heard Jerry Gude laugh. She heard the television murmur.

'Florence?' she heard him call. 'What about my proposal? What's your answer?'

Quietly she shut the door.

'Hurry up,' Gude shouted to the empty flat. 'You're missing the best bits. Just another little drink, Florence. There's still a long way to go.'

Arena

☐ The History Man	Malcolm Bradbury	£2.95
☐ Rates of Exchange	Malcolm Bradbury	£3.50
☐ The Painted Cage	Meira Chand	£3.95
☐ Ten Years in an Open Necked Shirt	John Cooper Clarke	£3.95
☐ Boswell	Stanley Elkin	£4.50
☐ The Family of Max Desir	Robert Ferro	£2.95
☐ Kiss of the Spiderwoman	Manuel Puig	£2.95
☐ The Clock Winder	Anne Tyler	£2.95
☐ Roots	Alex Haley	£5.95
☐ Jeeves and the Feudal Spirit	P. G. Wodehouse	£2.50
☐ Cold Dog Soup	Stephen Dobyns	£3.50
☐ Season of Anomy	Wole Soyinka	£3.99
☐ The Milagro Beanfield War	John Nichols	£3.99
☐ Walter	David Cook	£2.50
☐ The Wayward Bus	John Steinbeck	£3.50

Prices and other details are liable to change

ARROW BOOKS, BOOKSERVICE BY POST, PO BOX 29, DOUGLAS, ISLE OF MAN, BRITISH ISLES

NAME..

ADDRESS..

....

....

Please enclose a cheque or postal order made out to Arrow Books Ltd. for the amount due and allow the following for postage and packing.

U.K. CUSTOMERS: Please allow 22p per book to a maximum of £3.00.

B.F.P.O. & EIRE: Please allow 22p per book to a maximum of £3.00

OVERSEAS CUSTOMERS: Please allow 22p per book.

Whilst every effort is made to keep prices low it is sometimes necessary to increase cover prices at short notice. Arrow Books reserve the right to show new retail prices on covers which may differ from those previously advertised in the text or elsewhere.